DEATH
CAME CALLING

DEATH
CAME CALLING

by
Donald Webb

A Division of Bold Strokes Books

2014

DEATH CAME CALLING

ISBN 13: 978-1-60282-979-4

This Trade Paperback Original Is Published By
Bold Strokes Books, Inc.
P.O. Box 249
Valley Falls, NY 12185

First Edition: January 2014

Credits
Editors: Greg Herren and Stacia Seaman
Production Design: Stacia Seaman
Cover Design by Sheri (graphicartist2020@hotmail.com)

Acknowledgments

First of all, I would like to thank all the dedicated people at Bold Strokes Books for their help and support in bringing this, my first mystery novel, to fruition. Secondly, a special thanks to Greg Herren for his fantastic editing job.

My never-ending gratitude goes to Andre, my lifelong partner, for his support and encouragement.

PROLOGUE

DEATH CAME CALLING
THE INCITING EVENT

Gale-force winds roared across the wide San Sebastian beach, rocking David Earl Warren's car like a rubber duck caught in the wake of a speeding cigarette boat. Warren stared through the shimmering windows of his vehicle. He'd never encountered a storm with such velocity. The rapid back-and-forth movement of wiper blades—barely coping with the downpour—had a mesmerizing effect.

Breathing a sigh of relief, Warren turned off Ocean Boulevard into the underground parking at his upscale condominium. He took the elevator to the penthouse floor and let himself into his suite. He threw his briefcase onto a chair in the master bedroom and stripped down to his briefs. He'd been feeling shaky and listless all day, and had trouble concentrating on his job. A vague feeling of impending disaster had been with him all day.

The guys at work are probably right, he thought, *I must have the flu*. He poured a glass of water and swallowed a couple of NyQuil capsules. He noticed the bottle of Ambien in the cabinet. It had been a while since he'd used them. *I'll take some so I can get a good night's sleep*, he decided. He swallowed a couple of capsules with another glass of water. Still thirsty, he downed another glass of water, and for the fourth time that afternoon, he emptied his bladder.

He dropped the toilet seat and sat down on the lid. He could feel his heart pounding in his chest. *What's the matter with me? It can't be my blood sugar. I haven't eaten anything different today, and I had my usual dose of insulin this morning before heading for the office. I better check my glucose level.* He felt so tired and lethargic he could barely stand. Using the towel rack for leverage, he staggered to his feet and went into the bedroom. He pulled his blood glucose monitor out of his briefcase, went back into the bathroom, pricked his finger, and placed a drop of blood on a test strip. His glucose level was dangerously high. His hands shook when he picked up an insulin pen, dialed in an appropriate amount of insulin, and injected it into a fold of skin on his abdomen.

He stumbled into the bedroom and collapsed on his bed. Ten minutes passed. *Something's not right* flashed through his mind. *I should be feeling better by now.* A sudden attack of nausea overcame him. He crawled into the bathroom and heaved over the toilet. Nothing came up. He crawled back onto his bed and closed his eyes. He knew he was going into a coma. It took a while for his befuddled mind to reach a decision. He reached over to his bedside table and tried to pick up the phone, but all he succeeded in doing was knocking it to the floor. He tried to retrieve the phone, but couldn't move. He closed his eyes. The bed felt like it was tilting over backward into a deep void.

A noise penetrated the confusion surrounding his brain. When he managed to open his eyes, he vaguely perceived the outline of someone at his bedside.

"Help me," he managed to croak through his parched lips.

"Don't worry, asshole, I'll help you," the person said.

That was the last thing David Earl Warren heard before slipping away permanently.

CHAPTER ONE

It was 9:20 on Monday morning and Katsuro Tanaka was on his second cup of coffee. He'd come into his office early to complete the paperwork on his last case. When the report was completed, he opened the morning edition of the *San Sebastian Gazette* and started completing the crosswords.

The telephone disrupted his concentration. He lifted the phone, hooked it between his chin and shoulder, and said, "Tanaka Investigations."

"Tanaka, this is Prescott Harrington."

Wow, Tanaka thought, *this must be important; he's never spoken directly to me before. I hope he's not firing me.* "Yes, Mr. Harrington. What can I do for you?"

"I've got a special request for you, Tanaka. My neighbor, Winifred Ross, has a problem that I'd like you to look into."

Tanaka dropped his feet off his desk and opened his notebook. Harrington was the President and CEO of San Sebastian Insurance. Most of Tanaka's income came from work he did for Harrington's firm.

"Her nephew," Harrington continued, "died under unusual circumstances. She'd like someone independent to look into it. Manuela Ruiz, the head of our claims section, tells me you're our best investigator, so I'd like you to look into it for me."

Tanaka was quiet for a few moments. Most of his cases were mundane investigations of negligence, missing persons, missing property, employee background checks, and insurance fraud. Occasionally something different and challenging came along. The words *died under unusual circumstances* sent an ominous chill up his spine.

"What kind of unusual circumstances?" he asked.

"I don't know the details, Tanaka, just that her nephew's death was unexpected. I told Winifred I'd have someone look into it."

"Would I be working for you, or her?"

"Definitely for Winifred. This isn't company business."

Tanaka was quiet for a few beats.

"You'll do it?" Harrington asked.

Do I have any choice? he thought. "Yes, Mr. Harrington, I'll look into it for you. You have her address and phone number?"

He did. Tanaka recorded the information in his notebook.

After Harrington disconnected, Tanaka put his feet back on his desk. What did Harrington mean by "Her nephew died under unusual circumstances"? If the circumstances surrounding her nephew's death were unusual, why weren't the police investigating?

After his spouse, Patrick, was slaughtered, Tanaka had left the San Sebastian police to get away from violence. Now he was being asked to look into a suspicious death again.

CHAPTER TWO

Tanaka drove home and changed before driving to Winifred Ross's house on Mountain View Drive. He nosed his car between the open wrought-iron gates and drove down the bird-of-paradise-bordered cobblestone driveway. Bright red and pink poinsettia and hibiscus bushes dotted the landscape. Two Latino gardeners—one mowing the extensive lawn and the other trimming magenta and white bougainvilleas—watched Tanaka as he drove up to the house.

They're probably wondering what a common Honda Civic is doing in the neighborhood, Tanaka thought, smiling when the driveway circled a replica of the Brussels *Manneken Pis* fountain. It brought back memories of a trip he'd taken to Brussels. At that time, the statue had been in judo attire. This replica was naked. The driveway ended at a porte cochere on the north side of the sprawling mansion. The red-tiled roof, white walls, and ornately barred windows of the mission-style home blended into the lush surroundings.

After parking behind a silver convertible Mercedes SLK 350 Roadster, Tanaka stood on the granite steps and pressed the bell. Melodious chimes echoed inside.

A tall, gaunt, gray-haired woman who appeared to be in her seventies opened the door.

"Ms. Ross?" Tanaka asked.

"Yes?"

"I'm Katsuro Tanaka."

She blinked. "Oh, sorry…I was expecting…"

Tanaka smiled. "You were expecting a Japanese guy?"

"Well, frankly, yes."

"I get that all the time. My father was Japanese American, but my mother's pure Irish."

"Please come in, Mr. Tanaka."

They shook hands as he stepped into a space bigger than his office. Sunlight entering the narrow fenestrations on either side of the doorway sent prisms of light flashing through a crystal chandelier hanging from the vaulted ceiling. The terracotta-tiled floor added a warm glow to the ambience.

Her property taxes are probably more than my net income, Tanaka thought as he followed her down a central hallway into an expansive room. Two groupings of sofas and wing chairs sat on Persian rugs. Gleaming coffee tables displayed crystal vases filled with sweet-smelling red and yellow roses.

"Would you like some coffee?" Ms. Ross asked.

"Please."

"Have a seat. I'll be right back."

While he waited, Tanaka examined a collection of Steuben figurines displayed in a walnut cabinet. A movement on one of the wing chairs caught his attention. A pepper-and-salt schnauzer was watching him.

"Don't worry, I'm not going to pocket any," Tanaka said.

Ms. Ross returned with a tray containing two mugs of coffee and cream and sugar. She placed the tray on a coffee table and he sat at the end of a sofa, and she took an adjacent wing chair. When they were sipping their coffee, Tanaka said, "I understand you want me to look into your nephew's death?"

"That's right, Mr. Tanaka, there's something fishy about his death." Winifred Ross sat erect in her wing chair, as if she were posing for a graduation photo at a Swiss finishing school. "Some people might say I'm crazy, Mr. Tanaka, but I'm as sane as a judge."

Tanaka remained silent.

Her graceful hands toyed with the three-strand pearl necklace adorning her swanlike neck. "It couldn't have happened like they say it did. My nephew was always so particular about taking his insulin."

He knew he should tell her he couldn't help her, but she spoke with such certainty, and he could also detect that underneath her brave front, she was utterly forlorn, so instead he said, "Why don't you start at the beginning and tell me everything?"

She sighed and rearranged her skirt. "The police say David drowned in his tub while in a diabetic coma and there's nothing to indicate foul play." She raised a lean arm in an elegant, fluid motion and brushed a few strands of gray hair from her forehead. "The coroner ruled his death was accidental, so they closed the case. But David couldn't have died that way. It's just not possible. It couldn't have happened the way the police say it happened."

After a deep breath, she shook her head and continued, "He was too careful about his health to let that happen. I know he always tested his blood every night before retiring. If his blood sugar wasn't right he would've looked after it." Her lips compressed in a moue. "I'm really quite annoyed with the way the investigation was handled, Mr. Tanaka."

Tanaka hated when older people called him Mr. Tanaka—it reminded him of his deadbeat father—so he said, "Please...call me Kats."

"Kats?"

"Yes. It's short for Katsuro."

She nodded and leaned back in her chair. "Only if you'll call me Winifred. That's what David always called me."

Tanaka smiled back at her and nodded.

"The police are not entirely to blame, Kats," she said. "I guess in some ways it's my fault."

"How's that?"

"Well, when the police started the investigation, I insisted David's death had to be accidental."

"They would still have investigated thoroughly," Tanaka said.

"I can't help blaming myself."

The schnauzer let out a loud snort. They both looked at him. He regarded them with his bleary eyes for a few seconds, shifted around, and went back to sleep.

Winifred shook her head. "Spoiled rotten," she said. "Can't do a thing with him."

"You say your nephew's name was David?"

"Yes. David Earl Warren. You may have seen his death notice in the *Gazette*?"

Tanaka was stunned. *Earl Warren* was a name he never wanted to hear again.

After a few beats, Winifred asked, "You feeling okay, Kats?"

"Yes, I'm fine," he managed to get out. "I'm sorry…you were saying?"

"I was asking if you'd seen David's death notice?"

"No. I don't recall seeing it," he said.

"I'll be right back." She rose and left the room. A few moments later she returned carrying a huge leather purse. She rifled through it, pulled out a photograph, and handed it to Tanaka. "That was taken a few months before David died."

He studied the portrait. Warren, dressed in a three-piece suit, looked to be in his late thirties. His piercing eyes and slicked-down dark hair gave him the look of 1920s Valentino.

"He was a nice-looking man," Tanaka said, thinking, *He's more handsome than you are, and he certainly didn't have your nose.*

When he tried to return the photograph, she said, "You can keep it."

He couldn't see a reason for keeping the photograph, but placed it in his pocket.

She sighed. "I feel so…so alone. He was my only living relative and he's been taken from me."

"I can imagine you must be pretty upset by his death, then?"

"I've never been one to show my emotions…but yes, I am."

"That's not always the best way to handle grief, I'm told."

"I know, but it's my way."

They were silent for a short while. Tanaka was trying to decide how to deal with her request, and she was watching him with her hazel eyes.

"I'm not sure why you're telling me this," Tanaka said.

An involuntary spasm, like a wince, crossed her face, and her back straightened. "Why am I telling you this? I want you to find out who murdered him, that's why."

CHAPTER THREE

Tanaka was silent for a few moments. "PIs generally don't investigate murders, Winifred, that's a job for the police. I generally work for a group of personal injury attorneys and an insurance company. I don't think I'm the right person for you."

"Prescott told me you do work for him. He said you used to be a policeman, so you would know what to do."

Tanaka appraised her for a long moment. *Thank you, Mr. Harrington, for volunteering my services* flashed through his mind, but he said, "Why don't you tell me about David."

She closed her eyes for a beat or two before speaking. "David's parents were killed in a plane crash when he was seven years old. He was staying with me at the time. He had no other relatives, so they appointed me his legal guardian and trustee of his estate. I was thirty-five when I gave up my career and devoted my life to him…and now I'm a seventy-year-old with nothing to show for my life. Not that I'm complaining, Kats. I would do it again without a second thought."

Winifred took a deep breath, pulled a white linen handkerchief out of her purse, and blotted her eyes. The scent of lavender drifted across to Tanaka. She looked out of a window and kneaded her hands.

"David and I were always close and I loved him dearly," she said as tears began streaming down her wrinkled cheeks.

Winifred's distress was contagious. Tanaka had to take a few deep breaths and force himself to suppress thoughts of Patrick's violent death. He leaned over and covered Winifred's hand with his. She placed her other hand over his hand. They sat like that for a few seconds. She patted his hand when she had herself under control.

"You're a softy, just like David was," she said.

·

They smiled at one another, and she continued. "David was a teenager when we found out he had diabetes. For a few years, he was in denial and carried on as though he was still normal and refused to wear an alert bracelet. One day an off-duty paramedic found him unconscious in Lighthouse Park. He called an ambulance. When David woke up in the emergency room, he finally realized he had to take care of his diabetes. He was good after that and always kept his blood sugar under control. He'd never've been in that tub unless his blood sugar was normal."

Tanaka picked up his mug. It was empty.

"Would you like some more coffee?"

"That would be nice, thank you," he said.

She left the room and returned with a pot of coffee and a plate of hermits.

She filled his mug, then asked, "Would you like a cookie?"

"Thanks," he said. "They look homemade."

"They are." She reached for one. "I'm a little hungry—didn't have any breakfast."

The schnauzer bounded off the chair, scampered over to Tanaka, sat on his rump, and rested his forepaws on Tanaka's thigh.

"He wants a cookie," Winifred said.

"Can I give him one?"

She nodded. "Rudolph, ask nicely."

Rudolph sat back and raised his paws in the air. "Good boy," she said.

Tanaka placed the cookie in Rudolph's mouth. Rudolph devoured it and looked at Winifred.

"No more," she said, shaking her head.

Rudolph climbed back onto the wing chair and stretched out on his back.

Tanaka took a sip of his coffee. "How old was David when he died?"

"Forty-two, about the same age as you, if I'm not mistaken."

Tanaka smiled. *Here I thought I didn't look a day older than thirty-five.*

"What happened?" he asked.

"We'd spoken the night before his death. He said he wasn't feeling well and was going to have an early night. I promised I would be over the next morning to look after him."

"What date was that?" Tanaka asked.

"How could I forget? It was Friday, January the thirteenth, when I last spoke to him."

"This year?"

Winifred nodded. "Yes. Last month."

She blotted her eyes and blew her nose, while Tanaka jotted down notes in his notebook.

When he looked back at her she said, "The next morning I phoned him. He didn't answer, so I left a message telling him I would be over with coffee. When I got there, I found him in the tub. I knew right away it was too late, but I called 9-1-1 anyway. I was right. They didn't even try to resuscitate him. They said he'd been gone for a while."

CHAPTER FOUR

In a flash, he was back in his bedroom, feeling Patrick's lifeless body in his arms, and once again he had to fight to control his emotions.

"You must've been devastated," he finally said.

"You've no idea. I still have nightmares about it."

"Believe me," he said after a few moments, "I've also lost someone close to me, so I know what you're going through."

Winifred gave Tanaka a long, appraising look. "I'm sorry to hear that, Kats. Was it someone in your family?"

"Yes. I lost my spouse two years ago, but it still feels like it was yesterday. They say that I'll get over it, but I'm not sure if that's true."

"It's hard to lose someone you love, isn't it?"

Tanaka nodded.

"So you can see why I'm anxious to get to the bottom of this?"

He nodded again.

"You have any children?" she asked.

"Yes, I've got a seven-year-old son."

He took out his wallet, withdrew a photograph of his adopted son, and handed it to her. "He's called Tommy."

She examined the photograph. "He's a cute little thing. He's going to be a handsome man, just like his daddy."

"Thank you," Tanaka said. He wasn't about to tell her Tommy was actually Patrick's son, and he'd adopted Tommy after he and Patrick had married during the short window when same-sex marriages were legal in California before Prop 8 passed. When Tanaka and Patrick first met, Patrick was recovering from a disastrous marriage to Tommy's mother. Shortly after she deserted Patrick and Tommy, she was killed in a car accident.

"It's hard bringing up a child on your own, isn't it?" she said, returning the photograph.

"I'm lucky. My mother lives with us and takes care of him when I'm not home."

She adjusted the silk Hermès scarf draped around the shoulders of her tailored emerald-green jacket. "You *are* lucky. I had no one to help me."

"You were telling me about David," he prompted.

She dabbed her eyes and resumed the account of her nephew's death. "At the time, I accepted the coroner's verdict of accidental death. However, the more I think about it, the more certain I am it couldn't have been accidental. It just doesn't feel right."

"Was David depressed?"

"What do you mean?"

"Could it have been suicide?"

"Oh no! You can forget that. When I saw him a few days before his death, he was his usual self."

"You're sure of that?"

Winifred lifted her pointed chin. "Of course I'm sure. You think just because I'm an old lady I don't know what's going on?"

"Sorry. I just—"

"Good. Now let's get on with it."

"Do you know if he had any enemies, someone who'd want him dead?"

Her chin dropped and she leaned back in the chair. "Not really. The only person who comes to mind is Margaret, his ex-wife. I hate to say this, Kats, but she's not top-drawer, if you know what I mean. I could never figure out what David saw in her. I wouldn't be surprised if she had something to do with his death. She was so nasty during their divorce. She even threatened to shoot him."

"When was the divorce?"

"About eighteen months ago."

"They have any children?"

"No, Margaret didn't want any. Said it would ruin her figure."

Tommy brought such joy to his life Tanaka couldn't imagine anyone not wanting children.

"Was your nephew living alone at the time of his death?"

"Yes, he's lived alone ever since the divorce."

"Any other enemies come to mind?"

She shook her head, closed her eyes, and rubbed her temples. "He was an attorney…perhaps he had a problem with a client?"

Tanaka took a mouthful of coffee and then wrote some notes in his book. "Was there anyone special in his life since the divorce?"

Winifred played with the clasp on her purse and glanced out of the window. "No. The divorce hurt him, and he didn't want to get involved with anyone."

"Any close friends?"

She thought this over. "The only ones that come to mind are Jeremy Townsend and Michael Easton. Jeremy's been a friend of ours for a long time, and Michael's a partner in the law firm where David worked. David and Michael shared an apartment in L.A. while they were in law school, and I know David looked after the Eastons' house when they were on vacation. David also attended office functions and met with some of the other attorneys from Pratt James Easton after hours, but I don't think he ever considered them real friends."

"No one else comes to mind?"

She shook her head. "I can't think of anyone else. Even though David and I didn't live together, we saw each other at least once a week."

"What about a will? He have one?"

"Yes. He left Jeremy five hundred thousand dollars, but he left the residue of his estate to me."

"Five hundred thousand?"

She straightened up. "Yes. It might sound strange to you…but it's not. If David had had other close friends, I'm sure he would've included them in his will. That's the kind of person he was."

Tanaka had questions about Jeremy Townsend, but he let them slide for the moment. "When was the will written?"

"A week before he died."

"Any idea why he'd written a new will?"

"Not really. He was probably just taking Margaret out of it."

"Who had custody of the will?"

"David had given a copy to Jeremy, but he named me executrix. Being a lawyer, he had written the will himself. Two people at his office had witnessed his signature." Winifred sighed. "Of course, Margaret is contesting the new will. She said she had a will that left everything to her."

Tanaka thought for a few moments. "How were you related to David?"

"David's mother was my sister."

Tanaka could feel her appraising him as he made some more notes.

"Did you say you don't have a family of your own?" Tanaka asked.

"Yes, I don't have any relatives, and I've never been married. Mind you, I've had many proposals, but I never met anyone I wanted to share my life with."

"I bet you had a lot of suitors, Winifred."

Her neck reddened. "Of course, when I was younger my career came first."

It was the second time she had mentioned her career. "What was your career, Winifred?"

Her cheeks flushed. "You may find it hard to believe, but I was once on the stage...a dancer. I started with a ballet company, but of course, I was too tall, so I ended up in musicals. I eventually left the stage and started my own modern dance school in L.A., and was doing very well until my sister's death." Winifred straightened in her chair. "I still exercise at the barre every morning. It keeps me fit and supple."

"I don't find that hard to believe, Winifred. You still have a dancer's figure."

She smiled. "You're full of the blarney, young man—I guess it's part of your heritage—but I appreciate the compliment."

"Is there anything else you think I should know?" Tanaka asked.

She toyed with the diamond solitaire on her right ring finger and glanced about the room. She looked back at Tanaka and said, "No...I can't think of anything right now. Please, say you'll help me."

Tanaka hesitated. *She's holding something back. She's not telling me everything.*

"It's really not my kind of case." He was also thinking, *I'm not sure if I want to help anyone with the name Warren.* "I'll have to think about it."

"I'm sorry to hear that, Kats. You're my last hope."

He slipped his notebook and pen into his jacket pocket and stood. "I'll get back to you when I've made a decision, Winifred."

She led him to the door and watched him climb into his car.

"I'll be waiting for your call, Kats," she called out, and closed the door.

She has everything money can buy, he was thinking as he drove away, *and yet she's all alone in that huge mansion.*

CHAPTER FIVE

B ack in his office chair, Tanaka closed his eyes and thought about his session with Winifred. *She's trying to pull me into a possible homicide. If it is a homicide, will I be able to handle it? On the other hand, if I don't take the case, and Warren was murdered, then the killer will get away with it. Maybe I should do a little digging before making a decision.*

He called the San Sebastian Police Station and made an appointment to see Sergeant Richard Sadowski.

"Kats, what's up?" Sadowski asked when Tanaka walked into his office that afternoon.

Tanaka lowered himself onto the chair next to the desk. "Well, nice to see you too, Rick."

"Nice threads," Sadowski said. "How come you're all dolled up in your Sunday best?"

Tanaka adjusted the lapels of his suede jacket. "You like it? I bought it at Nordstrom."

"It must've been on sale."

"It was. Got two for the price of one."

"So, you dressed up just to impress me?"

Tanaka shook his head. "I had a meeting with a new client."

"How come you wanted to see me at work? You missed me so much you couldn't wait till Thursday?"

"It's business."

"I thought for a minute you'd come to tell me you had to back out of Thursday's squash match."

"No way...the game's still on. I have to win back the twenty you won last week."

Sadowski smiled. "Fat chance, I could beat you blindfolded. So what's this all about, then?"

"I'm looking into David Earl Warren's death."

"You're kidding? Who hired you? No, don't answer that. It could only be that aunt of his. I guess she still hasn't given up on the idea of foul play?"

"Yeah. She just can't let it go. I told her I'd look into it."

"Oh well, hopefully you can set her straight and get her off our backs. Mind you, that'll be pretty hard. She's one determined old broad, that one."

Tanaka nodded. "He was her only relative. What do you expect?"

"I don't know if she told you, but Warren's death was investigated right from the get-go. The preliminary walk-through pretty well convinced everyone involved that his death was accidental, but the suite was still checked from end to end to make sure foul play wasn't involved."

"I know the routine."

Sadowski pulled a spring-loaded tension hand exerciser out of his drawer and started exercising his right hand.

No wonder he's so good at squash, Tanaka thought. *I'll have to get myself one of those.*

"So...what do you want to know, then?" Sadowski asked.

"It sounds like you're familiar with the case. Were you the investigating officer?"

"No. The only reason I know about the case is because I'm the one she came to see after the coroner's report came back."

"Who was the investigating officer?" Tanaka asked.

"Frank Smith."

The answer didn't exactly thrill Tanaka. Smith wasn't renowned for exemplary investigations. When Tanaka had worked with him he'd had to clean up after the detective on a number of occasions.

"Can you review the findings with me?"

"Sure...what do you want to know?"

Tanaka checked his notes. "Was Warren submerged in the tub?"

"From what I remember, by the time Smith got there, the

paramedics had already removed him from the tub to try to revive him. They said Ms. Ross found him fully submerged. She had drained the tub and was giving him mouth-to-mouth when they arrived."

Tanaka felt a heaviness in his chest. The image of Winifred leaning over the tub, desperately trying to breathe life into her nephew, brought back the horrifying memories of him doing the same to Patrick after finding his bloody, lifeless body on the bedroom floor.

He took a few deep breaths. "Could you go over the case file with me, Rick? I'd like to know what the autopsy findings were."

"I don't know about that…I could get canned if anyone found out."

"Please, Rick. No one's going to know."

Sadowski chewed at his bottom lip and rubbed his chin. "Just last month Gonzales demoted someone for opening a file for an outsider," he said.

"He'll never know, Rick. I'm certainly not gonna tell him."

Sadowski dropped the exerciser on his desk. "Hang on, I'll get the file."

When Sadowski returned, he lowered his tall, muscular frame into his chair, sat back, propped his huge feet on the desk, and paged through the file.

"Gonzales isn't in the office, so we better hurry up and get this over with."

Tanaka nodded.

"Okay, here we go," Sadowski said. "At autopsy Warren's lungs were full of bathwater. His vitreous glucose level was six hundred and fifty-something or other. Which, I'm told, is way above normal. The pathologist decided the cause of his death was accidental drowning, precipitated by diabetic ketoacidosis."

"What a mouthful. You'll have to interpret for me."

Sadowski grinned. "Not as bright as I thought you were."

"You always were the smarter one, Rick. Now, Mr. Smartass, what does vitreous mean?"

"I must confess, I had the same question. That's the fluid in the eyeballs. They say it's the best way to check postmortem blood-sugar levels."

This was all new to Tanaka. "What was the other? Keto… something?"

Sadowski laughed. "Ketoacidosis. That's when there's a lack of insulin in the body. Apparently acid builds up in the blood until the body can't cope, and the person goes into a coma."

"So there's no doubt he died from a lack of insulin?"

"You got it," he said. "For some reason Warren hadn't given himself a shot."

Tanaka jotted some notes in his book. "Were there any other findings?"

Sadowski picked up the grip and resumed exercising his hand, paging through the file with his free hand. "The pathologist noted that the deceased was alive at the time of submersion. No signs of injury. No penetrating wounds. The only other thing noted was an abrasion on Warren's lower back—over the sacrum—that couldn't be explained, otherwise he was a healthy male."

"What about time of death?"

"He was alive at eight p.m. because he spoke to the concierge at that time, and they know he was dead at ten a.m. the next day when his aunt found him. When the team got to him, his core body temperature was eighty-eight degrees, and there was some rigor mortis of the upper torso, so the coroner determined he'd been dead for about eleven hours."

"So that puts it at about eleven p.m. on January the thirteenth?"

"Yeah, give or take two hours. Between ten and twelve, somewhere. Of course being submerged in water also affected his body temp, but that was the coroner's best estimate."

A deep voice boomed down the corridor outside Sadowski's office.

"Someone's been smoking in here again!" the voice bellowed. "If I find out who it is I'll make their goddamn life a misery."

"Shit," Sadowski said. He dropped his feet and threw the file he'd been reviewing into his desk drawer.

Lieutenant Gonzales, a big bear of a man dressed in a charcoal-gray suit, strode into Sadowski's office.

A sneer covered his face when he looked at Tanaka. "What's he doing here?" he said to Sadowski.

"Morning, Lieutenant," Tanaka said.

Gonzales ignored Tanaka.

"I hope you're not providing this private citizen with police information?" Gonzales said to Sadowski.

"I wouldn't do that, Lieutenant. He's looking for a missing person, and I was just telling him we don't have any John Does."

Tanaka hadn't seen Gonzales since he'd left the police force. His hatred for Gonzales had not abated. Gonzales, knowing Tanaka was gay, had always treated him with contempt. He could never forgive Gonzales for his blasé attitude during the investigation of Patrick's death.

Tanaka knew he should keep quiet and ignore Gonzales. He couldn't. "You not get a piece last night, Lieutenant?"

Gonzales took a few steps toward Tanaka. "What the fuck's that mean?"

"Well, you're more miserable than usual...I just thought that might be the reason."

Gonzales's face turned dark red and he took another step toward Tanaka. "Watch your mouth!"

Tanaka jumped up from his chair. "I don't have to take your bullshit anymore, you asshole."

Sadowski shot out from behind his desk and pushed his way between them. "Take it easy, Kats," he said.

Gonzales and Tanaka glowered at one another. Tanaka felt like pushing Sadowski out of the way and punching Gonzales. But he knew that would make things worse.

I can't let this continue, Tanaka thought. *My job depends on my having a good working relationship with the cops.* He took a few deep breaths and sat down. "Sorry, Lieutenant, I shouldn't have said that."

Gonzales glared at Tanaka for a few moments, then glanced at Sadowski and said, "Get rid of him. I don't want to see him in here again. I'll see you in my office when he's gone."

Tanaka's heart was still pounding when Gonzales turned to leave Sadowski's office.

"I'll be right in, Lieutenant," Sadowski said.

"Fuck," Tanaka said after Gonzales left the office, "I hate that horse's ass."

"You shouldn't've let him get to you."

Rick's right, Tanaka thought. "Sorry if I've landed you in the shit, Rick."

"No problem."

"Can we finish going over the file?"

"No, Kats. I'm going to do exactly as he says. Sorry, but you'll have to go."

Tanaka stood. "Thanks, Rick. I'll see you on Thursday."

When he left the police station Tanaka thought about the questions he still had. Maybe Rick would answer them on Thursday.

On his way back to his own office, Tanaka thought about the autopsy results. He'd need to dig deeper to find out what had really happened to Warren.

CHAPTER SIX

Tanaka stopped at the Subway restaurant on the corner of Caballeros and Castillo, picked up a foot-long ham sandwich, and took it back to his office.

He sprawled in his office chair, took a bite out of his sandwich, and phoned Sadowski.

"What now?" Sadowski asked.

"How'd it go with Gonzales after I left?"

"Never said a word. I think he was embarrassed by it."

"Good. I should've kept my big trap shut, I—"

"That would've been a nice change."

"I was scared I'd landed you in shit."

"What's the matter with your big trap? Trying to disguise your voice?"

"I'm chewing on a sub."

"I should be so lucky. You just called to ask about Gonzales?"

"Yeah, just wanted to check."

"You mean I can get back to real work? You're finished with me?"

"See you Thursday," Tanaka said, and hung up.

Tanaka was halfway through his sub when Karen Lange, his thirty-five-year-old part-time assistant—dressed in tight black jeans and white T-shirt—came bursting into his office in her usual gung-ho style. Tanaka hadn't seen her in over a week.

"Morning, Katsuro," she said, flopping down onto the wing chair beside his desk.

"It's about time you got here," Tanaka said.

"Sorry. Got held up."

"Just kidding. I know you've been busy."

Karen was a student in the criminal justice program at San Sebastian College. Tanaka and Karen had first met when they'd both enrolled in a computer course at the college. When she'd found out Tanaka was a PI, she'd begged him to take her on as an assistant. She had worked for three years as a claims investigator for a Los Angeles–based company prior to moving to San Sebastian to join her partner, so becoming a PI was a logical move for her. He didn't really need any help, but he gave her a chance anyway. She'd become a valuable asset and he'd learned to trust her sharp mind.

"How are classes going?" Tanaka asked.

"Great. I'm learning a lot."

"I could do with a refresher. Maybe I should sign up."

"You could teach the classes."

"Gimme a break."

"How are things at home?" she asked. "I bumped into your mom and Tommy down at the harbor on Saturday. They were visiting the aquarium, and he was having a ball."

"I bet he was. She spoils him rotten."

"How's he doing? He still talk about Patrick?"

"Sometimes—when I mention him—but he's slowly forgetting."

Even though Tanaka was her boss, Karen and Tanaka were close friends. When she'd joined him—a year after Patrick's death—Tanaka was awash in rage and self-pity. She'd forced Tanaka to deal with his grief and helped him focus on bringing up Tommy.

"Last week I took him to see the tae kwon do competition, and now he wants to join. I'm not sure if I should let him."

"Why not? It'll do him good."

"What if he gets hurt?"

She regarded him with her large soulful eyes. "Did you ever get hurt?"

"No, not really."

"Well, what's your problem, then? You have to untie the apron strings, Kats. You can't mollycoddle him forever. Now, what about work? Have I missed anything?"

She jotted down some notes while Tanaka told her about Winifred Ross and his talk with Sadowski. He didn't mention the clash with Gonzales.

Karen looked up at him when he paused. "Does Winifred live in the area where your grandparents used to farm?"

"Their farm was a little farther north."

His grandparents had lost their land, most of their possessions, and irreplaceable personal property in 1942 when they were forced into a relocation camp. Even though they were American citizens, they had to sell their property in a matter of days for pennies on the dollar. The government eventually made reparations, paying his father $20,000, a fraction of his grandparents' loss. The injustice still infuriated him when he thought about it. If the family hadn't lost everything, maybe he'd be living on Mountain View Drive.

"Doesn't the name Earl Warren ring any bells?" Tanaka asked.

"Well, duh…wasn't he the chief justice of the Supreme Court?"

"Yeah, and what else?"

She screwed up her face and thought for a few moments. "Oh, yeah, I remember. He was also governor of California."

"He was also the California state attorney who had the Japanese removed from the coast in 1942."

"Oh-oh."

"Oh-oh is right. When she told me her nephew's name was Warren, I wanted to get up and walk out of there. I felt like I'd been kicked in the gut."

"Does that mean you're not going to take the case?"

"Not necessarily. Maybe he wasn't related to the famous Warren."

They sat quietly for a few moments, then Tanaka handed Karen the photograph. "That's him."

Karen sat back and examined the photograph while Tanaka finished his sub.

"He was a hunk. If I were straight I'd have gone for him," she said.

"If you were straight all the women would have to watch their men."

She smiled, struck a pose, and ran her hand through her spiky blond-streaked hair. "You think so?"

"I know so. I've seen the guys at the gym giving you the eye."

"I've seen some of them giving you the eye," she said.

"Really? Which ones?"

She rolled her eyes and returned the photograph. "Like you don't know. I've seen you preening. So, what's next?"

"I want to do a little more digging before I make a final decision. I think I'll check Warren's condo, see if I can find anything amiss."

"What do you want me to do?"

"You still working on that insurance fraud?"

She nodded. "I'll have it cleared up pretty soon."

"Keep at it, then."

Tanaka phoned Winifred. When she answered, he said, "I want to have a look at your nephew's suite. Is that possible?"

"Does this mean you're going to help me?"

"I haven't made up my mind yet. I'm still thinking about it. I'll make a decision when I've looked at a few more things."

"I'm just about to leave for downtown. I can bring the keys to his suite with me, if you like."

"Good. Can I meet you somewhere and pick them up?"

"Where's your office?" she asked.

"On East El Centro near Castillo."

"I'll meet you at the parkade entrance on El Centro in fifteen minutes."

"See you there."

Tanaka was waiting at the entrance when Winifred drove up in the Mercedes he'd seen at her house.

She handed him the key, and he wrote down Warren's address.

"Does anyone else have a key?" he asked.

"As far as I know the only other people are Jeremy and the condo management company. I wouldn't be surprised if Margaret still has a key because David didn't change the lock after she moved out."

Tanaka couldn't believe Warren hadn't changed the lock. It would've been the first thing he would've done.

"I'll let you know my decision."

"I'll be waiting. You can call me on my cell phone."

Tanaka recorded the number in his notebook.

He went back to his office and picked up his equipment.

CHAPTER SEVEN

Warren's upmarket condominium sat on Ocean Boulevard overlooking San Sebastian Harbor. Tanaka knew it was a new building, but it looked like a converted factory or brewery. It was going on four when Tanaka entered the lobby. A concierge, looking like an aging, dehydrated lounge lizard, slouched behind the counter.

The few strands of hair he had combed over his dome did little to hide his baldness. A network of broken capillaries was evident on his large nose. His gray-tinged skin appeared stretched over his facial bones. Tanaka checked his name badge. "Hi, Mr. Bernier, my name's Katsuro Tanaka. I'm a private investigator. Mr. Warren's aunt has asked me to look into his death."

Bernier's long, bony fingers trembled when he reached for Tanaka's business card. Tanaka could smell booze under the Listerine.

Bernier appraised Tanaka. "I don't understand. I heard the cops already said his death was accidental and the case was closed."

"That's true, but Ms. Ross is still pretty upset. She'd like to know how Mr. Warren spent his last hours. She tells me you're one of the few people she trusts, and hopes you'll assist me."

Tanaka hoped flattery might get Bernier to open up.

"Sure. She's a nice lady," Bernier said. "What can I do for you?"

"Were you on duty on the night Mr. Warren died? That would be Friday, January the thirteenth."

"I was on from four to midnight. I always work those hours."

"Did Mr. Warren have any visitors on the evening he died?"

Bernier sighed. "No. I already told the cops that. In fact, he rang me at about eight and said he wasn't feeling so good and he was going to have an early night. He didn't want no visitors."

"How did he sound?"

"He sounded…how do you say it? Hoarse, yes, hoarse, you know, like he had a frog in his t'roat, but otherwise he was the same as ever."

Tanaka looked around the lobby. "Is this the only entrance into the building?"

"That's right. No one gets in here without me knowing."

Bernier glanced at the door. He closed his eyes for a moment and sighed. A spindle-legged, well-coiffed elderly matron tottering on impossibly high heels, dragging a bichon frise behind her, approached the door. The dog kept stopping and smelling every bush on the way to the door.

Bernier sighed again. He unfolded his loose-jointed body from the chair and ambled over to open the door for her.

"Did you have a good walk, Mrs. Walsh?" he asked.

"Not really, Henri. Tootsie's been a naughty girl. She's not going to get a treat today. Did you hear that, Tootsie?"

Bernier sauntered over to the elevators and pressed the up button.

When the elevator door opened, she said to Bernier, "Be a darling and get rid of this for me."

She handed him a transparent plastic baggie containing dog poop.

Tanaka could see the blood rise in Bernier's cheeks. He glanced at Tanaka, checking to see if Tanaka had heard.

After the elevator door had closed, Bernier said, *"Vache!"*

Tanaka didn't think Bernier would keep his job for long if she knew he'd called her a cow.

Bernier walked around the counter carrying the baggie at arm's length, as though he'd discovered a bag of anthrax. He entered a door behind the counter, and Tanaka could hear water running.

When he came back out to the desk, drying his hands on a paper towel, he said, "When I win the lotto I'll tell her where to shove that bag of dog shit. Just because you work for them they think they can treat you like dirt."

"Yeah, I know what you mean. It sounds like you have to put up with a lot of crap."

"You got that right."

"I guess they can be demanding?"

"They're all the same, them rich bitches. What we need is a socialist government to put them in their place."

Tanaka played it cool and said, "I imagine you're right."

"Now, where was I?" Bernier asked.

"You were telling me about entrances."

"Right...this is it."

"What about the underground parking? Can't people get in that way?"

"Only the owners. You need to know the code to get in that way, and to be on the safe side, we change it every year."

"So, if someone knew the code they could get in without you knowing?"

"No, they couldn't. See the screen here?" he said, pointing to one of the consoles behind the counter. "There's a security camera down there, and I can basically see everyone going in and out."

Tanaka looked at the monitor. The gate was closing. "So, was that someone coming or going?"

Bernier's cheeks flushed again. "It's that cow's fault. If she didn't give me that dog shit I woulda seen."

Yeah, and if you're not in the back room having a shot of bourbon, Tanaka thought.

"I imagine it must be pretty busy at times. It's a lot of work for one person." Tanaka pointed to the door behind the counter. "What if you have to use the facilities back there?"

"What if I have to use the facilities?"

"Yes. What if you need to take a leak? Who keeps an eye on things?"

Bernier looked over his shoulder and scratched his ear. "Well, I rarely have to go in there. I basically hold it until my relief comes in."

"So there might be the odd time when you have to go in there?"

"All the other guys do it."

"Thanks, Henri. You've been helpful."

Tanaka couldn't believe such a classy condominium would have such a marginal character working as a concierge. How had Bernier managed to get the job? If he were on the homeowners association, Bernier would be looking for a new job.

So much for security.

❖

Tanaka took the elevator to the penthouse floor.

He always carried his bag of equipment with him since he never knew what he'd need when investigating a crime scene.

Before he inserted the key, he pulled a flashlight from his bag and checked the lock. It was a good dead bolt and—just as Sadowski had said—it hadn't been picked. He opened the door and checked the jamb. It was clean.

He thought the place smelled musty, like his did when he got back from an extended vacation. He opened all the vertical blinds and windows, then did a quick tour of the condominium. Antiques filled the spacious suite. There were no signs of a struggle. He unlocked the balcony door and went outside. It was big and private. Obviously, no one could've entered the suite from that direction.

The roar of an engine caught his attention. A huge catamaran loaded with tourists, headed for Santa Catalina, was making its way out of the harbor.

He went back inside and carried out a thorough inspection. It felt strange to have unlimited time. Normally he had to rush through the search, hoping the owner wouldn't walk in the door. It didn't look like the suite had been cleaned since Warren's death. A thin layer of dust had settled on all of the flat surfaces. Two full containers of Starbucks coffee—cold and forgotten—sat on the coffee table between two suede sofas.

If the cops tossed the place, Tanaka thought, *they must've put everything back, because it's too neat. Did Winifred clean up after them? If she did, why did she leave the coffee cups?*

A DVD player sat below a large flat-screen TV mounted above the gas fireplace. He checked the stack of DVDs. He could never fathom why people bought movie DVDs. Once he'd seen a movie, that was it. None of Warren's movies was to his taste. The king-size bed in the master bedroom was unmade, as though someone had just gotten up. Only one side of the bed looked slept in. Tanaka pulled the top sheet down. There weren't any bloodstains, or any other stains, on the sheets.

From the end tables, three framed photographs stared at him. One was Winifred, one was a young man, and another was a man and woman. The woman looked like a younger version of Winifred, so he assumed it was a photo of Warren's deceased parents.

An Audemars Piguet watch lay on the bedside table. *It's worth more than my car*, Tanaka thought. *If someone was in the suite, it wasn't to rob the place.* The dresser drawers contained socks, briefs, running shorts, and laundered shirts. Giorgio Armani suits and Givenchy jeans filled the closet. *He didn't shop at Walmart*, Tanaka thought as he went through all the jacket pockets. Imelda Marcos would've been impressed by Warren's collection of Gucci loafers, oxfords, and the three pairs of Adidas. It was an imposing wardrobe, but not Tanaka's style at all. He was a Levi's and boots kind of guy. He only put on a tie when he wanted to make an impression on someone, and that wasn't often.

He had not seen a cell phone and was unable to find one in the suite.

As Tanaka turned to enter the bathroom, he bumped his elbow on the doorjamb and dropped his pen. When the tingling in his forearm subsided, he bent down to retrieve the pen. A rusty-brown stain covered a protruding screw head on the metal strip between the tiled bathroom floor and the bedroom carpet. It was hard to see. If he hadn't dropped his pen, he wouldn't have noticed it. *It sure looks like dried blood*, Tanaka decided. He got his digital camera out and took a number of shots from different angles. He washed and dried a knife from a kitchen drawer and then scraped the dried blood onto a clean sheet of paper. After folding the paper, he placed it into an envelope and wrote the details down on the envelope. The envelope went into his bag.

The bathroom vanity held the usual toiletries. Sitting on the counter were a box of unused disposable needles and a box of alcohol wipes. An empty biohazard container sat inside the lower vanity. A bottle of Ambien capsules, a package of NyQuil, and a bottle of Tylenol were in the medicine cabinet. The garbage can was empty. He found two more garbage cans in the suite, and they were both empty. The washer and dryer were empty. A shirt, a pair of socks, and a pair of Jockeys were the only items in the clothes hamper. There were no bloodstains on the shirt or shorts.

The smell of sour milk in the fridge was overpowering, so he emptied and rinsed the jug. The only unusual things in the fridge were a purple case and a gray case. Each case contained a different-colored gadget loaded with a cartridge of insulin. There were also two packages containing unused cartridges of insulin. One package held two new plastic-sealed cartridges while the other held one new plastic-sealed cartridge. He wrote down the names of the insulin. He felt out of his depth. He needed to do some research on diabetes and insulin.

In the second bedroom, all the drawers and the cupboards were empty. The den was set up as an office with a workstation in one corner, a StairMaster and treadmill in another. He opened the Murphy bed attached to one wall. The only thing in it was a mattress. The second bathroom was clean, and the cupboards were empty.

The answering machine was next. There were only three old calls. He recognized Winifred's voice, saying, "Hi, it's me, I'm on my way over with coffee." The other two were from the same guy. The first one said, "It's Jeremy. Hope you're feeling better? Call me when you can." In the second call the same voice asked, "What's happening? Why haven't you called? I'm worried, please call me."

The drawers in the desk yielded the usual utility bills, credit card statements, and a photocopy of a bill made out to Pratt James Easton from a car rental company, for a Lexus for two weeks in December of the previous year. Tanaka placed the credit card statements and the bill for the car rental in his bag. He couldn't find an appointment book, an address book, a checkbook, or a bankbook.

Tanaka turned on Warren's desktop computer. When it asked for the password, he called Winifred. "I'm at your nephew's condo. I need to get into his computer. Do you know the password?"

"As a matter of fact, I do. We had a good laugh when David told me what it was. We used to have a dog called Maverick, so he used that as his password."

Tanaka recorded the password in his notebook.

"Winifred, there are some other things I need to know. First, has the place been cleaned since your nephew's death?"

"No. Mrs. Perez used to clean David's suite every Friday, but I told her not to bother until I decide what to do about his condo. Do you think I should have her clean it?"

"No. Leave it for the time being. I'll let you know when I've finished checking it."

"Good."

"Do you know how I can get hold of her?"

"Well, actually she's my housekeeper, but I let her clean David's place every Friday. She'll be here all day tomorrow. If you'd like to speak to her you can come over."

"Good, I'll do that," Tanaka said.

"I won't be here tomorrow, I've decided to rejoin my bridge club, but I'll tell her to expect you."

"Were you here when the cops left?" he asked.

"Yes, I locked up after they were gone."

"Did you tidy up?"

"No. I didn't touch anything, I was too upset."

"Have the cops been back here?"

"Not to my knowledge—I think they would've discussed it with me, don't you?"

"Yes, I'm sure they would've."

"Was there anything else?" she asked.

"I can't find an address book. Do you know if David had one at home?"

"Yes, it should be in his briefcase. He always carried one around with him."

"How about an appointment book?"

"That would probably be at his office."

"I can't find a cell phone...I'm assuming he had one?"

"Yes. I tried calling him on it, but it was turned off."

"What's the number?"

He recorded it in his notebook. "Thanks. I'll look for the briefcase. One other thing. What did David do with his used needles?"

"He was always careful with them. He didn't want anyone accidentally sticking themselves, so he always used a sharps container... biohazard container. He dropped the full container off at the drugstore and at the same time, he picked up a replacement. It should be in the vanity of the en-suite bathroom."

"I'd like to find out more about diabetes and your nephew's insulin. Do you think it would it be possible for me to speak to his doctor?"

"I don't see why not. It's Dr. Hamilton-Jennings. I'll call her and set something up."

"Another thing, Winifred. There's a car key on the table in the hall. Is David's car still downstairs?"

"Yes, it's a black Lexus. It should be in stall thirty-four or thirty-five. He owned both stalls. I used to park in one when I visited him."

"Great. I think that's all for now."

"I'm anxious to hear what you think."

"I'll be in touch."

He tried calling Warren's cell phone, but there was no response. He looked for Warren's briefcase. It definitely wasn't in the suite.

Nothing in Warren's Microsoft Word files jumped out at Tanaka as being pertinent. He would have to take a closer look at them some other time. He clicked on the Outlook Express icon and opened Warren's address book. Warren hadn't entered any addresses, and his inbox seemed to be all spam. Tanaka wondered if there had been names in the address book and someone had deleted them.

Law-related tomes filled the bookcase. David Earl Warren's photo was in a yearbook from the UCLA School of Law. Tanaka stuck the yearbook in his bag. He paged through a photo album. One professional photograph, taken at a reception, showed Warren posing with another male and two females. The notation below the photograph stated *Margaret's fortieth birthday party—July 2007.* He placed the album in his bag.

After another quick look around to make sure he hadn't overlooked anything, Tanaka locked the suite and took the elevator down to the parking garage. He searched the dusty car. The only thing out of the ordinary was a door key, in a small envelope, in the glove compartment. Printed on the envelope was the number 9090. Tanaka checked the key against Warren's door key. It didn't match. He placed the envelope and key in his pocket.

As Tanaka walked back through the lobby, Bernier was completely engrossed in a real estate brochure, so he left without speaking.

Tanaka left the building thinking about the biohazard container. If Warren's suite hadn't been cleaned since his death, why was the biohazard container empty? Even if Warren had missed giving himself a shot the night of his death, wouldn't there be, at least, a used needle or two from the morning? *I definitely need to learn more about diabetes.*

CHAPTER EIGHT

The next morning Tanaka arose as usual at 6:00 a.m. and went for his daily jog along the trail around Lighthouse Point. His primary reason for jogging was to keep fit, but he also used the time to chew over work issues. His meeting with Winifred had opened up old wounds, so all Tanaka could think about during his jog was Patrick. Before Patrick's death, they had traveled all over North America competing in as many marathons as they could. Without Patrick's companionship and encouragement, jogging had become a lonely affair.

Tanaka arrived home after eight. There was a message from Winifred telling him she had made an appointment for 10:00 for him to meet with Dr. Judith Hamilton-Jennings, Warren's primary care physician.

He was in the waiting room for about five minutes before being shown into the doctor's office.

The lab coat and the stethoscope draped around her neck gave her a professional look. Her wrinkled face and silver hair made her look more like someone's seventy-year-old grandmother.

"So," Dr. Hamilton-Jennings said, "you want to know about David Earl Warren?"

"Please. Thanks for fitting me into your busy schedule."

"Winifred tells me you're looking into David's death, and I should answer all your questions."

"Yes. I'd appreciate your help."

"What do you want to know?"

"Can you tell something about diabetes so I can understand what happened to David?"

"It's a complicated disease, but I'll try to explain it to you in non-technical language." She settled back in her chair.

Tanaka opened his notebook and got ready to write.

"You know about insulin?" she asked.

Tanaka shook his head.

"It's quite complicated, really." She was silent for a few beats while she tried to decide how to explain it to Tanaka, then she said, "Insulin is a hormone secreted by the pancreas. The blood cells need insulin to convert our sugar intake into energy."

She paused while Tanaka took notes. "David was insulin dependent," she said when he looked up from his notebook.

"You mean he needed insulin to live?"

She leaned forward and rested her arms on her desk. "Precisely. We all do."

They stared at each other for a while. "Okay so far?" she asked.

He nodded.

"When diabetes goes untreated, severe complications can occur—"

"What kind of complications?"

"All bad, I'm afraid. Things like stroke, high blood pressure, heart disease, circulatory problems, and eye diseases, to name a few."

"It's a complicated disease," Tanaka said, jotting down the details.

"It certainly is."

Tanaka checked his notes. "What is ketoacidosis?"

"It's a severe complication of diabetes. Because the body cannot convert starches and sugars into glucose for energy, it breaks down fat into fatty acids and uses the fatty acids for energy instead. The fatty acids form ketones."

"Is this dangerous?" Tanaka said.

"Oh, yes. Untreated ketoacidosis leads to coma and eventual death."

"Do you know Winifred thinks David was murdered?"

"Winifred's a smart woman. She'd've made a great attorney—or a doctor, for that matter—so I think we should take it seriously."

"So you think it's possible?" Tanaka asked.

She sighed. "It's hard to imagine anyone murdering David. He was such a nice boy, and I was very fond of him." Tears welled up in her eyes. "What else do you want to know?" she asked.

Tanaka checked his notes. "There were two insulin gadgets and two types of insulin in the fridge. Was he on both of them?"

"He was on NPH and regular insulin. The gadgets you found are called insulin pens, they're much easier to use than syringes. Once you've loaded the cartridge, all you have to do is dial in the amount of insulin you want to inject and then inject it."

"What's the difference between them?"

"NPH insulin is long-acting. It takes about an hour and a half to start working and lasts for about eight hours. Regular insulin is short-acting. It starts to work faster and lasts a shorter time."

"How much did he take?"

"He was on a sliding scale. Every diabetic is different. The dose has to be individualized. It depends on the person's lifestyle, and more specifically, their diet and exercise."

"Was he well controlled?"

"Oh yes, very. I had trouble with him when he was a boy, but for years his blood sugar has been under control...so he must've been doing everything right. I find it hard to understand what went wrong. It doesn't make any sense."

"How did he know how much insulin to inject?"

She sighed. "He always checked his blood glucose in the morning and at night before retiring."

"How'd he do that?"

"He'd place a strip of paper in his glucose meter, prick a finger with a lancet, and put a drop of blood on the paper. The meter would then digitally display his blood glucose level."

"Glucose meter?"

She pulled a sheet of paper out of a drawer and handed it to Tanaka. "That's a glucose meter—the same as the one David used."

It was an advertisement for a glucose meter. Tanaka hadn't seen anything resembling the depicted meter in Warren's suite.

"You can keep that," she said, when Tanaka moved to hand it back to her. "I've got a stack of them."

Tanaka folded the sheet of paper and placed it in his pocket. "Say he checked his blood glucose at night and it wasn't normal, what would he do?" Tanaka asked.

"If his blood glucose was low he'd have a drink of juice to boost his glucose. If it was high, he'd give himself a shot of regular insulin. I'm making this sound simple, but in fact, it's not. Is it making sense to you?"

"Yes."

Dr. Hamilton-Jennings peered at him over the top of her reading glasses, as though she expected him to elaborate.

Tanaka didn't want to tell her what he was thinking. An alarm had gone off in his head. It wasn't just the absence of the glucose meter that had set it off, it was also the fact that Warren had neglected to properly monitor his blood sugar, which seemed totally out of character.

"If David hadn't taken his insulin, what would've happened?"

"If not treated, he'd have slipped into a coma and died."

Tanaka tried to absorb all the information she'd given him.

"Is there anything else?" she said.

"You're saying Warren was a well-controlled diabetic who looked after himself, and you have trouble understanding why he died in the manner he did."

"That's about it. However, of course, we weren't there and have only the forensic evidence to go on. I might add that at his checkup last month everything was fine. He was also in good spirits and there was no sign of depression, so if anyone's thinking suicide, I couldn't accept that. If his death wasn't accidental, then there's only one conclusion."

"I found a bottle of Ambien in his medicine cupboard, which you had prescribed. What was that for?"

She frowned, and briskly flipped through Warren's file. "Oh yes, I did prescribe Ambien some time ago. He was having trouble sleeping during his divorce."

Tanaka couldn't think of any more questions for the doctor. He tucked his notebook away. "Thank you, Doctor. You've been very helpful."

Tanaka left her office. His mind played back her words: *There's only one conclusion.*

CHAPTER NINE

Tanaka drove to Winifred's house to meet with her housekeeper. A short, stout Latina, probably about fifty-five years old and with her hair combed into a bun, opened the door.

"Señora Perez?" Tanaka said.

"*Sí?*"

"I'm Katsuro Tanaka."

"*Habla usted espanol?*" Perez asked.

"Sorry, señora. I don't speak Spanish."

"I speak not very well English," she said.

"We'll manage, I'm sure. Did Ms. Ross tell you I was coming?"

"*Sí*, Señora Ross tol' me you come see me." She held the door open for him. "I make the coffee...you wan'?"

"That would be great. I could do with a cup."

She led him out to a patio at the rear of the house. The backyard stretched up into the rugged terrain of the Sierra Madre Mountains. A grove of lemon, orange, and grapefruit trees formed a screen on the south side of the house, and on the north side, an extensive vegetable garden lay between the house and the white adobe wall surrounding the property.

An umbrella shaded four patio chairs and a table. Perez gestured toward the chairs. "I get coffee."

As he breathed in the sweet smell of citrus blossoms, Tanaka watched a young Latino fishing debris out of a kidney-shaped swimming pool.

When she returned, she poured him a cup of coffee. He added cream and sugar. "You want cookie?" she asked, indicating a plate of oatmeal cookies.

Tanaka took one and nibbled. It was still warm. "Nice."

"Today I make them. Jeremy, he like them."

"Jeremy?"

"*Amigo* for Señor Warren."

"They're delicious."

"The señora, she say you ask for Señor Warren."

"Yes, there are a few things I'd like to check."

She settled back in her chair, an expectant look on her face.

"How long did you work for Mr. Warren?"

She thought for a short while. "I work eight year soon."

"So you were with Mr. Warren before he married?"

"*Sí.* When the señor he move, the señora she say I clean for him Friday."

Tanaka picked up another cookie. "Can you think of anyone who might've harmed Mr. Warren, any enemies?"

A scratching sound at the patio door attracted their attention. They looked over. Rudolph sat with his nose pushed against the screen.

Perez rose and opened the door. Rudolph ambled over to Tanaka and rested his head on Tanaka's knee.

"He like you," Perez said. "He no like stranger."

"We know one another. It's the cookies. He thinks I'm a soft touch."

"Soft touch?" she asked.

"He thinks I'll give him a cookie."

"*Sí,* he like cookie."

"Can I give him one?"

"*Sí, uno.*" She held up a finger. "The señora, she say he no eat food for us."

Rudolph snatched the cookie out of Tanaka's hand. He begged for a while. When he realized he wasn't going to get another one he lay down, rested his head on Tanaka's boot, and closed his eyes.

"You ask for the señor?" she said.

"Yes. I was asking if Mr. Warren had any enemies."

"The señor, he very nice man, he no have enemy. He good to me and pay me good. He no have to, the señora she pay, but he like make me happy."

"How about Mrs. Warren? Was she also good to you?"

Señora Perez sipped her coffee as she considered his question. "I no like talk for her."

"I'm getting the feeling you didn't get along with her? You can be honest with me. It's just between the two of us."

She took another sip of coffee and set her cup down before responding. "I try hard, but she no like me. I not do nothing right. I wanna quit, but the señor he wan' me, so I stay."

"How did Mr. and Mrs. Warren get on?"

Tanaka could see she was having trouble with the question. She sighed. "Always they fight. It get big trouble before she go. She say bad things. A lady, she no speak like that."

"Did Mrs. Warren have any special male friends?"

Perez's faced flushed. She closed her eyes for a moment and sighed. "I guess I tell you, because you find out anyways."

"I can see you don't like talking about people, señora, but it will help me if you tell me."

She was quiet for a while, and then nodded, as if she'd reached a decision. "Señor one day, he telling the señora she...um, she screwing around." Her face flushed again.

"What did she say?"

"The señora, she laugh. She say he fine one talk."

"You think he had a girlfriend?"

"No, no. Not he, he never do that. But she...I think do it."

"Did you know the name of Mrs. Warren's lover?"

She shook her head. "I never hear name."

"I understand you cleaned Mr. Warren's suite on the day he died?"

"*Sí*, always Friday I clean. If I know he sick, I stay late. Maybe I help him." She pulled an embroidered handkerchief out of her apron pocket and dabbed her eyes.

"I can see you're upset, Mrs. Perez, but I'm sure there was nothing you could've done."

She sighed. "You right, I thinking."

The young man cleaning the pool approached the patio and said something in Spanish to Señora Perez. *"Un momento, por favor,"* she said, and walked over to him. They walked over to the vegetable garden. They chatted for a while and Perez pointed to some beds. She watched the young man rake the bed for a few moments before returning to the patio.

"He ask what he do," she said as she seated herself.

Tanaka checked his notes. "Can you tell me if there was a sharps disposal container in the bathroom that day?"

"A sharps...?"

"A can for his used needles."

"*Sí*, two he have in bathroom. The señor he tell me no touch, I no touch."

"Two of them?"

"*Sí, dos.*" She held up two fingers. "One he use, one he no use before one she is full."

"There were definitely two of them there that day?"

"*Sí, señor, estoy cierto.*"

"You saying you're certain?"

"*Sí, cierto.*"

Tanaka showed her the advertisement for the blood glucose meter Dr. Hamilton-Jennings had given him. "What about one of these, you ever see one?"

"*Sí*, I know that one. I buy same for the señor at drugstore. He keep in bathroom."

"Did you look in the fridge that day?"

"*Sí*, I clean Friday."

"Did you see the insulin?"

"*Sí*, she was there."

"How many were there?"

"They was two in one box and three in other one."

"You seem sure about that."

"Sure I sure. I check Friday. When he have one, I take paper to drugstore for more."

"A prescription?"

She nodded.

"You emptied the garbage cans?"

"*Sí*. Friday I put new bag."

"In all of the garbage cans?"

She nodded again.

Tanaka reviewed his notes. "Did Mr. Warren have many visitors?"

"I see only the Señor Jeremy, *y* Señor *y* Señora Easton."

"Did you notice any stains on the floor?"

"Stains?"

"You know...spots, like blood or something else."

"I vacuum and wash floors. Spots I no see. If spots, I use cleaner. I no see spots Friday."

"Did you notice any bloodstains on the sheets?"

"I no see blood. After to clean, I wash sheets and clothes for señor on Friday...everything she was fine."

Tanaka sipped his coffee. "Is there anything else you think I should know?" he asked.

She shook her head. "Why you ask these things? You no think he die...um, how you say, natural?"

"At this point I don't know. Ms. Ross has asked me to look into it, so that's what I'm doing."

Tanaka pulled out the key he'd found in Warren's car. "Do you recognize this key?"

She examined it and checked it against some keys she had in her pocket. She shook her head. "I no see before."

"Thank you, señora. I appreciate your help. I wish I spoke Spanish as well as you speak English." He stood up and shook her hand. "Mr. Warren was lucky to have had such a dedicated housekeeper."

"*Gracias, señor.* You very kind."

"*De nada, señora,*" Tanaka said.

She smiled. "You welcome, señor."

On the way out, he handed her one of his business cards. "If you think of anything that will help, please give me a call."

Why did someone remove one of the sharps containers, Tanaka was thinking as he climbed into his car, *and what happened to the other vials of insulin?*

CHAPTER TEN

Back at the office, Tanaka leaned back in his chair, pulled off his boots, and put his feet up on the desk. Sadowski's work phone number was on the speed dial, so Tanaka pressed the number.

"You again?" Sadowski said. "You calling to say hi?"

"No, there's something I need to know about Warren's condo."

"Thought so."

"Do you know if the investigating officer removed anything from the suite?"

"I had a look at the file after Gonzales finished with me. Figured you'd want to know more. Nothing was taken."

"Has anyone been back to the condo?"

"No. There was no reason to go back."

"Thanks, Rick. You're a lifesaver."

"Yeah, yeah," Sadowski replied before hanging up.

❖

The outside office door banged closed. Karen came bursting into the office. She threw her jacket at the coat rack, missed, swore, picked it up, and hung it on the rack.

"You get out the wrong side of the bed today?" Tanaka asked.

"My battery was dead."

"You talking about your car?"

"Smartass. I had to get the service station to replace it. Say, I had a thought, can I put the battery down as a business expense?"

"You think too much. You can try...but it won't fly."

"Wow! The man's a poet." She made a fist, raised a thumb in

the air, and winked. "How's your investigation into Warren's death going?"

While she was getting the coffee going, Tanaka gave her a detailed rundown on his talk with Bernier, about his findings in Warren's condominium, and about his subsequent meetings with Dr. Hamilton-Jennings and Mrs. Perez.

"I get the impression you think something's not right."

"There are too many loose ends and inconsistencies for me to accept the official verdict."

"Like what?"

"Okay. What happened to the used needles, and why was there less insulin in the fridge?"

"Hmm…Mrs. Perez sure they were there?" Karen asked.

"Yes, she confirmed they were there on Friday, so what happened to them?"

"Was she believable?"

"Yeah. She'd make a great witness if she had to testify."

"Warren may have thrown the vials of insulin in the glass recycling bin downstairs and taken the sharps container back to the drugstore."

"True…but he would've picked up a new container at the same time, and Mrs. Perez said she always looked after the insulin, so why would Warren suddenly change his routine?"

She nodded. "You also said his briefcase was missing, didn't you?"

"Yes, and his address book."

They were silent while she scribbled in her notebook.

She looked up at Tanaka. "What about the abrasion on Warren's back?"

"Think about it. Let me know if you come up with a reason for it."

She chewed on her delicately shaped lips. "Any ideas about what happened?"

"If foul play was involved, it must've been premeditated. I can't even figure how it could've been done, or what was done, for that matter. Someone could've entered the building—and not been seen by Bernier, in which case Warren would've either let them into his suite or they would've had a key."

"So it looks like the only people who gained from his death were Winifred Ross and Jeremy Townsend," she said.

"Right…except Margaret Warren assumed she was still in the will, so that doesn't let her off the hook. I think we can safely eliminate Winifred."

"I guess so."

"Of course, there could be other motives."

"Such as?"

"Revenge, love, jealousy, you name it. Perhaps to cover up another crime. Anything's possible. It doesn't have to be for financial gain. We need to determine who stood to benefit from Warren's death."

"You going to take on the case?"

"Yes…it'll be a nice change to have a client who won't care about the expenses."

She screwed up her mouth. "I think you're crazy. You left the police force to get away from this kind of violence, and now you want to get involved in a murder investigation?"

"I'll be okay," Tanaka said.

"I don't think so. Are you sure?"

"Yes, I'm sure. Now stop bugging me."

She shook her head. "I think you're crazy."

Tanaka knew she was right, but he wanted to do something different. He was tired of investigating insurance fraud. He missed the excitement of police work.

"It'll be all right," Tanaka said. He handed her the envelope containing the blood scrapings. "These are the scrapings from Warren's floor. Take them over to the lab and have them checked. If it's human blood, get the group type and call Dr. Hamilton-Jennings to see if it matches Warren's."

"Will do, Katsuro."

"Glad you came in today. I've missed your chitchat. Since Patrick died you're the only one who helps me cope with the downside of the job," Tanaka said.

Karen winked at Tanaka. "Does that mean I'll be getting a raise?"

He raised his eyebrows and turned his pockets out. The only thing in them was his keys.

"I guess not," she said.

"You got that right."

"Don't you and Steve discuss your cases?"

Tanaka thought about her question. Steve Hartman and Tanaka had been lovers for ten months. When they had first met, he had tried to discuss some of his cases with Steve, but Steve hadn't seemed interested. "He's not interested in them."

She never said anything, just looked at him.

"I'm going to drop in and see Margaret Warren," Tanaka said, "and I'll try to see someone at Warren's law firm."

"Anything else you want me to do?"

"I'll probably be tied up with this case for a while, so I'd like you to take over the other two cases I've been working on, and you might as well take a contract form to Winifred and have her sign it. You can collect a retainer at the same time."

"By the way," Karen said, playing with the Libra charm on her necklace, "I just read your horoscope for today. It says you've got a short fuse—so keep your mouth shut, unless of course it's to eat."

"I told you before, I don't believe that crap."

"I know, I know...but I do. I always plan my day around my horoscope."

"Well—if you insist, what else does it say about me?"

"Just the usual stuff, telling you to watch that stubborn streak you have."

"And what does it say about you?"

"That I'm going to be my usual pleasant and charming self," she said.

"I told you it was crap, didn't I? Now, where were we?"

Dimples appeared in her cheeks. "You've had enough? I should focus on the job at hand, you say?"

The aroma of freshly brewed coffee permeated the office. She poured coffee into two mugs and placed one in front of Tanaka .

"I need a caffeine fix. I was waiting for you."

She narrowed her eyes. "Like you don't know how to make coffee."

He reviewed the other cases with her and left them in her capable hands.

"Do you want me to pick you up for tae kwon do tonight?" she asked.

"Nah, it's okay," Tanaka said. "I'll see you there."

❖

Tanaka called Winifred. She was pleased to hear he was taking on the case. He informed her that Karen would be contacting her.

"While I've got you on the phone, Winifred, I'd like to speak to someone at David's law firm. Who do you think I should see?"

"Michael Easton would be the one. I mentioned before that David was friendly with him, and Michael became a partner in January, so he'll be able to tell you all about the firm. Do you want me to give him a call?"

"No thanks, I'll call and set up an appointment. I also want to see Margaret. You have her phone number and address?"

She did. Tanaka recorded it in his notebook.

Before hanging up he told her he'd be in touch when he had something specific to tell her.

Tanaka still wasn't sure if he was doing the right thing. He had a bad feeling—a premonition that things were going to go wrong. He hadn't thought about murder in a long time. The last homicide he'd been involved in was Patrick's, and he'd never gotten over that. If Warren's death turned out to be a homicide, would he be able to deal with the traumatic memories the process would evoke?

CHAPTER ELEVEN

While driving to Margaret Warren's condominium on the north end of Ocean Boulevard, Tanaka was formulating the questions he'd be asking her. He wondered if Margaret was as bad as Winifred maintained, or was it just that Winifred thought Margaret hadn't been good enough for her idolized nephew?

City work crews resurfacing the boulevard had parts of the road cordoned off, so traffic was heavy. As Tanaka waited for the flagman to wave him through, he watched two anchored sailing vessels gently bobbing about on the undulating aquamarine sea. The fog that had been around all morning was dissipating, slowly giving way to a bright, sunny afternoon. A tribe of Latino workers raked fallen palm fronds from the wide expanse of beach.

The rocks below the aquarium had become the temporary resting place for a group of homeless people. They'd parked two shopping carts loaded down with their worldly possessions at the rear of the building.

What a life, Tanaka thought as he relaxed in his car. *It's one thing to be homeless when it's warm and sunny, but an increased hardship during the winter. No wonder the poor bastards migrate here from the north. I'm glad I've never been in such a situation.*

Tanaka recognized Margaret Warren when she opened her door. She was one of the four in the photograph he'd seen in Warren's photo album. Today she wore her blond hair pulled back tightly into a plait that hung down her back. He knew she was at least forty-two. She looked a lot younger.

"Konnichiwa," she said.

"Konnichiwa to you," Tanaka said.

"Come on in," she said.

Her high-heeled knee-high black leather boots reverberated on the hardwood floor. He followed her down the hallway. *If she clomps around in those boots all day, I'm glad I don't live below her* went through his mind.

He took a seat opposite her on a black leather sofa.

"Well, Mr. Tanaka, you're quite the hunk. I was expecting an old oriental man, but you're what? Eurasian?"

"Something like that."

Her left eyebrow lifted, as if waiting for more.

She said something in Japanese.

"Sorry, I don't speak Japanese. *Konnichiwa* is the extent of it. I was born and raised in San Sebastian."

"That's a pity. I'm going on a trip to Japan next year, so I've been taking conversational Japanese classes. I thought I'd be able to practice on you."

"Thank you for agreeing to see me on such short notice," he said.

Her lips curled up as if she'd just sucked a lemon. "The only reason I agreed to see you was because I wanted to see what a PI looked like."

"Well," Tanaka said. "What do you think?"

"I wouldn't throw you out of bed. You're quite the hunk."

Lady, you'll never get the chance, he wanted to say.

"So tell me," she said, "do you have a big weapon?"

He didn't know her well enough to determine if she was serious or if it was a double entendre, so he said, "A big weapon?"

She smiled. "Is that a question, or an answer?"

"A question."

"Well then, I'll rephrase mine," she said. "Do you carry a big gun? Besides the obvious one in your pants, I don't see any other bulges."

This is not going to be an easy interview, Tanaka decided.

"I have a gun, but I don't carry it around with me all the time. I didn't think I'd need it today."

"What a pity. The thought of you carrying a gun turns me on."

He remained silent.

Margaret ran the tip of her tongue over her scarlet lips. "What exactly do you want to know about my dearly departed ex?" she asked.

"I've been hired to look into his death and—"

"I just knew that frustrated old cow was going to stir things up. What's there to look into? His death was accidental, so how come you're snooping about?"

"Sorry to upset you, but—"

"Who's upset? What makes you think I'm upset? I couldn't care less about his death."

"Sorry. I'm sure you're right, Mrs. Warren. His death was probably accidental, but I have to ask the questions. Perhaps if you help me I'll be able convince Winifred."

"Please, call me Margaret. I hate being called *Mrs. Warren*. It sounds like I belonged to that creep, and I certainly didn't."

"Sorry…Margaret. I wonder if you—"

She jumped to her feet. "I need a drink." She headed toward an antique Sheraton sideboard. "You want one?"

"No, not for me, thanks."

She poured herself a large Johnnie Walker Blue Label on the rocks.

Tanaka looked out of the picture windows. He could see her ex's building at the southern end of Ocean Boulevard.

She returned to her seat. "So what's Winifred been saying?"

Her short black leather skirt rode up her muscular thighs. He couldn't help staring at the cobra tattoo on the inside of her left thigh. She crossed her legs and winked at him when she saw him looking.

"Winifred seems to think David's death wasn't accidental and—"

"What crap. That horse's ass never looked after himself properly. He was a jerk. She's only doing this to get under my skin. She likes to put on a matronly look, but under the façade, she's basically a whore. I mean, what else do you call someone who has sex with her own nephew?"

Tanaka couldn't stop himself from laughing. "You can't be serious. Why would David want to have sex with an old woman like that? From the photos I've seen of him he looked like he could've had any woman he wanted."

Her voice rose an octave. "What? You've never heard of the Oedipus complex?"

"She seems like a nice old lady, I can't imagine her involved in something so tawdry."

"Boy, are you ever naïve. Where've you been hiding? You need to get out more. Trust me, Mr. Tanaka, they were screwing. He was always coming home late, smelling as if he'd just stepped out of the shower and refusing to tell me where he'd been. I knew he'd been to see her."

She rearranged her legs. This time he didn't look.

"Of course," she continued, "then he'd be too tired for sex. Look at me. Do I look like a woman who doesn't know how to keep her man happy? Our breakup was all that shrew's fault."

"I take it you were really pissed off at them?"

Her eyes darkened and narrowed. "Pissed off? That's putting it mildly. If I'd ever caught them in the act I would've killed both of them."

Usually Tanaka tried to maintain his cool during interviews and be as non-directive as possible. But because Margaret Warren was so obnoxious, he decided to give her the gears. "Are you trying to tell me you sat around moping while David was out screwing his aunt? I don't believe it."

A grimace crossed her face. "Who cares if you believe it?"

She'd stopped flirting.

"I would've thought an attractive woman like you would've had men falling over themselves to get to you?"

"You got that right."

"And yet you expect me to believe that while David was cheating on you, you were sitting at home twiddling your thumbs?"

"Who cares what you think?"

"So you're saying the divorce was all his fault?"

"That's what I'm saying. Do you have any other insights you'd like to share with me?"

"I'm wondering if some guy wanted to please you so much, he got rid of David for you."

"Why would anyone do that? I didn't inherit anything."

"No...but maybe, you thought you were going to."

Margaret stared at him and clenched her jaw. "How many more times do I have to tell you David's death was accidental? Are you thick or what?"

Tanaka just gazed at her calmly. Her jaw tightened and her hands gripped the chair arms.

"I take it your divorce wasn't amicable?"

"Amicable. That's the understatement of the year. I had to fight for every penny I got from that bastard."

"Did you contest the will?"

"You're damn right I've contested the will. I should've got everything, including the house, not that shrew, and on top of that, some unknown entity that he'd befriended gets a big chunk."

"Didn't Winifred own the house?"

She shook her head. "Warren didn't want to live there after we got married, so he bought the condo and let her live in the house."

"I can see why you'd be upset," Tanaka said.

"I'm glad you finally understand something."

Tanaka looked around the room at the expensive furnishings and original artwork. Some dump. He should be so lucky.

"Can you think of anyone who might've wanted David dead?"

Margaret emptied her glass and went for a refill.

She returned and sprawled back in her chair. Her skirt rose high enough for him to get a glimpse of her black panties. "What were you saying?" she asked.

"I was asking if you knew of anyone who'd want David dead." He felt like adding, *Besides you, that is.*

"I'm sure there must be a long list."

"Anyone specific come to mind?"

"Why don't you ask his assistant? I'm sure they were screwing around. Mind you, why he'd want to screw that mousy little thing when I was available defies logic."

"Do you mind telling me where you were on the night David died?"

She banged her empty glass on the coffee table. "What! You serious? You think I killed him?" she said, pointing to her chest.

"You're not a suspect, Margaret. I'm asking everyone the same question."

Margaret leaned back into her chair and placed the index finger and thumb of her trembling right hand over her closed eyes.

"What a crock of shit," she finally said, "but if it'll get you off my back I'll tell you. I spent that weekend at Pacific View Resort with a friend, and don't ask me his name because I won't tell you. When I got home I heard about David's death." She clamped her fists, as if she was ready to punch him. "Are you finished?"

"Just one more question. Do you still have a key for his condo?"

"A key? Shit, you don't give up, do you? If I were going to kill him I wouldn't have drowned him, I would've shot him."

She looked out of the window and tapped her foot on the floor.

"Well...do you?" he asked.

"Do I have a key? No, why would I have a key?"

"Because Warren didn't change the locks, and you had one."

She shook her head. "I threw it out."

Tanaka showed her the key he'd found in Warren's car. "You recognize this key?"

She examined it. "No. Should I? It's not for my suite."

"Thanks for your time, Margaret. I appreciate your assistance." Tanaka handed her his business card. "If you can think of anything that might help, please give me a call."

She dropped the card on the hall table and sneered, "Sure, but don't hold your breath."

What a bitch, Tanaka thought as he made his way back to his car. *I can see why Winifred thinks she's capable of murder.*

CHAPTER TWELVE

Tanaka had made an appointment to see Michael Easton, so he left Margaret Warren's condominium and drove to the law offices of Pratt James Easton, located in a high-rise on South Castillo close to Tanaka's own office.

Easton's corner suite on the tenth floor was three times bigger than Tanaka's. His shoes sank into the plush teal-colored carpet when he walked over to Easton's desk. The furnishings in the office were all teak. A sofa, two club chairs, and a coffee table were arranged in one corner of the room, and centered in front of a large picture window were a desk and a credenza.

Easton rose to meet Tanaka.

Tanaka recognized him. He was one of the foursome in the picture Tanaka had seen in Warren's photo album. Easton looked like he was dressed for a spread in *GQ*. His coal-black hair—probably touched up—was stylishly short and stiff. Not a blemish or wrinkle showed on his face, which looked tight as a new drum. He was at least forty-three but looked thirty.

Maybe I should save my money for future plastic surgery, Tanaka thought. *I wonder what he would say if I asked him for the name of his plastic surgeon?*

"Have a seat, Mr. Tanaka," Easton said, pointing to the chair in front of his desk.

I guess I'm not important enough for the seating area, Tanaka thought.

When Easton sat down behind his desk, six feet separated the two of them.

"My secretary tells me you want to talk to me about David."

"Yes."

"I'm wondering why a private investigator would be interested in him."

"I've been hired to look into his death."

Easton raised one eyebrow and grimaced. "His death? By whom?"

"I'm afraid that's confidential."

"This doesn't make any sense. David's death was ruled accidental and the case closed, so what could you possibly hope to gain by this investigation?"

"My client would like to be assured the police thoroughly investigated."

Easton leaned back and peered at Tanaka through his half-lowered eyelids. "I see. Okay, fire away."

"Would you mind telling me about the firm and about Warren's role here?"

"Certainly. We're a small firm of trial attorneys dealing mostly in criminal law. There are three partners and five associates…sorry, four."

Easton leaned forward, straightened the files already centered on his desk pad, and placed his gold Montblanc pen onto the pile. "I'd known David for a long time. He was the same age as me, but we went to different schools. We were never friends as children. The only time I saw him was when his parents visited mine. We did become friends in law school and shared an apartment. David was a good attorney, one of the best. He usually won his cases. If he'd lived he would've made partner."

Easton swiveled around in his chair and opened a drawer in the credenza.

While Easton was occupied, Tanaka checked the framed diplomas arranged in a grouping on a wall. A portrait of Easton and a woman hung alongside the degrees. She was the fourth person in the picture he'd seen in Warren's album.

Easton turned back to Tanaka and handed him a framed photograph. "That's David and I at our alma mater." Easton shook his head. "I put it away in the drawer because it upsets me to look at it."

The photo showed the two of them dressed in graduation regalia, arms around one another's shoulders and big smiles on their faces.

Easton closed his eyes for a moment. "It still saddens me to talk about David. I can't believe he's dead...I still expect to see him come walking into the room."

Tanaka knew the feeling. He often expected Patrick to walk into their bedroom.

Easton played with his monogrammed cufflinks and adjusted the Windsor knot on his regimental tie. "David and I were close. All of the attorneys and staff here will miss him. It was a real shock when I got back from Carmel and heard the news."

Tanaka waited a beat before asking, "You were in Carmel on January the thirteenth?"

"Yes. My wife and I drove there on Friday evening and we didn't drive back until Sunday night. I attended an educational session sponsored by the State Bar Association at the Carmel Rendezvous."

"That's a beautiful place. You stayed there?"

"Yes...only the best for members of the Bar."

"I understand David wasn't feeling well that Friday?"

"That's true, David wasn't his usual self. He felt bad all morning... thought he was getting the flu. He had the sniffles and had trouble concentrating. He thought it was because of the cold medicine he was taking. We managed to convince him he should go home and get to bed."

"Did you know he was a diabetic?"

"Of course. Everybody in the office knew he was a diabetic. It wasn't a secret. Nor was it a problem. I can't recall him ever being sick in all the years I've known him."

"Given the fact he was a well-controlled diabetic—and had been for many years—don't you find it a bit strange he died the way he did?"

Easton tilted his head to one side. "You find it strange?"

"Yes."

"Well, I don't."

Tanaka was quiet for a few moments.

"Is there anything else I can help you with?" Easton asked.

"Can you think of anyone who might've harmed him?"

Easton tapped his lacquered nails on the desk. "I'm not denying Warren had problems with some of his clients, that's the nature of our business. All criminal attorneys have some unhappy clients."

"So it's possible a client might've harmed him?"

Easton sighed. "I don't understand this insistence of yours that his death was not accidental. The coroner has already made a ruling and the case is closed. I do not, not for one minute, imagine David's death was anything but accidental. To be frank, Tanaka, you're wasting your time. I suggest you tell your client that."

"So you don't know of anyone with a grudge against him?"

Easton started paging through the top folder on his desk and let out a long sigh. "If you're wondering why I'm not enthusiastic about your investigation, Tanaka, it's because I can't believe anyone would've harmed David. He was a good friend, so stop trying to complicate a simple case of accidental death. Leave it alone and let him rest in peace."

Easton placed his forearms on his desk and leaned toward Tanaka. He was smiling. "Now, is there anything else?" His voice lacked warmth. He lifted his shirt cuff, looked at his Cartier watch. "I'm a busy man, Tanaka."

"Is it possible for me to speak with Warren's secretary?"

"Warren didn't have a specific secretary—the associates share legal secretaries—but he did have a young research assistant."

"Can I speak to her?"

Easton tapped his fingers on his desk for a moment. Tanaka thought he was going to refuse and was surprised when Easton said, "I don't see why not. But make it short. We run a tight ship here."

Easton pressed a button on his desk. "Miss Gray," he said when his secretary entered his office, "please take Mr. Tanaka over to Sally Ferguson. He'd like to speak with her."

"Yes, Mr. Easton," Miss Gray said, and backing out of Easton's office, bumped into an elderly-looking man. Her face reddened. "Sorry, Mr. Pratt, I didn't see you there," she said.

"That's quite all right, Miss Gray," he said.

Pratt looked at Tanaka. Tanaka extended his hand. "I'm Katsuro Tanaka, Mr. Pratt. I'm a private investigator. I'm looking into the death of David Earl Warren."

Pratt shook Tanaka's hand and withdrew it quickly, as if he'd been burned. "Archibald Pratt," he said.

Archibald Pratt was about five-eleven and two hundred pounds. His bald head, circled with a band of gray hair, gave him the appearance of a friar. Only the brown robe was missing. His sagging jowls, wrinkled face, and numerous liver spots put him in his early eighties.

Tanaka guessed that when you were the senior partner in a law firm, you weren't required to retire.

Pratt stepped away from Tanaka and looked at him through the bottom half of his horn-rimmed glasses. "I thought the police had put his death to bed," Pratt said.

Tanaka explained why he was there.

Pratt shrugged. "Well, I'm sure Michael gave you all the information you needed." He turned away and walked into Easton's office.

Nice meeting you too.

Miss Gray coughed. "This way, please," she said.

Margaret Warren had described Ferguson as mousy. *It must've been jealousy on her part*, Tanaka decided, *because she's not at all mousy—she's cute.*

Ferguson looked about eighteen years old. Her emerald-green eyes, mop of red hair, and smiling freckled face made Tanaka's day.

As soon as Ferguson heard why Tanaka was in the office, tears welled up in her eyes. "I'm sorry. I miss him so much. He was such a nice person."

"I'm trying to figure out what happened on his last day."

"How come?"

"My client doesn't believe his death was accidental."

Her eyes opened wide. "They don't?"

He shook his head. "I wonder if I can have a look at Mr. Warren's appointment book."

"It's not here. Mr. Warren must've taken it with him."

"Can you remember if anything unusual, besides his illness, took place on that day or the days preceding his death?"

Sally considered his question for a few moments. "No, not really. Nothing unusual."

"Any problems with clients?"

"Oh no, nothing like that."

Her gaze moved in the direction of Easton's office. Tanaka looked over his shoulder. Miss Gray was staring at them. "Sorry, but I have to get back to work."

"Sure," Tanaka said. "Just one thing more." He showed her the key he'd found in Warren's car. "Do you know if this key's for the office?"

"No, we don't use keys here. We have key pads and special codes for all of the doors."

"Would this be the code for the office?" Tanaka asked, showing her the envelope from Warren's glove compartment.

She shook her head. "Our codes are all five digits."

Tanaka gave her his business card. "If you can think of anything, Sally, please give me a call."

She glanced at the card and slipped it into her pocket. "Sure, Mr. Tanaka, I'll give it some thought."

Tanaka felt drained. Nothing he'd learned had changed his mind. He still felt Warren's death was fishy. He'd need to keep digging.

He decided to call it a day and went home.

❖

Tanaka's mother was in the kitchen when he arrived. The wonderful aroma of baked apple pie hung in the air. She was busy tossing a salad when he entered.

He gave her a light peck on the forehead. "You're spoiling us," Tanaka said.

"Nothing's too good for my two boys," she said, pulling some placemats out of a drawer and going into the dining room.

"I'll do that," Tanaka said, following her into the dining room. "You look tired. Why don't I pour you a glass of wine? Then you can put your feet up."

She smiled, ran a hand down his cheek, and said, "Thanks, Katska…you're spoiling me too."

She was relaxing in an easy chair when he took her a glass of chilled Pinot Grigio. She took a sip and smiled.

"You look like you've had a busy day," Tanaka said.

"Not really. I went to the library this morning, picked up Tommy after school, and we walked over to the harbor. The sailboats fascinate him."

"Maybe when he's older I should let him take some sailing lessons."

"That sounds like a great idea, Katska. He'd love that."

"I don't know what we'd do without you," Tanaka said. "Tommy must tire you out."

"Oh, Katska. How can you say that? I'd do anything for you and Tommy…after all, he is my only grandchild," she said, adding with a smile on her face, "and I don't think I'll be having any more…will I?"

Tanaka smiled. "He upstairs?"

"Yes…you going to tae kwon do tonight?"

He nodded.

"Dinner won't be long."

If she weren't in our lives, Tanaka thought, *how would Tommy and I cope? She provides a stable environment for us and gives Tommy the feminine input a growing boy needs. I need to tell her more often how much we appreciate her.*

He set the table and went upstairs.

Tommy was in his bedroom laying out the tracks for a train set. Tanaka was stunned when Tommy looked up at him and smiled. With his violet-colored eyes and mass of curly red hair, Tommy was a miniature Patrick.

"Hi, Daddy," Tommy yelled. "Look what Grandma bought me. You gonna help me?"

Tanaka sat down next to Tommy and gave him a hug.

"You're squeezing too hard," Tommy said with a giggle. "When I start tae kwon do we'll be matched."

They wrestled around on the rug for a short while, and then Tanaka let Tommy pin him.

"I love you, Tommy," Tanaka said.

A lump rose in Tanaka's throat when Tommy giggled and said, "I love you too, Daddy."

Tanaka wondered if Patrick would be pleased at the way he was bringing up their son. He hoped so.

"You wanna see my train?"

"Gran's just about ready to serve dinner," Tanaka said. "Let's wash our hands. I'll help you after we've eaten."

"Choo, choo, choo," Tommy yelled, and disappeared into the bathroom.

CHAPTER THIRTEEN

The next morning Sally Ferguson phoned and asked Tanaka to meet her at the Starbucks on the corner of Caballeros and Castillo.

While Tanaka waited, he sipped his cappuccino and watched the passing parade.

A couple of street kids with rings through their lips, noses, eyebrows, and who knew where else, carrying bulging backpacks and stuffed garbage bags—probably containing all their worldly belongings—crossed against the light with a dog of unknown heritage trailing behind them. They paid no heed to the traffic, and when one motorist honked his horn, they gave him the finger.

Sally took a seat at his table.

"You like something to drink?" Tanaka asked.

"No, thanks. I don't have time."

She looked around while she toyed with an onyx cameo suspended on a gold chain around her neck. She slipped an appointment book out of her purse. "I found this yesterday, after you left, when I was going through Mr. Warren's desk. He must've put it in there before leaving. I just assumed he'd taken it with him."

Tanaka leafed through the book. It looked like Warren kept a busy schedule.

"Mr. Pratt asked me to clean out Mr. Warren's desk and get the office ready for a new attorney."

"Thanks, Sally. I appreciate your help."

"You're welcome. I just can't understand why you're interested in Mr. Warren's appointment book. I know your client says there's something suspicious about his death, but I just can't believe it. He was such a wonderful man."

"Bad things sometimes happen to good people, Sally."

She nodded. "I guess so."

"It seems you were very fond of him, Sally."

Her face turned scarlet. "I must admit, I did like him—he was so cool and all—but he wasn't interested in me."

"Did he have any non-client visitors…someone special?"

"No, with him it was strictly business."

Tanaka watched her for a few moments. It was obvious she'd been besotted with Warren. She'd be a good source of information. "I think my client is right, Sally. There does seem to be something fishy about his death."

Tears filled her eyes. "You're not suggesting he was murdered, are you?"

"Things just don't add up, Sally. I do believe that's what happened."

"Who did it?" she asked.

"It's too early for that. I'm still looking into it."

"You think it was one of his clients?"

"Could be. What's your take on it?"

"I don't know…I can't really believe it. It's too far-fetched."

"There were never any problems in the office with clients?"

She thought for a moment. "Something weird did happen a few weeks before Mr. Warren died, but I'm not sure if it was with a client. It's probably not important."

"Please, tell me about it, Sally."

"Mr. Warren was working late. He needed some research done for the next morning, so he asked me to come in. When I arrived I could hear him shouting."

"Could you hear what he was saying?"

"Yes. He was saying something like, 'You're not going to get away with it. I haven't decided what to do yet, but believe me, I intend to do something.'"

"Who was in his office?"

"He was alone. I heard him bang down the phone." She looked around the coffee shop. "After he hung up, I waited for a few moments before going into his office. His face was red and he was breathing hard. He looked surprised to see me. He apologized and said it was just something he had to deal with."

"You don't know who it was he was talking to?"

"No, he never mentioned it."

Tanaka opened the appointment book to January 13, the day of Warren's death. He turned the book sideways so they could both read the entries.

"I've checked the whole book," Sally said. "Most of the appointments were routine, but there are two I'm unsure about."

"Which ones are they?"

She pointed to one on the evening of January 10. "That's one."

He couldn't read the notation. "What does it say?"

She laughed. "That's Mr. Warren's writing. I was always asked to decipher his writing. I guess because we were both southpaws it was easier for me."

She turned the book toward her. "It says Stanley Pearson at his place."

"Do you know Pearson?"

She shook her head. "I don't recall seeing that name before."

"You said there was another one?"

Her hand shook when she turned the page. "Here it is, on January ninth. This one says Robert Sadler at Lighthouse Point."

"You don't know that name either?"

"No, that one doesn't ring a bell either. It's weird too. I mean, why would he meet someone at Lighthouse Point at eight o'clock at night?"

Tanaka thought for while. It's one thing for an attorney to meet a client in his home, but in a park?

"Did you come across an address book in Mr. Warren's desk?"

"No, he usually kept that in his briefcase."

"He didn't leave his briefcase in his office, did he?"

"No, I'm sure he took it with him, he always did."

"Do you know if Mr. Warren rented a car for two weeks in December? I found a bill made out to the firm for a rental."

"No, I think…" She glanced around the coffee shop. Her eyes opened wide. "Oh, shit."

Tanaka followed her gaze. Miss Gray, Michael Easton's officious secretary, was walking toward the counter.

"I'm in for it now. Mr. Pratt told us he didn't want us talking to the media—or any one else—about Mr. Warren. He said all enquiries were to be referred to him. The Dragon Lady's sure to tell him about seeing me with you."

"Sorry if I've caused you problems, Sally. Do you want me to call and explain?"

"Oh, no. That would only make it worse. I better get going."

Sally pushed the appointment book toward Tanaka and left.

Tanaka watched her dash across the street. When she got to the sidewalk on the other side of the street, she made a wide detour around a fiddler wearing a Darth Vader mask and a black leather outfit.

The joys of living in paradise, Tanaka thought as he sipped his cappuccino.

He paged through Warren's appointment book and thought about the entries. *Who are Saddler and Pearson? Why did Warren meet with them outside his office? I'll have to find out.*

CHAPTER FOURTEEN

Winifred had arranged to meet with an official at Warren's bank, so on Wednesday afternoon, they entered the office of Cindy Merrill together.

"I was sorry to hear about your nephew, Ms. Ross. He was a fine man. I'm sure he'll be missed by all who knew him," Cindy said.

"Thank you, Cindy."

"What was it you wanted to know?" Cindy asked.

"I know David's account has been closed," Winifred said, "but we wondered if we could review his transactions for last December and January? Is that possible?"

"We can do that. Do you have his old bank card?" Cindy asked.

Winifred shook her head. "No. Can you do it without the card?"

Cindy nodded. Her fingers flew over the keyboard. "As you know, Ms. Ross, Mr. Warren had a number of investments with us, and a checking account."

"Could you look at his checking account and see if there were any unusual withdrawals for those months?" Tanaka asked.

"Sure...let's see..." She scrolled through the data. "It looks as though Mr. Warren had his monthly salary deposited and had automatic withdrawals for all his monthly costs including his utilities and credit cards. There are also routine debit card and ABM withdrawals. Oh, here's an in-branch withdrawal for ten thousand dollars on the ninth of January."

"Does it say anything else?" Tanaka asked.

"No, just cash."

"Any other withdrawals?" Tanaka said.

She continued her search. "Here's one. A check for one thousand dollars cashed on the fifth of January."

"Does it indicate who the check was made out to?" Tanaka said.

"No. I'll have to go through his file and pull his checks."

"Before you do that, would you please look at November and December?"

She tapped the keys. "The one-thousand-dollar check shows up every month, but there are no other large amounts."

"Can you find out who the payee was?" Tanaka asked.

"Sure. Give me a few minutes."

When Cindy came back into the office she said, "They were all made out to a Daniel Mitchell."

Tanaka wrote the name in his book.

"Anything else I can help you with?" Cindy asked.

"Did Mr. Warren have a security box?" Tanaka asked.

"I don't know," Cindy said. "I'll check for you."

When Cindy left the office Winifred said, "I never thought about it. I should've checked before. Did you find a key?"

"No, the only key I found was a door key I found in his car. It definitely wasn't a security box key. It's not for his condo or for your house, either."

"You found it in his car?" Winifred said.

Tanaka explained.

Cindy returned. "He does have one. Would you like to access it?"

"Yes, please, but we don't have a key," Winifred said.

"That's okay, I'll get someone to open it," Cindy said.

Winifred had to sign some legal forms and show her identification before they gained entry to the box.

The box was empty.

According to the records, Warren had accessed the box two weeks before his death, and on January 16, three days after his death and the first business day following his death. Someone had obviously forged his signature.

Winifred gasped. Tanaka and Winifred stared at each other.

Cindy looked at them for a few moments, then she said, "Is there anything else you'd like to know?"

"No, I can't think of anything else at the moment. Thanks for your help," Tanaka said.

As they left the bank, Winifred said, "Isn't that strange? I guess this proves someone wanted him dead."

"It looks that way."

"I've heard the name Daniel Mitchell before," she said. "I'm sure David did his undergraduate degree with him at the University of San Sebastian."

"Can you remember anything more about him?"

Winifred thought for a while. "Not really. There was something about him, though…"

"Can you think of any reason for the ten thousand dollars?"

"No. Why would David need that amount of money in cash? It was only four days before his death. What do you think it means?"

"I'm not sure. I didn't find any money or his wallet in his suite. It could be blackmail…but we shouldn't jump to conclusions."

"Blackmail! I find that hard to believe. I'm sure there wasn't any reason for him to be blackmailed."

"You're probably right, but we need to keep an open mind. When you spoke to David on the night he died, how did he sound?"

"Just tired."

"You're sure it was him?"

"Yes, it was David. Why do you ask?"

"I just want to make sure it wasn't someone impersonating him."

Her eyes narrowed and she tilted her head to the side. "Are you getting anywhere?"

"It's too early. There are still a number of leads I need to follow up. I'll give you a call next week."

"Thanks, Kats. I'm glad you decided to help me. I don't know what I'd do without you."

"Tell me, Winifred, did David ever talk about a Robert Sadler or a Stanley Pearson?"

"No, I don't think I know them. Are they involved?"

"I'm not sure. Just two names that showed up in David's appointment book I need to check out." Tanaka showed her the key and envelope he'd found in Warren's car. "This is the key I was talking about. Do these numbers mean anything to you?"

She examined them. "No. Do you think it's an alarm code?"

"Could be…I'm not sure."

She shook her head. "I don't know…I hope I've done the right thing?"

"Sure you have. We'll find out what happened to David."

❖

Tanaka was on the way to the parkade to pick up his car when the City Hall chimes reminded him he hadn't eaten all day. He was just about to cross the street when Karen appeared on the sidewalk.

"Where are you off to?" she asked. "You not working today?"

"I'm going to pick up my car and drive to the Seafood Shack for lunch. You eaten?"

"No, I was going to give it a miss. I need to lose weight."

"Oh, please," Tanaka said. "Like you need to lose weight. Join me. I could do with some normal company."

"You're the boss."

They picked up Tanaka's car and drove to the wharf.

While they waited for their food—a salad for Karen and fish and chips for him—Tanaka told her about his visit to the bank.

"So, it looks as though Warren was being blackmailed. But surely the blackmailer wouldn't have killed him. I mean, why would he do that? That would be like cutting off the hand that feeds him," she said.

"Or her. It didn't have to be a him."

They stopped talking while the server delivered their food.

"What if Warren threatened to turn him in? He might've decided that was the only way out," Tanaka said when they were once again alone.

She smiled. "Or her."

"Touché."

"I wonder what was in his security box?" Karen said.

"It must've been important for him to take that chance," Tanaka said.

"Aha," she said.

"Okay, I agree. A male must've been involved."

"Yeah, but there could've been two of them, a he and a she."

Tanaka nodded. "You have a security box?" he asked.

"Yeah."

"What's in it?"

"My will, my passport, and insurance papers…the usual stuff."

"There we go," Tanaka said.

She leaned over, snatched two of his French fries, dipped them in the ketchup on his plate, and shoved them into her mouth.

"I thought you were on a diet?" Tanaka said.

"I am, but there's less calories when it's on your plate."

Tanaka pushed his plate over to her. She tucked in.

"Here comes another big shot," she said, pointing with a red-tipped French fry.

Tanaka looked in the direction she was pointing.

A cutter, over forty feet long, the Stars and Stripes fluttering at its stern, inched up to a mooring.

"I could go for a life like that," Tanaka said.

"Not me, I prefer terra firma."

They watched for a while, and then she said, "Did you ask about security cameras while you were there?"

Tanaka smiled when he saw she had eaten all the French fries. "No. I wanted to think about it first. I wasn't ready to point out to Cindy that Warren was dead on the sixteenth, so he couldn't have accessed the box."

"Well—with your stomach full, are you ready to ask her now?"

"I want to talk to Winifred first. Anyway, the bank will probably ask for a court order before letting me review their tapes. You know how touchy they are about privacy."

Tanaka paid the bill and they left the restaurant.

On the way to the car, a black cat meandered across the sidewalk in front of them. Karen stopped dead in her tracks. "That's a bad sign."

Tanaka shook his head. "It's a cute little cat."

"I'm not taking any chances," she said, grabbing Tanaka's arm and dragging him across the street.

When they were in the car, Tanaka said, "I'm not hanging around this afternoon. I'm going out to Steve's. I haven't seen him this week."

"I'm going to a psychic reading tonight," Karen said. "I want to see what's in store for me. You want to come?"

Tanaka shook his head. "No way. I'll see you in the morning."

CHAPTER FIFTEEN

Tanaka called his mother to let her know he wouldn't be home for dinner, picked up a couple of bottles of Merlot from his favorite wine store on Amado, and headed to Steve Hartman's house.

Steve's house in Pacific Heights, built in a Frank Lloyd Wright style, overlooked the San Sebastian Harbor. It was the kind of home you'd expect a successful attorney to own—especially one with a rich father. The side of the house fronting the road was single level; however, the side overlooking the harbor was two stories, with a den and guest room below the main floor. A cantilevered deck jutted out over the cliff. A glass solarium covered the south end of the deck, and on the north end, wooden stairs descended to the lawn.

There was at least five hundred yards between Steve's house and his closest neighbor, and it was quiet and lonely. A variety of pine trees and deciduous broadleaf trees surrounded the house, blocking out the sunlight. Tanaka shivered when he exited his car. It was always a few degrees cooler here in Pacific Heights than in the center of the city.

When Tanaka opened the front door, Steve's black Lab, her leash between her teeth, came bounding up, nearly knocking him off his feet with her exuberance.

He bent down to scratch her neck. "No, we're not going for a walk, Sheba. I've got things to do. I'll let you out for a while."

As he watched her scamper around, circling and circling until she found the right spot, a gold-colored '79 Pontiac Trans Am crept past the driveway entrance. Tanaka recognized the make and model because he'd owned an identical car before he'd hooked up with Patrick. He wondered if the driver was casing the joint. The car was too far away for him to get a glimpse of the driver or the plates.

Probably just my suspicious mind, he concluded.

After he'd let Sheba back in, he went into the kitchen to prepare dinner. Steve had asked him to cook. Tanaka didn't like cooking, but Steve liked macaroni and cheese, and knew it was one of the few things Tanaka didn't mind preparing.

Once the dish was in the oven, Tanaka opened a bottle of wine to let it breathe and made a salad. While he was setting the table, the garage door opened and closed. Sheba scrambled toward the connecting door, her paws slipping and sliding on the tiled floor.

Tanaka turned to watch Steve enter the dining room. In many ways, he reminded Tanaka of Patrick. However, he was unique. He had the same muscular body and at five-eleven was the same height. His most striking feature was his red hair, which he styled in the not-combed look, and his electric-blue eyes. Like Patrick, he used Calvin Klein's Obsession. The distinct scent had immediately attracted Tanaka when they had first met at the courthouse.

He often marveled at how they'd connected. Their backgrounds were polar opposites. Steve had been raised in the upper echelons of San Sebastian society, whereas he was a scrapper from the south side.

Steve smiled at Tanaka, kicked off his loafers, ran a hand through his hair, dumped his briefcase and jacket on a chair, and said, "You're supposed to be naked and barefoot when you're in the kitchen."

"I'm scared I'll burn my dick."

"If only it were that long," Steve said.

"You've never complained before."

Steve smiled, bent down and scratched Sheba's neck.

"You look tired," Tanaka said.

He nodded. "I am. It smells good in here."

"I thought I'd shower and use some deodorant for a change."

"Not you, silly, the food. Mind you, you don't smell too bad yourself."

They hugged and kissed. Tanaka placed his hands on Steve's butt and pulled him close.

"Let's forget dinner and go straight to bed," Tanaka said.

"My, aren't we impatient," Steve said.

"What do you say, Stevie?"

Steve broke away. "Stevie says he's going to take a shower, and you're going to behave yourself."

Resisting the urge to join Steve in the shower, Tanaka carried the open bottle of wine and two glasses out to the solarium and relaxed on the sofa. As he pulled off his boots, he watched a white sloop, blue sails billowing in the breeze, tack back and forth as it made its way toward the harbor.

When Steve joined Tanaka in the solarium, he stood at the windows and looked out over the harbor. "I love watching the fishing boats bringing their day's catch into harbor," he said after a few moments.

The plaintive cawing of seagulls disrupted the silence.

"Look at the gulls waiting for a handout," Steve said.

"They're noisy and messy."

He joined Tanaka on the sofa, tasted the wine, and snuggled up to him. "Nice. I've been looking forward to this all day."

"Me too," Tanaka said. He felt completely relaxed. Steve often had a calming effect on him.

Steve sipped his wine.

Tanaka massaged Steve's neck and rested his face on Steve's damp hair. "You have a busy day?" he asked.

"Uh-huh. I've been in court most of the day. The two cases I told you about."

"How'd it go?"

"The Bergen case has been remanded, and Wesley has to be in court again tomorrow. What about you…been busy?"

Tanaka told him about Winifred hiring him to look into Warren's death.

"I read about his death in the *Gazette*," Steve said.

"Did you know him?"

"No."

"How about Easton? You know him?" Tanaka asked.

"Yeah. I've spoken with him and his wife at social gatherings. They seem like a nice couple. He received some kind of award a few months ago. I think it had something to do with him donating funds to a women's center. Rumor has it he's going to be appointed to the state appellate court."

"How does one get appointed? I thought you had to be elected."

"The governor appoints people to fill vacancies that occur mid-term. He has to appoint someone to replace a judge elevated to the superior court."

Steve rested his head against Tanaka's shoulder. "What else have you been up to?" he asked.

"Nothing much."

"I was expecting a call from you last Sunday. You sure you didn't go out?"

Tanaka pulled away from him. "I feel like you're cross-examining me, Stevie. You're spending too much time in court. I told you I'd be spending the weekend with Tommy."

"Sorry, I didn't mean for it to sound that way—I missed you... that's all."

He nestled against Tanaka.

As they sipped their wine, they watched the amber sun disappear below the horizon. The buzz of the oven timer disturbed the tranquility of the evening. They carried their glasses into the dinning room and sat down to dinner.

❖

After dinner, flashlights in hand, they took Sheba for a walk around Pacific Heights.

When they were back home, Steve put on a Gershwin CD, and they settled down on the den sofa.

Steve lay back, his feet resting on Tanaka's lap. He liked having his feet rubbed, so Tanaka obliged.

Sheba lay on the floor dozing, her eyes occasionally opening when they spoke.

Steve rubbed the sole of his foot against Tanaka. "It feels like something big's come up. Do you want to go into the bedroom and fool around?"

Tanaka laughed. "I haven't heard that expression since high school."

Steve held Tanaka's hand and led him into the bedroom.

Afterward, when they were relaxing on the bed, Steve asked, "Did Patrick do the things to you that I do?"

What the hell, Tanaka thought. *Why does he always have to bring up Patrick?*

"Stevie, please—"

"Sorry. I know you don't like talking about him. I won't bring it up again."

It was too late. The mood was broken. All Tanaka could think of was Patrick.

"Have you thought any more about moving in?" Steve asked.

Here we go again went through Tanaka's mind. He didn't want to get into the same old discussion with Steve. Maybe he could steer the conversation away from the topic.

"You should see Winifred's mansion. She must really be loaded," Tanaka said.

"Did you hear what I said?" Steve asked.

"Yes."

"And?"

"Aren't you happy?" Tanaka asked.

"I just think things would be better if we lived together," Steve said.

"I'm not ready for that kind of commitment, Stevie. I wouldn't want to move Tommy. He's had enough problems in his young life without having to adjust to a new environment. What about my mother? I was Tommy's age when my mixed-up old man took off and left her to bring me up alone. I'm not about to move and leave her all alone. She'd be devastated. After Tommy, she's the most important person in my life."

Steve lifted his head and gazed into Tanaka's eyes. "So we should carry on this way?"

"I'm happy with the way things are. I'm sorry if you're not."

"I guess I'm being greedy. I just want you here all the time."

"Can we leave things the way they are for a while?"

"Sure," Steve said. "But promise me you'll think about it."

"Anyway, you know me, Stevie. I like visiting you up here in the clouds, but I'm a city boy. I can walk everywhere from my house in North Beach, but you have to drive everywhere, even for milk."

Steve gave him a long, appraising look.

He never mentions he could move in with me, Tanaka thought. *Maybe he's not into raising children? I'm not going to ask him. I better change the subject.*

"Have you decided what you want to do about your birthday yet?" Tanaka asked.

"Not really. I'm just as vain as you are. I don't want to celebrate the fact I'm turning thirty-five."

Tanaka laughed at him. "You're still a baby...wait till you get to my age. Give it some thought. Maybe we should go to Vegas for a few days."

"I'll think about it."

Steve lay on the bed, watching him dress. He slipped into a robe when Tanaka was ready to leave.

They embraced at the door.

"See you Saturday?" Steve asked.

"Yeah, I'll be over. Don't forget to set the alarm, Stevie. I worry about you being here on your own."

"Oh please," he said, "I'm a big boy, I can look after myself. Anyway, I always put it on. Besides, Sheba is here to protect me."

"Some protection. She'd probably lick an intruder. By the way, the alarm wasn't set when I got here, so be careful."

❖

When Tanaka arrived home, he went into Tommy's room to check on him. Tommy looked so tiny curled up in his bed, clutching his G.I. Joe.

Tanaka stared at the framed photo of Patrick on the bedside table. He picked it up, and examined it. *Why did you have to leave us, Patrick? We miss you so much.*

He watched Tommy for a few moments, kissed him on the forehead, and went into his own bedroom.

Tommy would always come first with him.

CHAPTER SIXTEEN

On Thursday morning, Karen and Tanaka were in the office reviewing the case. Tanaka took a sip of coffee and reached for another doughnut. They were devouring them at a rapid rate. He took a big bite. Tanaka didn't ask her about her diet.

"Delicious," Tanaka said between chews. "I'll have to jog an extra mile tomorrow."

"You got that right. You know the old saying, 'Short on the lips, long on the hips.'"

"Well, you certainly don't have to worry," Tanaka said as he reached for another one. "Not with your skinny body. You seem to burn off the calories faster than you eat them."

She narrowed her eyes. "Skinny? I'll have you know I'm all muscle. I'm butch."

He didn't really think she was skinny, and she certainly wasn't butch. She was feminine and had the kind of body many women strive to achieve.

"How did the psychic reading go?" Tanaka asked.

"Not good."

"Why?"

"The Grim Reaper appeared twice in my Tarot card reading. It's supposed to mean the conclusion of an area in my life, and the beginning of a new area, but I see it as death."

Tanaka sighed. "I wish you wouldn't put so much faith in those psychic readings, Karen. They'll drive you crazy."

She shrugged. "I believe in them, okay? We haven't talked about your interviews with Margaret and Easton yet. Did you manage to see them?"

"Yes." He paged through Warren's photo album and showed her the group portrait of David Earl Warren, Margaret Warren, Michael Easton, and Easton's wife.

"Nice cozy group," she said.

"It looks that way, doesn't it—but it didn't last."

They talked about his meetings with Margaret Warren and Michael Easton.

"She sounds like a real bitch," Karen said. "I wonder what sign she is?"

"There's a sign for bitchiness?"

She rubbed her chin. "Do you think Margaret could've done it?"

"At this point I haven't even figured out what was done. I'm just sure something was done."

"So we're looking at means and opportunity for something?" she said.

"Right. I know that's vague, but that's all we have. I'm sure Margaret could've killed him. She obviously hated him, and I had trouble believing her. Something was off. Her body language didn't jibe with her verbal cues, and she often stalled before answering my questions."

"Does she have an alibi for the time?"

"Yes, she says she was at Pacific View Resort that weekend. We'll have to verify that."

"What about Easton?"

"He seemed genuinely upset about Warren's death—they went to law school at UCLA together—but he also came across as controlling."

"Maybe that was just the attorney in him?" she said.

"He's probably practicing for when he's a judge."

"A judge?"

"Yeah," he said, and told her about Steve's comments.

"What was the name of the guy who was getting a thousand a month from Warren?" Karen asked.

Tanaka leafed through his notebook.

"Mitchell...Daniel Mitchell. We need to find out who he is. Can you look into it?"

She nodded. "You know anything about him?"

"Winifred thinks Warren did his undergraduate degree with him. Give her a call and see what she can tell you."

"Will do, Katsuro."

He told her about his get-together with Sally Ferguson and showed her the two names Sally identified.

"You've been busy," Karen said.

"I have. I'll check them out with Sadowski."

"You spoken to Winifred yet about the security tapes at the bank?"

"I'll do it now."

Tanaka picked up the phone and called Winifred. He explained about the security tapes. She agreed they should try to review them, and she'd call the bank to speak to Cindy.

"Why didn't you ask her about Mitchell?"

"Oops, must be getting senile in my old age."

She shook her head, rolled her eyes, and said, "So, what's next?"

"I'll arrange for Stevie and me to spend Saturday night at Pacific View Resort to confirm Margaret's alibi. I'll meet with Jeremy Townsend next week to see what that's all about."

When Karen went into the outer office, he called Sadowski and asked him if he could check to see if Townsend, Mitchell, Sadler, or Pearson had any priors.

Sadowski called back later. "You owe me big for this. Sounds like you're keeping good company these days. There's no record for a Daniel Mitchell or a Jeremy Townsend, but the other two characters both have sheets." The sound of shuffling papers came across the line. "Pearson beat up and robbed a gas station attendant. He's also been arrested a couple of times for operating a grow-op and for dealing. His last stint inside was for possession. He's been out for six months. Seems to have been clean since then, but I doubt it."

"He doesn't sound like the reforming type, does he?"

"Never met one yet," Sadowski said. "Sadler assaulted and robbed a couple of gays. He served eighteen months. He's been out on parole since September."

"You have their ages?"

"Pearson's twenty-eight and Sadler's twenty-five. They've both got many years of crime ahead of them, I'm sure."

"Any current addresses on them?"

"You could try Sadler's probation officer."

"Do you know who it is?"

"Uh-huh. You remember Jack Turner?"

"Sure. The tall guy with the shaved head?"

"That's him," Sadowski said.

"Thanks, Rick. I owe you. I'll take you out to McDonald's one of these days."

"What. You think I'm easy? It'll take more than a meal at McDonald's to keep me happy. The San Sebastian is more my style."

"Sure. I can see us at the Sebastian. People will start talking about us."

"Has this got anything to do with Warren's death?"

"At this point, all I have are names that've surfaced in the case. If something comes up I'll let you know."

Tanaka couldn't help smiling. The old turn-of-the-century hotel was definitely not their style. There was no way he could see them sitting in the Sebastian—with pinkies raised, sipping tea from fragile china cups. Sipping ale and chomping on peanuts in Skipper's on the wharf was more their thing.

Maybe I should come clean and tell Sadowski about my suspicions? Tanaka thought. *But then he might take the case away from me, and I don't want that to happen. I'm enjoying myself too much.*

CHAPTER SEVENTEEN

On Thursday afternoon, Tanaka found his way to the office of Jack Turner, the probation officer.

"Hi, Kats," Turner said. "Long time no see."

"Yeah, it's been a while."

Turner shook Tanaka's hand. "How's it been, going private?"

"Great. Nothing like being your own boss."

"You got that right." He cleared a chair for Tanaka and sat behind his desk. "I was sorry to hear about Patrick, Kats, he was a great guy."

"Thanks, Jack."

Turner closed a file he'd been reading. "As you can see," he said, pointing to the pile of file folders on his desk, "things haven't changed."

"I guess you'll always have a job."

"That's true. Now, what can I do for you?"

"I'm on a case, and the name Robert Sadler has come up. What can you tell me about him?"

"Don't tell me he's violated the conditions of his parole."

"At this point I don't know," Tanaka said. "I'd just like to find out something about him."

Turner retrieved a file from a filing cabinet and leafed through it. "He's a nasty character. Beat up a couple of gays in Lighthouse Park."

"Just for the fun of it?"

"The usual story. He says they tried to pick him up, and because he's straight, he flipped. They say he joined them in a threesome and demanded money. When they refused to pay him, he went berserk, gave them both a severe beating, and took off with their wallets."

"Sounds like a real winner," Tanaka said.

"You got that right."

"You know where I can find him?"

"Well now, you know my files are confidential."

"I won't divulge my source," Tanaka said.

Turner tapped his pencil on his desk for a few beats. "I'm going down to pick up my mail. I know you're not going to do anything illegal while I'm away from my desk."

When Turner left his office, Tanaka scanned the file and wrote down Sadler's home address and his place of employment.

Tanaka was standing at the door when Turner returned.

"Nice seeing you, Kats. You'll let me know if you discover any violations?"

"Sure," Tanaka said, shaking Turner's hand. "And I'll try to get his address some other way."

❖

That evening, Tanaka was in the underground parking garage where he usually stowed his car. As he approached his parking spot, he noted the area around his parking stall was in darkness. It was usually well lit, so he went on high alert. He checked between the cars in the area and went down on his knees to check under them. The place was silent and deserted. He shivered when a sudden gust of wind blew through the garage.

Tanaka straightened up and inched closer to his car.

Headlights appeared out of nowhere, blinding him. The growl of a V8's exhaust and the squeal of rubber on the concrete floor set his heart into overdrive.

He leaped between two parked cars. He wasn't fast enough. The passenger side of the speeding car brushed against his leg, sending him reeling over the hood of a parked car.

He spun around. A gold-colored Pontiac Trans Am—still accelerating—tore down the exit ramp. It was going too fast for him to see the plates or driver.

The smell of burnt rubber and exhaust hung in the air.

Luckily I wasn't seriously injured, Tanaka thought. *I'll need to be more vigilant in the future or I'll end up dead like Warren.*

❖

At 7:00 p.m., Tanaka drove to the squash club to meet Sadowski for their regular Thursday-night game. Tanaka was hoping to win back the twenty dollars he'd lost at their last encounter, but he knew that wasn't going to happen. Sadowski was unbeatable. Sadowski won the toss, and knowing Tanaka's backhand wasn't good, he elected to play from the left service box, putting Tanaka at a disadvantage right at the start.

Sadowski was an excellent all-round player, particularly good at attacking, while Tanaka tended to be a retriever. Sadowski dominated the "T" and, being a master at placing the ball, had Tanaka running around the court, keeping him off balance until Sadowski had him worn out.

After three games, they went into the restaurant, perched on some stools, and ordered a couple of energy drinks.

"Well, I guess you owe me another twenty," Sadowski said.

"This is getting too expensive for me. I don't think I'll place any more bets for a while."

Sadowski grinned. "How's your investigation going?"

"Haven't come up with anything solid yet."

"I've been doing some thinking about the case, and I've reviewed the file. It does sound a bit fishy when I think about it. Maybe if the coroner hadn't been so hasty we would've dug some more."

"I don't want to get you in trouble, Rick, but do you mind me asking you some questions about Warren?"

"I knew you still had questions. What are they?"

"Were there any drugs or alcohol involved?"

Sadowski shook his head. "No. They found some traces of Ambien in his blood, and he was taking an over-the-counter cold medicine, but the pathologist didn't think they contributed to his death. No trace of drug paraphernalia or other drugs in the suite."

"Anything else I should know?"

"Not really. There was no evidence of foul play."

"Thanks a lot, Rick. I appreciate the info."

"You just make sure you let me know if you come up with anything. I'll reopen the case if I have to."

"Will do, Rick."

Tanaka's muscles were aching when he finally got home. He took a couple of Tylenol and had a hot shower, after which he went into Tommy's room. He watched him for a few minutes, kissed him on the forehead, went into his own room, and climbed into bed.

The incident with the Trans Am kept playing in his mind. *Who was driving the car? Why did he try to run me down?*

It took a while before Tanaka slept.

CHAPTER EIGHTEEN

The next morning Tanaka drove to the garden center where Robert Sadler worked.

A middle-aged woman singing "Hey Jude" watered hanging plants in the store. The flower pinned in her long gray hair, with the large hoop earrings and ankle-length denim granny dress, gave her the look of a 1960s Haight-Ashbury hippie frozen in time.

"Hi. How you doing?" she said in a melodic voice. "You after some flowers for your honey? I've got some really nice roses. Or maybe you'd like a mixed bunch?"

"Sorry, I'm not looking for flowers. I'm looking for Robert Sadler. Is he working today?"

The smile disappeared from her face, and she gave a long sigh. "What's he been up to now? I hope he's not in trouble again?"

"No, I just need to speak with him. Will that be a problem?"

She shook her head. "Like I could stop you from speaking to him. What's he done this time?"

She probably thinks I'm a cop, Tanaka realized, and decided not to disillusion her.

"It sounds like you know him quite well?" Tanaka said.

"I should. I'm his mother." Tears formed at the corners of her eyes.

"He's been a handful?"

"Maybe if he'd had a father to keep him in line things would've been different."

"It must've been hard for you—I know what it's like being a single parent."

She nodded and blotted her eyes with a paper towel.

"Maybe if you talk about his problems it'll help."

"I told the social workers about everything, but it didn't help."

"What kind of problems are you talking about?"

"Why should I tell you?"

"It would help me to understand him."

She toyed with the glasses hanging on a cord around her neck, looked over her shoulder, and said in a quiet voice, "He didn't have it easy growing up."

"I can imagine it must've been hard for you."

"Oh, yes. I had my hands full, let me tell you."

Tanaka remained silent.

Mascara-laced tears flowed down her cheeks. "It was all my fault."

"Your fault?"

She blew her nose on the paper towel. "Yes. I didn't know a male friend of mine was abusing him."

"You mean sexually?"

She nodded.

"I can see why you'd feel guilty, because he was a friend of yours, but surely you can see it wasn't your fault?"

"I keep telling myself that, but it doesn't make it any easier." She began arranging a vase of lilies.

"What happened to your friend?" Tanaka asked.

"He committed suicide. Bobby feels cheated. He wanted him punished." She closed her eyes and took a few deep breaths. "Listen to me. Pouring out my sorrows to a complete stranger."

"That's okay…I understand."

She sighed. "Go easy on him, will you? He's basically a good boy."

Tanaka nodded.

"You'll find him out back watering the shrubs."

❖

It was like an oasis out back. Shrubs and bushes of all sizes filled the area. Different-colored blooms glinted amongst the leaves.

The familiar skunky aroma of marijuana overpowered the natural scent of the blooms.

Dressed in a pair of ragged denim shorts, tight white T-shirt, and Dr. Martens boots, Robert Sadler sat on an overturned planter watering some shrubs, puffing on a joint. When he saw Tanaka approaching, he dropped the joint and ground it out with his boot. His biceps muscles flexed when he reached up and checked the rubber band around his long blond ponytail.

"Robert Sadler?" Tanaka said.

Sadler rubbed a hand over his chin and appraised Tanaka with his drowsy cobalt eyes.

He must've been smoking for a while, Tanaka decided. *If I breathe in enough of the secondhand smoke, I'll probably get a cheap high.*

"Who's asking?" Sadler said.

Tanaka handed Sadler his business card.

Sadler shrugged when he'd finished reading the card. "Whadda you want? Can't ya see I'm busy?"

The uncultured voice didn't match the façade.

"Your mother says it's okay to speak with you. I just need to ask you a few questions."

"What, I'm supposed to speak to you 'cause my mother says it's okay? I'm not a kid. Get lost. I don't need to answer none of your questions."

"That's true. I don't care one way or the other. If you prefer, I could get the cops to ask them."

Sadler continued watering the shrubs for a while. He threw down the garden hose and turned off the water.

"You guys make me sick. Just 'cause I was convicted for something I didn't do, you think you can walk all over me. Whadda you want now?"

"I understand you know David Earl Warren?" Tanaka said.

Sadler's eyes blinked rapidly. "David…Warren, you say? Never heard of the dude. What makes you think I knew him?"

"I've got evidence to prove you knew him, so cut the crap," Tanaka said.

"What evidence?"

"I'm asking the questions, not you."

"I'm telling you the truth, dude. I don't know what you're talking about."

"Well, if you're telling the truth, how come you were seen talking to Warren at Lighthouse Point on January the ninth?"

Sadler's eyes started blinking again. "January the ninth, you say? Let me think." He rubbed his eyes as though he was deep in thought.

Tanaka waited.

"Lighthouse Point? In January? Oh yeah," he said, with a forced laugh, "it's coming to me now. I forgot all about it. I drove up there to see if there were any chicks hanging out. You know what it's like, don't you? I was sitting in my car—minding my own business—when this dude comes over and starts talking to me. I figured he was trying to pick me up, you know, a fag, so I told him to get lost. Was that him?"

"You know damn well it was him. You'd arranged to meet him there."

"That's crazy, dude. Why would I lie to you? I'd never seen him before."

"Why were you blackmailing him if you'd never seen him before?"

Sadler's jaw tightened and his fists clenched. He turned abruptly and started walking away from Tanaka. "Get lost, creep. I'm not answering any more of your goddamn questions."

Sadler walked into a shed and slammed the door.

Tanaka pushed open the door and said, "I'll get lost when I'm good and ready."

Sadler turned and faced Tanaka. He leaned against a potting table and folded his arms across his chest. "I told you I didn't know the dude."

He shoved past Tanaka and left the shed.

Tanaka pursued him. Before he could speak to Sadler, an elderly couple approached Sadler.

"We're looking for some ground-cover plants," the man said. "Do you have any?"

A sweet smile appeared on Sadler's face. "We sure do," he said. "They're over here. What kind were you looking for?"

Tanaka noted the change in Sadler's demeanor and waited while Sadler took his time showing the couple the plants.

Sadler ambled over to Tanaka after they'd left. "You still here?" he asked.

"Yes, and I'm not leaving until I get some answers," Tanaka said.

Sadler sighed. "What now?"

"Where were you on Friday, January the thirteenth?" Tanaka asked.

"Minding my own business, which is what you should be doing."

"I'm going to find out one way or another," Tanaka said. "Maybe the police will have better luck with you."

Sadler was quiet for a few moments. "You're an asshole."

"Well, this asshole wants to know what you were doing on that day."

"Who remembers that far back? If it was a Friday, I was probably screwing some chick," he said.

"You're a real charmer, aren't you?"

Sadler shoved past Tanaka and pulled a joint out of his pocket.

Tanaka left the garden center and drove back to his office.

At 3:00 p.m., Tanaka drove back to the garden center and parked where he had a view of the back lot. Using his binoculars, he watched Sadler working amongst the flower beds. At four, Sadler smoked another joint.

Tanaka shook his head. *The guy's gotta be flying.*

Using the zoom on his digital camera, Tanaka took a number of shots of him. At 5:00 p.m., Sadler came out of the front door. He climbed into a rusty old Nissan truck.

Tanaka followed him downtown.

He wasn't surprised when Sadler parked on Caballeros, then entered Andre's, the only gay bar in town.

While he waited, Tanaka paged through a forensic sciences book.

At 7:45, Sadler came out of the bar with a well-dressed older man. The older guy climbed into a shiny new Lexus. Sadler followed the Lexus in his truck. Tanaka followed them to a house on Mountain View Drive.

There didn't seem to be any point sitting in the car waiting for Sadler to finish business. Anyway, Tanaka wanted to spend time with Tommy. Tanaka's mother had told him Tommy tended to fret when Tanaka wasn't home for dinner. Tommy had asked her once if he had gone to stay with Patrick.

Tanaka closed the forensic sciences book.

On the way home, he thought about Sadler blackmailing Warren. What had Sadler known about Warren?

CHAPTER NINETEEN

K aren was working at the computer when Tanaka dropped into the office the next morning.

"How come you're working on a Saturday?" Tanaka asked.

"You told me money wasn't a problem. Anyway, I have some work to catch up on."

She poured two mugs of coffee.

"What, no Krispy Kremes?" Tanaka said.

"I told you I'm on a diet...so don't you be buying any either. Anyway, what are you doing here? You're supposed to be on your way to Pacific View Resort."

"I've just come in to pick up a photo of Margaret."

She followed Tanaka into the inner office. "What's happening with the case?"

He told her about Robert Sadler.

"Sexy Sadler," she said.

"You've got him pegged."

"Sounds like Warren was definitely being blackmailed, doesn't it?" she said.

"Yes, but why? We'll have to see if we can come up with a connection between Warren and Sadler." Tanaka checked his notebook. "What about Mitchell? Have you found anything on him?" he asked.

"I checked with Winifred to find out what year Warren graduated, and phoned the University of San Sebastian. A Daniel Mitchell definitely graduated with Warren. I couldn't find anything until I called my pal at Social Services. They have a forty-two-year-old Daniel Mitchell listed. He's been on a disability pension for years. He's the same age as Warren, so it's probably him."

"Did you get an address?"

She opened her notebook and read off the address.

"Lovely area," Tanaka said. "I'll have to pay him a visit."

She handed him a photograph. It showed Warren and another male in cap and gown. "I got this from Winifred. It's Mitchell and Warren."

"Great. Let's hope he hasn't changed too much," Tanaka said.

"Everyone you've interviewed so far seems to be covering up something."

Tanaka told her about his narrow escape with the Trans Am on Thursday evening.

"Shit. You think someone wants you off the case?"

"No doubt in my mind."

"You're going to have to be more careful."

"It looks that way."

"What's next?"

"Steve and I have already booked to stay at Pacific View Resort tonight, so I'll be able to verify Margaret's alibi."

"I'm glad you two are getting away for the night. You need a break."

"You got that right. Stevie is good for me."

She raised an eyebrow. "Sounds like it's getting serious."

"Stevie wants me to move in with him."

"How do you feel about that?"

"It's not going to happen. I couldn't do that to Tommy. Maybe when he's older…but not now."

"And you think Stevie's going to hang around waiting for you?"

"Probably not."

"Anything you want me to do while you're lazing around?" she asked.

Karen was preparing for the Bureau of Security and Investigative Services examination, so Tanaka said, "You probably need to spend time studying, so please, take the rest of the weekend off. We'll get back to the case on Monday."

"Yeah, I do have a lot of policies and procedures to review."

He handed her his camera. "Before you leave, can you download the photos and print some copies of Sadler? I might need them on Monday morning."

"Will do. Have a great time, you lucky thing. I've always wanted to visit that place."

Tanaka paged through Warren's photo album and removed a portrait of Margaret.

He was looking forward to the trip. He only hoped Steve would relax and enjoy their time there without pestering him again about moving in with him.

CHAPTER TWENTY

Tanaka was driving Steve's Mercedes, and Steve was relaxing in the passenger seat. Tanaka took US 101 north out of the city and exited on El Camino Real. According to the Weather Channel, it was going to be sunny and warm all weekend.

"I've been looking forward to this trip," Steve said, resting his hand on Tanaka's thigh. "It's been ages since we managed to get away."

Tanaka covered Steve's hand with his hand. "I'm looking forward to it too, Stevie. It'll be nice spending the whole night together."

"I hear they have private hot tubs," Steve said.

Tanaka smiled. "Have you ever done it in a hot tub?"

"No...what about you?"

Patrick and Tanaka had spent a glorious weekend at the resort. He wasn't about to bring that up, so he said, "I've been in a hot tub, but I've never done it in a hot tub."

"So, tell me honestly. Is this going to be all pleasure, or will there be any business involved?" Steve asked.

"Well, actually, I do have to confirm something."

"Thought so. It's not like you to take time off in the middle of a case."

"It won't interfere with the weekend, I promise, just a few questions, and then the time is all ours."

It was just before noon when they checked into their cabin, which consisted of a large sitting room with a wood-burning fireplace, a bedroom with king-size bed, an en-suite bathroom, and a kitchenette. The sliding glass doors opened up onto a broad deck. Loungers encircled the hot tub.

They had a quick lunch in the restaurant. While the server was clearing their table, Tanaka pulled out the photograph of Margaret Warren.

"I wonder if you could help us," he said to the server. "We're trying to arrange a surprise getaway for someone, but we think she might've been here recently. Do you think you could take a look at this photo and see if you recognize her?"

The server held the photo toward the light. "Oh yes, *she's* been here before," she said.

"That's a shame. Was it some time ago?"

"No, fairly recently. It was a weekend in January...a winter getaway special."

"You sound pretty sure about that," Tanaka said.

"How could I forget her?"

"What do you mean?"

She looked around, as though checking to see if she could be overheard. "Well...I don't like talking about our visitors, but the reason I remember her was because of the scene she made. She didn't like the service and had her server in tears. I had to take over."

"So I guess it's not a good idea to arrange anything for her."

"She said she'd never set foot in the place again, so yeah."

"Thanks for being so frank," Tanaka said.

As they were leaving the restaurant Steve said, "Was that the answer you wanted?"

"Yes and no. She's given Margaret an alibi."

"So it wasn't her, then."

"I guess not. I feel like I'm going around in circles," Tanaka said.

"Do you want to talk about it?"

"No, not really. I've got what I came for, so for now, let's enjoy ourselves."

After a long hike along the shore, they returned to their cabin and settled down on the private sundeck overlooking the water. The crash of the waves pounding on the rocks below was rhythmic, hypnotic, and soothing. In the distance, Tanaka could see cargo ships and tankers on the calm Pacific.

They spread a blanket on the sunny deck. Tanaka stripped and lay on the blanket. The sun felt good on his naked body. Steve wanted to wear his bathing suit, but Tanaka managed to persuade him to strip.

"What if someone sees us?" Steve asked.

"Who cares? If they want to watch, let them."

Tanaka opened a bottle of Merlot and poured two glasses. They clinked glasses and sipped the wine. Later, they climbed into the hot tub and drank the rest. At five, they climbed out of the tub and soaped each other up under a hot shower.

While Steve dressed for dinner, Tanaka phoned home.

Tommy answered. "Hi, Daddy," he said. "Grandma said it was you."

"You and Grandma behaving yourselves?" Tanaka asked.

Tommy giggled. "Grandma always behaves."

"I was thinking about you today," Tanaka said. "We saw some big ships passing."

"Can we go on one, Daddy?"

"Sure. How about one to Alaska?"

"Oh, boy. We can go sledding with dogs, you know, like the Idita."

Tanaka laughed. "You mean the Iditarod dog sled race?"

"Yeah. When you get me a dog we can take him with."

"We won't be going at that time of the year…if we go."

They chatted for a while. Tanaka told Tommy he had to dress for dinner and would see him Sunday night.

When Tanaka and Steve sat down to eat, they were both famished. As they ate, they watched the burnt-orange sun drop below the horizon. The bed was turned down and the wood fire was giving off a cedar aroma when they returned to the cabin.

The next morning, they made their way back to the city.

When Tanaka stepped out of Steve's Mercedes and climbed into his Honda Civic, he felt like he'd been downgraded. He felt energized from the getaway with Steve and was ready to get back to work. He was relieved Steve hadn't brought up the subject of him moving in with him again. *Maybe he's accepted that it isn't going to happen, because we're good together.*

CHAPTER TWENTY-ONE

Tanaka needed to see why Warren had left Jeremy Townsend half a million dollars, so on Monday morning he called and arranged to meet with Townsend.

Townsend's apartment building on San Roque overlooked Lighthouse Park.

He greeted Tanaka with a big smile and a firm handshake. Tanaka was trying to figure out why Townsend looked familiar, then realized he'd seen Townsend's photograph in Warren's bedroom. Townsend was about six-three and was probably about thirty-five. His toned body had the definition only achieved after many hours in the gym. Dark hair, now damp, topped his tanned body.

Quite the hunk, Tanaka was thinking, *he's just my type.*

Townsend showed Tanaka into a living room furnished in a contemporary Ikea style. When Tanaka looked out the window, he could see the tops of huge fir trees swaying in the light breeze.

Two love seats separated by a pine coffee table occupied the center of the room. Townsend sat in one and Tanaka claimed the other.

"Thanks for seeing me on such short notice, Mr. Townsend."

"Please, call me Jeremy."

Tanaka nodded.

"Winifred told me she'd hired you, so I've been expecting your call," Townsend said.

"What do you think about Winifred hiring me?"

"Well, I know she thinks David's death wasn't accidental, so I guess it's a good thing."

"Do you think it was accidental?"

"I'm not sure. I mean…I agree with her that the way David died was strange, but I just can't understand why someone would want to harm him."

"You don't think David had any enemies?"

"Not in his private life. David was a wonderful person. He went out of his way to help people. He often did cases pro bono and did all kinds of volunteer work."

"You said not in his private life. What do you mean?"

"Well, I know he was having problems with one of his former clients."

"What kind of problems?"

"One time when I was over at his place he received a phone call. I could see the call upset him. When I asked him what the problem was, he told me a guy he'd defended on a drug possession charge had been found guilty and was now out on parole and harassing him."

"You know the name of this guy?"

"David did mention it. Let me think." He closed his hazel eyes.

"Take your time."

"It was foreign sounding," he finally said. "Franco? No. Francelli, yep, that's it. Joey Francelli."

"Any idea where I might find him?"

He shook his head.

Tanaka wrote down the name. "You'd known David for a long time?"

"Oh, yes. For years. We met when he was in for eye tests."

"What kind of work do you do?"

"I'm an RN. I work at the medical center."

"So you'd know all about diabetes and insulin?"

"For sure. If David had any questions about his diabetes, he'd ask me."

"Did he check his blood sugar and take insulin when he needed it?"

"Oh yes, he was fanatical. He didn't want to end up with any complications, so he was always careful about his diet and blood sugar. He exercised regularly. We used to go to the gym together."

"Can you tell me how you came to have his will?"

"Well, that was a bit strange. He said he didn't want to leave it at home or the office. When I asked why, he just said he'd feel better if I kept it."

"Did you know you were mentioned in the will?"

"Did I know I was mentioned in his will?"

"Yes…did you?"

"It was kind of sealed. He never talked about the contents."

"You said kind of sealed. Was it, or wasn't it?"

His face flushed. "Well, it was in an envelope, but the envelope wasn't sealed."

"So if you'd wanted to you could've looked at it?" Tanaka said.

"Why would I do something like that?"

"Why do you think he left you that much money?"

Townsend's face colored even more. He shifted in his seat and pulled at the earring in his left earlobe. "To be honest with you, I've no idea. It probably looks odd, but he basically didn't have any other friends."

"It sounds more than odd to me, Jeremy. I've never heard of anyone leaving five hundred grand to a friend."

Townsend shrugged. "I was really surprised when I found out about the money."

"Could you tell me where you were on January the thirteenth?"

"January the thirteenth?" Townsend asked.

Tanaka sighed. *Does he have to repeat every question I ask before answering?* "Yes."

"You mean where was I when David died? You're not suggesting I had anything to do with his death, are you?"

"Did you?" Tanaka said.

"Of course not. What kind…what kind of question is that?"

"A routine question. One I'm asking everyone. I'm just trying to sort things out."

"Oh, sure. I'm the only one besides Winifred who inherited, so I guess you think I had something to do with his death?"

"I'm trying to figure things out, Jeremy. I'm not accusing you of anything."

"Do I need an attorney? Maybe I shouldn't answer any more questions."

"That's up to you. But why would you need an attorney if you've nothing to hide?"

Townsend closed his eyes and rubbed the bridge of his nose. "I've got nothing to hide. What is it you want to know?"

"I asked where you were on the day Warren died."

"I was in Palm Springs that weekend," he said.

"Where did you stay?"

"Where did I stay?"

"Yes."

"Let me see…oh yes, I stayed at the Royal Columbia on Indian Canyon."

"When did you get back to San Sebastian?"

"On Sunday afternoon."

"How did you find out about Warren's death?"

"Winifred called and told me," he said.

"You live alone, Jeremy?"

"Yeah."

"You have a girlfriend?"

"What's that got to do with anything?"

"Just one other thing, Jeremy."

Tanaka pulled out the key he'd found in Warren's car. "You any idea whose key this is? Is it for your door?"

Townsend's hand shook when he examined the key. "No, it's not for my place. Where did you find it?"

"What about these numbers, you recognize them?"

"No, what are they?"

"Anything you think I should know that might help me with the case?"

Townsend hesitated for a brief moment. "No, sorry."

Tanaka stood up and walked toward the door.

He's definitely covering up something, Tanaka thought as he entered the elevator. *I'll have to dig deeper.*

CHAPTER TWENTY-TWO

On Monday afternoon, Tanaka drove to Daniel Mitchell's low-income subsidized-housing unit located in the south side of the city.

Assorted characters lounged around the complex's lobby. Some were in wheelchairs, some on motorized scooters, and others relaxed on two broken-down sofas. Their heads swiveled in his direction when he entered the door and crossed to the elevator. Conversation ceased, but started up again as soon as the elevator doors started closing.

Graffiti covered the ancient elevator walls.

Tanaka knocked on Mitchell's door. It opened a crack and one eye peered at him.

"What do you want?"

"I'm looking for Daniel Mitchell," Tanaka said. "Is that you?"

The eye blinked. "What if it is?"

"I'd like to talk to you. Can you open the door?"

The door opened a little wider. Mitchell had changed quite a bit since the graduation photo, but Tanaka could still recognize him. He had a wild and unkempt look. His ragged clothes were dirty. His thick black hair was uncombed. Nicotine stained his overgrown mustache and beard. The odor of stale sweat and cigarette smoke wafted out the door.

"I wondered how long it would take before you got here," Mitchell said.

"You were expecting me?"

"What do you take me for? Do I look stupid?"

"No, not at all...I was just wondering how you knew I was coming."

"What do you mean?"

What the hell! Tanaka thought. *What's with this guy?*

"You said you knew I was coming."

"Oh yeah. As soon as that broad moved in next door, I knew there would be trouble. Anybody can see she's been put in here to spy on us. Why else would she get the best suite in the place?"

"Do you mind if I come in for a minute, Mr. Mitchell? I'd like to ask you a few questions."

Mitchell held the door open for Tanaka.

The furnishings in Mitchell's small apartment consisted of an unmade single bed, a small table—cluttered with dirty dishes—and one straight-back chair. A small kitchenette and bathroom completed the appointments. A patina of nicotine covered the window, and dirty clothes lay on the floor.

What a dump, Tanaka thought. "Thanks for letting me in."

"As though I could stop you if I wanted. You guys just come and go like you own the place. What's she been telling you?"

Mitchell walked back and forth like an expectant father in the waiting area of a delivery room.

Tanaka handed him one of his business cards.

Mitchell read it and smirked. "Anybody could have one of these printed. I know you're from Social Services, man. So whadda you want?"

"You're wrong, Mr. Mitchell, I'm not from Social Services."

Mitchell sat down. "I know you're out to get me, man, so quit the shit."

Ah, man, this guy's psychotic, Tanaka decided. "I can hear you are wondering if you can trust me. Let me assure you that you can. I've got no connection with Social Services, and anything you tell me will be confidential."

"So? What then?"

"I've been hired to look into David Earl Warren's death."

Mitchell gave a wild cry and his eyes darted manically. He jumped up from the chair, did a little jig, and sat down again. He tried to roll a cigarette with his trembling nicotine-stained fingers. His head bobbed around on his neck like a doll on a car's dashboard. "She's saying I'm going to be punished for what I did."

"Who? Your neighbor?"

"Yep...the snitch."

"Punished? For what?"

"Never you mind," Mitchell said a sly grin on his face. "It's none of your business."

"Is your neighbor talking to you now?"

"Can't you hear her?"

"No. I can't hear her, but I can hear how threatened you feel by her."

"Don't patronize me, man. Whatcha think you are? A shrink?"

I guess I didn't learn enough on the crisis line, Tanaka thought.

"So, what can you tell me about Warren's death?" Tanaka said.

"I don't know anything about his death. What makes you think I knew him?"

"Well, I know you went to the University of San Sebastian together, and I know Warren was paying you one thousand bucks a month. What was that for?"

Mitchell locked eyes with Tanaka. "I thought you weren't from Social Services? No way, man. I never got any extra cash from anywhere."

"When was the last time you saw Warren?"

"I told you I didn't know the guy, so leave me alone. You government workers are all the same. You think just because you give me a crummy place to live in, that you can come in any time you want and give me shit. You're just trying to get me out of here so you can move one of your friends in. I'm not stupid, man. I know my rights."

There didn't seem to be any point in continuing the conversation.

Tanaka placed his hand on Mitchell's shoulder. "Take it easy, Daniel," he said. "Do you mind if I come back and see you sometime?"

"Like I could stop you."

Tanaka sighed. It was obvious Mitchell was having problems coping.

Mitchell needed help, so when Tanaka was in his car, he called an acquaintance at the mental health clinic. They had Mitchell on their books. The receptionist gave him the name of Mitchell's case manager.

When Tanaka called the case manager and informed her about Mitchell's mental status, she promised to visit Mitchell later that day.

❖

It was still light when Tanaka parked his car in the driveway at the side of his house.

Tommy poked his head out of the door.

"Can we go for a drive, Daddy?" Tommy yelled.

"Sure…see if Gran wants to come with us."

Tommy disappeared for a few minutes.

"She's busy," he said when he reappeared, pulling on his jacket. His L.A. Dodgers cap was pulled low on his brow. "She says not to be late for dinner."

Tanaka opened the car door for Tommy.

"Aw gee, Daddy, can't we go in the Mustang?"

Tanaka smiled. The restored 1965 Ford Mustang convertible was Tanaka's pride and joy, and he only took it out on special occasions.

"Sure, we haven't had it out for a while."

Tanaka backed the Mustang out of the garage and waited until Tommy put on his seat belt before backing out of the driveway. On the drive to Lighthouse Point waterfront trail, Tommy asked, "When can I start driving the Mustang, Daddy?"

"Not for a while, Tommy. After you've grown another two feet we'll talk about it."

It seemed everyone was out walking dogs. Tanaka and Tommy walked hand in hand along the cliff-side path.

Tommy stopped to play with a miniature white poodle.

Tanaka, ignoring the sign that read *Danger—Stay Away from Cliff Edge*, walked over to the precipice to watch two surfers in their shiny black wet suits riding breakers in the chilly breeze.

"Daddy!" Tommy yelled. "You're going too close! It's dangerous."

Tommy ran over to Tanaka, grabbed his hand, and pulled him away from the edge. Tanaka knew Tommy was only repeating something his grandmother had probably said to him, but it felt strange to have Tommy acting like the parent.

When Tanaka saw the concern in Tommy's eyes, he knelt down and gave him a hug. Tanaka wished he knew more about child rearing so he'd know how to deal with Tommy's anxiety.

"It's okay," he said. "I wouldn't go too close to the edge. I know it's dangerous."

"I'm scared you could die like my daddy Patrick."

Tanaka took a deep breath before saying, "I'm not going to die, Tommy. I'll always be with you."

Tommy was quiet. Tanaka was wondering what else to say when Tommy bounded off onto the grass and started running around with the dogs.

"When can I get a dog, Daddy?" he asked when Tanaka joined him.

"We'll talk to Gran about it," Tanaka said.

Tanaka let him romp for a while, then said, "We better get going, Gran's probably got dinner ready."

Tommy was still talking about getting a dog when they sat down to dinner. Tanaka decided he would have to discuss the issue with his mother when Tommy wasn't around, since she would probably end up taking care of the dog.

CHAPTER TWENTY-THREE

The next morning on the drive to his office, Tanaka noticed a gold-colored Trans Am following him as he turned onto Ocean Boulevard. He made a few more turns to see if it was still on his tail.

It was.

It looks like the same car that tried to run me down, Tanaka thought. He opened his phone and called Karen. After a few rings, Karen answered her cell phone.

"Where are you?" Tanaka said.

"I'm in the office. Why?"

"The Trans Am that tried to run me down is tailing me. I'll be parking on El Centro in about fifteen minutes. Can you be in your car, ready to tail it?"

"I'll be ready."

Tanaka found a vacant parking meter on El Centro and was busy looking for change when the Trans Am—its windows all heavily tinted—rolled by. Tanaka was able to get the plate number. Karen was right behind the Trans Am.

When Tanaka got upstairs, he called Sadowski, who said he'd get right back to him.

As promised, Sadowski called back. "I might've known. First you call and ask about him, and now you want his plates checked."

"Who are we talking about?"

"Stanley Pearson...like you didn't know," Sadowski said.

"I didn't know it was him, Rick. I've never met him. He's been following me around and I don't know why."

"Yeah, tell me another...it wouldn't be the first time you've withheld info from me."

"Not this time, Rick. I'm still trying to figure out what's going on. As soon as I have something definite I'll let you know."

"You probably want his address?"

"Please."

Sadowski gave him an address in southeast San Sebastian. Tanaka wrote it down in his notebook.

"At this rate you'll really owe me, and I don't mean a burger either," Sadowski said.

"Sure. When this case is over, I'll make it up to you. How does a night at Andre's sound?"

"That would be great. I've always wanted to spend a night in a gay bar. Should I invite Gonzales? I'm sure he'd enjoy spending a night surrounded by a bunch of queens."

Sadowski disconnected before Tanaka could think of an appropriate rejoinder.

Karen walked into the office and dumped the mail on Tanaka's desk.

"I followed the car to a run-down auto body shop on East Cabrillo, next to the railway tracks," she said, taking off her coat. "It was driven around the back, so I wasn't able to get a look at the driver. I've got the plate number, though."

"I've already checked on it. Sadowski says it's registered to Stanley Pearson."

"Stanley Pearson? That's one of the names in Warren's appointment book, isn't it?"

"Uh-huh. This case just gets more confusing by the minute. I wonder how he fits into it?" Tanaka said.

"What are you going to do?"

"I think I'll pay him a visit. Shake him up and see what happens."

She poured a mug of coffee and sat next to his desk. "You and Stevie have a good weekend at Pacific View?"

"Sure did, it's a fantastic place to relax."

"Did you find out if Margaret was there?"

"Yeah. She was there all right, so that puts her in the clear."

"That's one off the list. What about Mitchell, did you get to see him?"

Tanaka told her about Mitchell and his phone call to Mitchell's case manager.

"So he's schizoid. I guess that rules him out?"

"Not necessarily. His case manager says Mitchell functions quite normally when properly medicated. Then again, perhaps he was paranoid enough to do the deed if he thought Warren was out to get him."

"And he did say he was going to be punished," she said.

"Yes, but I don't think we can take anything Mitchell said as fact. I'll wait for a few days, then see him again."

"I guess I better review my psychology notes. We've been discussing abnormal psychology in class."

"That's a good idea. I could do with a refresher myself."

She sipped her coffee. "What about Townsend, were you able to see him?"

Tanaka brought her up to date.

"So he had the means and the motive. It would've been a piece of cake for him to doctor the insulin," she said.

"I wasn't satisfied with his answer about the money, and he seemed evasive when I asked where he was when Warren died, so we need to see if he had the opportunity."

"It does sound weird. I mean leaving Townsend five hundred grand. I should be so lucky," she said.

"There's more to it than that."

"Whadda you mean?"

"I'm sure Townsend's gay, and they were probably a couple."

"Oh-oh. So that means he's not the perp."

"Why not? He knew he was going to inherit the money. Maybe he needs the cash."

She closed her eyes and rubbed her temples.

"I'll go to Palm Springs to verify his alibi," Tanaka said.

"You have a photo of him?"

Tanaka paged through the album and found a photograph of Townsend. He was dressed in a soccer outfit and had a soccer ball tucked under his arm. Tanaka showed it to Karen.

"He looks familiar. Can't remember where I've seen him, but I'm sure I have. Who could forget a hunk like that?"

She headed into the outer office.

He shouted after her, "Will you see if you can find anything on Joey Francelli? I think I better pay him a visit."

She poked her head back in the doorway and saluted. "Will do, Katsuro."

❖

Tanaka sorted the mail. One letter stood out. His name and address were typed on a plain business-size envelope. There was no return address on the envelope, but the postmark indicated it had been mailed in San Sebastian.

He opened the envelope and pulled out the letter.

Printed in a large red font on a sheet of plain white paper were the words:

STOP SNOOPING AROUND OR YOUR KID GETS IT
IF YOU NOTIFY THE POLICE YOU WILL NEVER SEE
HIM AGAIN

He read the words repeatedly before the message sank in.

An icy fist encircled Tanaka's heart. The sky became dark, as though someone had thrown a cover over the sun. He shivered, reached over, and turned on his desk lamp.

The sheet of paper fell on the desk.

He couldn't think clearly. What should he do? Was it too late? Had he already taken Tommy?

"Karen," he yelled, "take a look at this."

She ambled back into his office and flopped down into the chair.

"Don't touch it…just read it."

"Oh, God!" she said when she was through. "The bastard!"

Tanaka read the letter again.

"What are you going to do? Are you going to call Rick?" she asked.

"No, I'm going to do like the letter says."

It took a few moments before Tanaka was able to clear his head and think logically.

He grabbed the phone and called his mother.

"Is Tommy at school?" Tanaka asked when she answered.

"Yes…what's wrong, Katska?"

Tanaka tried to keep the panic out of his voice. He didn't succeed.

"I'll tell you about it later. If he gets home before I speak to you, keep him inside."

"Katska! What's going on?"

"I can't talk now…I have to go."

"So?" Karen asked when he hung up.

"He's still at school. I'm going to pick him up."

"I'll come with you. I don't think you should drive."

They locked up the office and hurried to her car.

When they arrived at Tommy's school Tanaka dashed into the administrative offices. He explained that he'd come to pick Tommy up because of a family emergency. After checking his ID and their records, the secretary led him to Tommy's classroom.

Tanaka breathed a sigh of relief when he saw Tommy sitting at one of the desks. The teacher went over to Tommy and spoke to him. He screwed up his face, looked toward the door, and waved.

"Hi, Daddy. What's up?" Tommy said when he came out of the classroom.

Tanaka knelt down in front of him. "Something's come up, and we need to go home," he said.

"Aw gee, Daddy, do we have to? We're learning about the moon and stuff."

"Sorry, honey, but we need to go."

"Aw gee," he repeated. "This sucks." He glanced at Karen. "Karen, what're you doing here?"

"She drove me over," Tanaka said.

They went to his locker and collected his backpack.

As they drove home, Tanaka turned around and watched Tommy open his backpack and take out his lunch pail.

"I didn't even eat my lunch yet," he said. "What's the big deal?"

"We'll talk about it later," Tanaka said as Tommy devoured a Pop-Tart. When Tommy asked, "You wanna bite?" Tanaka just shook his head, too emotional to speak.

Tanaka's mother, a concerned look on her face, came dashing outside. Tanaka shook his head and placed a finger over his lips.

"Hi, Gran," Tommy said.

She gave Tommy a hug and looked at Tanaka.

"Karen," Tanaka said, "can you take Tommy upstairs? I need to talk to my mom."

Karen nodded. "Come on, Tommy. Why don't you show me your room? I hear you've got lots of toys."

"You wanna see my train?" Tommy was saying when they disappeared inside.

Tanaka sat his mother down and told her about the letter.

Tears formed in her eyes. "Oh, God," she said. "What are we going to do?"

"First of all, we'll have to be strong. We don't want Tommy to know about the threat, so you'll have to put on a brave face."

Covering her mouth with her hand and strangling a sob, she nodded.

"I've been thinking about it on the way home. I think you and Tommy should go and spend some time with Mary and George in Chicago until we catch the person responsible. Could you do that?"

She thought for a few moments. "That's probably the best thing. George'll protect Tommy."

George, Patrick's father, was a retired Chicago police officer. *She's right*, Tanaka thought, *George will know how to protect Tommy.*

"I'd like you to leave in the morning. Is that enough time for you?"

"I'll phone Mary and let her know, then I'll book a flight."

Tanaka put his arm around her shoulder. "I'm sorry about this. I'll try and get it sorted out as soon as possible."

"You'll take care of yourself while we're gone?"

Tanaka nodded. "I don't want anyone to know where you're going, okay? It's important."

"I'll go and call Mary now," she said.

"Mom, I love you," Tanaka said, holding her arm to keep her from leaving. "I don't know what I'd do without you."

She smiled and kissed him on the cheek. "I love you too, Katska."

"When you're finished talking to Mary, I want to speak to George."

❖

The next morning, after watching his mother and Tommy depart on a flight for Chicago, Tanaka dragged himself into the office.

Karen was waiting for him. "You still think it's a good idea not to tell Rick?"

Tanaka nodded.

"What are you going to do?" she said.

"I'm going to carry on. When I get my hands on the bastard, I'll kill him."

"I'll hold him while you do it," she said.

"You'll hold the fort while I go to Palm Springs to check on Townsend's alibi?"

"Of course."

Tanaka called the Royal Columbia Hotel in Palm Springs and reserved a room. Then he went home and packed a bag.

To Tanaka, the house felt cold and deserted.

He missed them already.

CHAPTER TWENTY-FOUR

Traffic was heavy all the way from San Sebastian to Palm Springs. The wind picked up when the I-10 threaded its way between the San Bernardino and San Jacinto Mountains. Hundreds of windmills twirled as they generated needed electricity. To the south, snow-covered Mount Jacinto sparkled in the last rays of sunshine. It was dark by the time he exited the expressway.

The Royal Columbia Hotel, recently refurbished, was a boutique hotel catering to the yuppie crowd. Tanaka had stayed there in the past, so he knew his way around. After checking into his room, he went back down to the lobby and spoke to the man behind the front desk.

"I wonder if you can help me," Tanaka said, putting on the saddest expression he could muster. "A friend of mine has gone missing and we are trying to find him. He was supposed to check in here on Friday, January the thirteenth, and we haven't heard a thing since then."

The desk clerk frowned. "We're not supposed to give out that kind of information."

"Please, it's important. His mother is devastated."

The clerk looked around the lobby. They were alone. "Give me his name and home address and I'll look into it for you. You won't tell anyone about this, will you? I could get fired."

"Thanks, I appreciate your help. I definitely won't tell anyone."

Tanaka wrote down Jeremy's information and handed it to the clerk. He pulled Jeremy's photo out of his pocket and showed it to him.

"Do you recognize him?" Tanaka asked.

The clerk took his time. "No," he finally said. "I don't recognize him."

"Were you working that day?"

"Yes. I always work from three to eleven on the weekends. Peter works the night shift on weekends. He'll be in at eleven. If you show him the photo maybe he'll recognize your friend."

"Thanks, I'll do that."

"Come back at about ten forty-five, and I'll let you know what I've found...but don't let on to Peter."

Tanaka strolled over to Palm Canyon and had a burger and Coke at Hamburger Mary's. With his belly full, he walked to the Spa Resort Casino and settled down in front of a video poker machine. He was down one hundred bucks when he realized it was time to head back to the Royal Columbia.

At 10:45, he was back in the hotel lobby. The same clerk was still behind the desk.

"I've checked, and we don't have any record of that name for December or January."

Tanaka slipped him a twenty. "Thanks for your help. I really appreciate it."

"You don't have to do that," the clerk said.

"I know, but I'd like you to have a drink on me."

The clerk was putting the twenty in his pocket when an elderly gray-haired man came through the door.

"Peter," the desk clerk said. "This is Mr. Tanaka. He's wanting to know if his friend was here in January. Can you look at the photo and see if you recognize him?"

The old guy nodded.

Tanaka showed him Townsend's photo.

He let out a long whistle. "What a cutie. He your boyfriend?" He took his time examining the photo. "No, I'm sure he wasn't here. I'd definitely remember him."

Tanaka thanked them and retired to his room. He wanted to get back to San Sebastian before lunch, so he'd have to be up early in the morning.

What's Townsend up to? Tanaka thought. *Why did he lie to me? I'll have to pay him another visit.*

CHAPTER TWENTY-FIVE

After arriving back in San Sebastian, Tanaka drove to the auto body shop where Karen had last seen the Trans Am that tried to run him down.

It was a rusty corrugated iron building and didn't look like the kind of place the Better Business Bureau would accredit. A number of automobile carcasses filled the space behind the building. The shell of a Honda Accord lay beside the Trans Am.

To Tanaka, the place looked like a chop shop.

A mean-looking pit bull with scars on its snout and a ripped ear, tied to a stake in the ground, growled and lunged at Tanaka.

A muscular guy with a greasy blond ponytail pounded at the front end of a jacked-up Honda Civic, one scuffed Dr. Martens boot braced against the car's right bumper. The rolled-up sleeves of the blue denim shirt he wore under his dirty overalls exposed bulging biceps and forearms covered with jailhouse tattoos.

A car engine swung from a block and tackle above his head.

With his small head and muscular body, Tanaka thought, *the guy looks like he's taken a few too many steroid shots*.

"Pearson?" Tanaka said.

The guy jumped—bumping his head on the suspended motor—and turned in Tanaka's direction. The hammer he'd been using dropped to the floor. His eyes widened. "Whadda you want?" he said in a squeaky voice.

"What? No pleasantries? I guess you know who I am?"

A sneer crossed Pearson's pitted face. He bent his arms and hooked his thumbs under the bib of his overalls. Tanaka thought for a moment

Pearson was going to beat his chest like a gorilla—which wouldn't have surprised him.

Pearson rubbed the area on his head he'd bumped. "How would I know who you are? Never seen you before."

"Is that right? Not even after trying to run me down?"

"You're crazy."

"I'm investigating the death of—"

"You're not a co—" Pearson cut himself off.

"Oh, is that right? I thought you didn't know who I was?" Tanaka said.

"I don't have to talk to you. Get the fuck out of here before I set my dog on you."

Stanley Pearson walked over and stood in front of Tanaka. They were eye to eye. Tanaka's were clear; Pearson's were red and watery. Pearson's pupils were so widely dilated Tanaka could hardly see his irises. With his crooked nose and his ragged left ear, it looked like he'd been in a fight and come out second best. He placed both hands on Tanaka's chest and tried to push him toward the door.

Tanaka raised his hands between Pearson's arms and knocked Pearson's hands off his chest.

"I'm supposed to shake with fright? You don't scare me," Tanaka said.

An ugly scowl grew on Pearson's face.

It's true what they say about owners resembling their dogs went through Tanaka's mind. *It's hard to decide who looks more vicious, Pearson or the dog.*

Pearson's voice rose. "This is your last chance, buddy. Get going before I really get mad." He kept sniffing and wiping his nose on the back of his hand.

"Maybe I'll leave after you tell me why you tried to run me down and why you've been following me around. Did somebody send you? Or is this a private grudge?"

Pearson's piggy eyes narrowed and his jaw tightened. "You're full of shit. I told you I never saw you before, so fuck off."

Tanaka stood his ground.

Pearson took a swing at Tanaka.

Tanaka's muscles stiffened. He sidestepped, moved back, pivoted on his left foot, and delivered a roundhouse kick to Pearson's right knee.

Pearson landed on his backside. He bared his teeth and snarled like a cornered hyena. Pearson was back on his feet and swinging again, his big fist colliding with Tanaka's left ear.

Tanaka felt dizzy. He lashed out. Unfortunately, Pearson ducked away and his fist just grazed Pearson's shoulder.

Pearson's muscular arms encircled Tanaka's torso. Tanaka's stomach heaved. Pearson smelled as if he'd attended a floater autopsy and hadn't bothered to change his clothes.

Tanaka managed to break free and backed away. He had to keep his distance from Pearson. In a wrestling match, Pearson would have him beat.

Pearson punched him in the chest, knocking him down. Pearson picked up the hammer and came at Tanaka. Tanaka kicked out Pearson's legs. He fell on top of Tanaka, winding him. The crash of the hammer on the concrete floor next to Tanaka's head spurred him to greater efforts. He gasped as he fought for control of the hammer. He managed to roll over on top of Pearson and jump up to his feet.

Tanaka kicked Pearson. This time, the pointed toe of his western boot connected with Pearson's solar plexus. He picked up the hammer and threw it into a corner of the garage.

Gripping his abdomen and gasping for breath, Pearson got to his knees. The dog growled and lunged at Tanaka. The tether held.

After a few moments, when he was breathing normally, Pearson glanced to his right and to his left, as though looking for something.

"Don't even think about it," Tanaka said. "That was just a taste of what I can do. I've got a black belt that says you won't win."

Pearson got to his feet and moved over to the dog.

Tanaka picked up a long steel rod. "If you let that dog loose, I'll kill it," he said.

Pearson stopped. His lips curled. "You're going to regret this, asshole. I don't take no shit from no one."

"Where were you on January the thirteenth?" Tanaka asked.

"Get lost."

"I'm staying until I get an answer."

Pearson went back to the car, leaned into the engine compartment, and began working. "Shit!" he suddenly shouted. He dropped the wrench he was using, sucked his thumb, and jumped up and down like a two-year-old in the midst of a tantrum.

"You made me do that," he yelled.

Tanaka took a seat on a pile of old tires. "Too bad…but I'm not leaving until I get some answers."

Pearson leaned against the car and glared at Tanaka. "Whadda you want again?"

"I asked you where you were on January the thirteenth."

"Okay, okay!" he screamed. "I was in Ventura, visiting a friend— now fuck off!"

"Why have you been tailing me?"

"I told you I never seen you before." Pearson turned toward the car.

"So how much are you making selling stolen vehicle parts?" Tanaka said. "I think I'll give my friend Sergeant Sadowski a call. I'm sure he'll be interested."

Pearson snarled at Tanaka. "Don't threaten me, asshole. You can tell your pig friend anything you want. He won't pin nothing on me."

He's right, Tanaka thought. *It's not all that hard to grind off vehicle identification numbers.* Tanaka stood and turned to leave.

Pearson shouted after Tanaka. "Next time you come out here I'll kill you!"

Just in case Pearson decided to let the dog loose, Tanaka carried the steel rod out to his car. His ear was still ringing and his hand shook as he opened the car door. Pearson had tried to run him down once. Now he was even more dangerous.

Tanaka went home and got ready for his weekly squash game.

CHAPTER TWENTY-SIX

Early the next morning Tanaka was jogging through the park along Lighthouse Point trail. He hadn't run the day before, so he felt the need to push himself more than usual. The sun struggled to penetrate the early morning fog. Goose bumps covered his sweaty body when the mournful sound of the Cabrillo Point foghorn penetrated the ghostlike silence.

Tanaka perched on top of the wooden barrier erected to keep people away from the crumbling cliff face and massaged his left calf muscle. He smiled when he remembered how Tommy had yelled at him when he'd gone too close to the edge. He was glad Tommy wasn't around to see him so close.

He didn't see or hear anyone approaching. Two strong hands landed in the center of his back and launched him over the edge of the cliff.

He landed with a thud, the breath knocked out of him, on a sandy projection about ten feet from the top. As his body continued its downward slide, he grabbed at bushes protruding from the vertical slope. The first bush gave way but the second one held. His legs dangled over the edge of the overhang. His head spun and his heart raced. This was his worst nightmare come true. As a teenager, he'd lost his grip while climbing Avalanche Gulch on Mount Shasta and had fallen about thirty feet. He hadn't been injured, but had to be extracted by a rescue team. That had been his last mountain-climbing experience.

And now, here he was, once again in the same predicament.

Tanaka could smell rotting vegetation and damp earth all around him. He kept still and forced himself to breathe deeply. He knew he should've been watching his back. Now it was too late.

If I get out of this, Tanaka promised himself, *I'll kill Pearson. I should've listened to Tommy. If I die, he'll be an orphan. How will my mother and Tommy cope without me?*

When the spinning sensation abated in Tanaka's head, he turned and sought additional anchors. A sturdier bush was just out of his reach. As he contemplated his next move, he was forced into action. The bush he was grasping was slowly uprooting.

His respiratory rate increased.

He lunged for the new anchor and managed to get a grip. Dislodged soil came sliding over him, nearly burying his upper torso.

The new anchor felt firmer. He slowly moved his legs, looking for a toehold. He couldn't locate anything solid. He could feel icy sweat trickling down the sides of his body. His arms were beginning to ache from the strain of supporting his weight. He knew the only way out was to pull himself up onto the narrow projection, or he would plummet to his death.

It seemed to take forever. Finally, with dirt sticking to his sweaty body, he was lying on his back on the overhang. He lifted the waistband of his sweatshirt and wiped his face. The cool air on his moist skin sent a shiver through his body. He knew he wasn't out of trouble yet, but for the moment, he felt relatively safe.

Tanaka didn't know how long he lay on the ledge...it seemed an eternity. When his heart rate and breathing were back to normal, he plucked up enough courage to attempt to move. He slowly rolled onto his abdomen and pushed himself to his knees. He kept his body flat against the cliff side and came to his feet.

The precarious ledge suddenly gave way and he was once again sliding down the face of the bluff.

His heart rate soared as raw adrenaline shot through his veins.

He grabbed at anything he could to stop slipping. In the end, gravity won and he was in a terrifying free fall that ended with a jarring thump.

He didn't move for a short while, amazed he was still alive. A searing pain in his butt was the only apparent injury he'd sustained.

He rose to his feet and staggered over rocks toward the closest stairway. A couple of homeless people, unaware of his existence, lay huddled together under a makeshift shelter.

Tanaka inched his way up the rickety wooden stairs. Blood trickled down his leg. His leg muscles ached with the effort. He was exhausted and out of breath when he reached the top.

Breathing a sigh of relief, he lay down on the grass.

An elderly woman walking her collie gave him a strange look.

"You okay?" she asked.

Tanaka nodded. "Did you happen to see anybody around here?"

"No. I thought I was alone until I saw you lying there. Quite a scare you gave me too, young man." She looked him up and down. "You look like my old man used to look when he worked in the coal mines back east."

"Sorry about that," Tanaka said.

"Are you sure you don't need any help? You look like you're bleeding."

"No, thank you. I had a fall, but I'll be okay."

"Well, if you're sure?" she said.

Tanaka nodded again. "Thanks, I'll be okay."

He sat up and watched her walk away. She glanced back at him a few times, as if to satisfy herself she was doing the right thing.

Tanaka waved.

She waved back and disappeared behind some trees.

The place was deserted.

He applied pressure to his posterior to stem the flow of blood and limped back to his car.

Tanaka's left side and butt ached, but as far as he could tell, he didn't seem to have any broken bones. He was lucky to have sustained only minor injuries. He didn't want to get blood on the car seat, so he took an old towel out of the trunk and tucked it under him.

He checked his face in the car mirror. It was filthy—no wonder the old woman had been concerned. Only his eyes and mouth were clear of dirt.

The only other vehicle in the parking area was a dusty bottle-green Dodge Ram pickup truck with an aluminum crossover toolbox mounted in the cargo area. It was the second time Tanaka had seen the distinctive truck parked in the same spot. In his rearview mirror, he could see the driver watching him. The truck backed out of the parking area and roared off. Tanaka was able to get a quick look at the tag number. He wrote it down and stuck the piece of paper in his wallet.

As he headed for the emergency room at the medical center, Tanaka thought about Pearson and ways to get even.

CHAPTER TWENTY-SEVEN

It was after ten when Tanaka finally arrived at his office.

"Well, it's about time," Karen said. "Where've you been? It's not like you to be this late."

She followed Tanaka into the inner office, watching as he cautiously lowered himself into his chair. "What's the matter with you? You look like you're in pain."

He pulled up his shirt and showed her the abrasions and bruises on his side.

"Oh my God," she said. "How did that happen? Did you fall? Were you in a fight? Were you in an accident?"

With her eyes wide open, she listened to the tale of his early-morning escapade.

"Did you get x-rays?"

"Yes, nothing was broken, but I had to have my rear end stitched."

"That's incredible. You're lucky you weren't killed." She smiled. "Are you going to show me your wound?"

"Not likely. I've shown my butt to enough people today, thank you."

"Did you see the person who pushed you?"

"No. The only people around were an old lady—and I'm sure she didn't push me—and a guy leaving in a hurry in a Dodge pickup… which reminds me…"

Tanaka phoned Sadowski and asked him to run the plates. Sadowski grumbled but promised he'd get back to him as soon as he could.

After Tanaka hung up Karen said, "Did the old lady see anything?"

Tanaka shook his head.

"I guess there's no doubt now someone wants you off the case," she said.

Tanaka nodded.

"What are you going to do? Are you going to report it?"

"No, there's nothing to gain by doing that. I'm just going to be more careful in the future."

"Maybe we should spend more time together so I can watch your back. You know I jog every morning," she said, "so why don't we do it together?"

"Are we still talking about jogging or something else?"

She smiled, shook her head, and rolled her eyes. "Hardly," she said.

"One of these days your eyes are going to stay like that," Tanaka said.

She rolled them again.

"Thanks for the suggestion, Karen, but I'm not going to let anyone force me into changing my lifestyle. We need to carry on as usual and show them we aren't intimidated. We can't be watching one another twenty-four seven."

"I guess you're right," she said. "Do you need to take it easy for the rest of the day?"

"No, I'm okay. It looks worse than it is."

With her head tilted to the side, she looked at him, as though she wanted to challenge his decision. "If you say so," she said.

"I do."

"Who do you think it was?"

"I'm sure it was Pearson."

Tanaka told her about his visit to Pearson's garage.

When he'd finished describing Pearson, Karen said, "Pearson the primate."

"That's a good description…I'll remember that one."

She smiled. "You should've kicked him in the nuts. That would've put him out of action for a while."

"He's a slime ball, and he's also a bully. I don't think the guy's playing with a full deck. His brain's probably fried."

"Do you think it was him in the pickup?"

"It didn't look like him, the guy had a normal head, but we'll know for sure when Sadowski gets back to me."

"I guess if we can figure out why Pearson the primate's after you," she said, "then we'll have the case solved."

Sadowski called back. "The truck belongs to a Clive Andrews. He's been in for assault, but he's on parole. What are you up to? Opening a rehabilitation center for ex-cons?"

"Just a name that's come up on a case," Tanaka said.

"Sure, I believe you. Don't bother me again today. I do have a job, you know."

"Before you go, do you have an age for him?"

"Yes, he's forty-six. Now leave me alone, please."

Shit, Tanaka thought, *all I need is another name to add to my list of suspects.*

He related the information to Karen.

"We'll have to figure out how he fits into the equation. Could you see if you can get an address on him?"

"Will do, Katsuro. Did you manage to get to Palm Springs to check on Jeremy Townsend's alibi?"

He told her about his trip to Palm Springs.

"So he's a liar," she said.

Tanaka moved around to relieve the pressure on his butt. "Why is it that everybody involved in this case feels the need to lie to me? Perhaps if one person decided to tell the truth we'd get somewhere."

"Do you think we should shake up a few more of them and see what happens?"

"Yeah, but there are a few more things I want to check on before that," Tanaka said.

"Like what?"

"I should've checked to see if there was any insurance on Warren's life, and I haven't done that yet. I also want to find out what the grounds were for the divorce."

Tanaka phoned Winifred to see if she had any answers.

Winifred wasn't aware of any insurance on Warren's life. She suggested Tanaka speak to Prescott Harrington. "I guess I haven't been thinking straight since David died. I should've looked into it."

"Do you know if David hired anyone to check on Margaret prior to his divorce?"

"Yes. David was sure she was cheating on him, so he hired Harry Whitfield," she said.

"Harry Whitfield?"

"Yes, he's a private investigator."

"I know him," Tanaka said. "He's not someone I would hire."

"I know David didn't like him, that's why I didn't even consider hiring him."

"What did she have to say?" Karen asked when he hung up.

Tanaka told her what Winifred had said. "I'll drop in and see if Harrington knows anything about insurance, and then I'll pay Whitfield a visit."

"Be careful," she said.

"Anything else?" he asked.

"As a matter of fact, there is. Jo and I went for a drink at Andre's last night. She knows the bartender. I showed the bartender the photo of Sadler. The bartender says Sadler likes to give the impression he's a breeder, but if the price is right, he'll go with anyone."

Tanaka smiled. "I hope he doesn't say anything to Sadler."

"It was a she, a transgender, to be more exact. She promised not to say anything. She and Jo are friendly, so I trust her."

"Good," Tanaka said. "Do you have anything else?"

"Yeah. I got the results from the lab. The scraping you collected was human blood, type O negative. I called his doc to verify. She says Warren was O negative. Do you want a DNA done?"

"No, I don't think we'll bother with the expense. Anyway, it'll take too long. I'm sure it was his blood."

"So…how did it get there?"

"You remember the abrasion on his back? I think he was dragged into the bathroom. It would've been easy because he was in a coma."

"Oh, God. You mean Warren was alive when someone dumped him into the tub?"

"Yes, that's exactly what I think."

"So, do you think the coma was accidental, and the perp took advantage of the situation?" she asked.

"No. I think it was premeditated. We've been on the wrong track. You remember there weren't any used needles or vials of insulin?"

"Sure. So the perp took them with him. But why?" she said.

"I think the thing started on the Thursday. Whoever was responsible doctored the insulin vials on Thursday the twelfth. Warren assumed he was taking insulin, but he was probably injecting something like sugar water," Tanaka said.

"He must've been confused when he didn't improve."

"Yeah. Poor sod. He never had a chance," Tanaka said. "I think the perp also dissolved some Ambien and put it into one of the vials of insulin. A combination of the injected Ambien and the oral NyQuil would've put him to sleep."

"So after Warren drowns, the perp walks out of there with all the evidence. If he'd left the used needles and vials, we would have known how it went down."

"We'll have to check alibis again to see who had the opportunity on the twelfth," Tanaka said.

"I guess we'll decide what to do after you speak to Harrington."

"Did you have any luck on tracing that Francelli character?" he asked.

"Yeah, I was lucky. I went and spoke to Jack Turner, the probation officer. He had Francelli on his books. He did the strangest thing. While I was in his office, he went to pick up his mail, leaving Francelli's file on his desk, so I took a quick look at it. Here's his address."

"Ventura," Tanaka said reading the address. "I wonder if he's a friend of Pearson's?"

"Right…Pearson the primate told you he was in Ventura. Maybe they're in it together."

"Could be. Did you happen to get an age?"

"He's thirty-nine."

"Thanks. I'll drive to Ventura tomorrow morning and talk to him, so don't expect me until late."

She went back into the outer office.

Maybe when she's finished college, Tanaka thought, *I'll ask her to join me full-time.*

CHAPTER TWENTY-EIGHT

Tanaka called and made an appointment to meet with Prescott Harrington. After welcoming Tanaka into his paneled inner sanctum, Harrington settled back in his huge black leather chair. He was the quintessential corporate man. His smoothly combed gray hair and three-piece dark-blue pinstriped suit wouldn't look out of place in any of the world's financial centers, Tanaka was thinking when he gingerly took a seat.

"I was glad to hear you had agreed to help Winifred, she's the salt of the earth," Harrington said. "Is there any substance to her claim of foul play?"

"I haven't finished my investigation yet, but I'm convinced her nephew's death wasn't accidental."

Harrington raised his eyebrows. "I didn't expect that. I thought you'd probably find Winifred was overreacting."

"I also assumed that at first, but there are too many inconsistencies surrounding Warren's death. There weren't any signs of a struggle in his suite, so I don't think he was killed in a rage. No, I'm sure it was premeditated murder."

"Do you have any suspects in mind?"

"Yes, but it's still too early to start naming them."

"What about the police? Have you got them involved?"

"Not yet, but I will when I have some specific evidence to present to them."

Harrington nodded. "Was there something specific you wanted to speak to me about?"

"I'm trying to find out if Warren had any life insurance, and if he did, who stood to gain?"

"Good point. I'm not personally aware of any insurance he had, but I'll see if we had a policy on him."

He picked up the phone and asked someone to check. "Ironic, isn't it?" Harrington said after he'd hung up. "Usually you're investigating insurance fraud for us, and now you're investigating a murder that leads you right back to us."

"Let's hope Warren didn't have any insurance with your company."

The phone rang. Harrington listened intently and made some notes. "Well, well," he said after he disconnected. "He did have a policy with us."

"How much?"

"Five hundred grand. However, the kicker is that there was a double indemnity clause, so we could be out a million."

"Who's the beneficiary?"

"It's a spousal life insurance policy on the lives of both Margaret and David, with the surviving spouse named as the beneficiary."

"So, that means if Margaret had died Warren would've benefited, but with him dying Margaret is the beneficiary?"

"That's right. Given the current death certificate, Margaret will be paid the million."

"Is there any way to prevent her from receiving that money?"

"We could prevent the money being paid to Margaret if she has acceded to the status of survivor by killing David."

"Any other way?"

"I'll have to discuss it with our legal experts. It's a bit strange, really. The policy may be null and void because they were legally divorced; however, I doubt it because she was apparently still keeping up the monthly payments."

"It sounds like you haven't paid Margaret yet?"

"No, we haven't. You think she killed him?"

"Let's put it this way. She's definitely on my list of suspects, so if you can delay paying her, it would be a good idea."

He stood up. "I'll talk to the legal department about it. Thanks for coming in. Do you have any idea how much longer it will take for you to reach a resolution?"

"No, it's too early. I'll let you know as soon as I can."

"Thanks, Tanaka. If you get us out of this there'll be a nice bonus for you."

CHAPTER TWENTY-NINE

Joey Francelli, the person Jeremy Townsend said had been harassing Warren, lived in an unincorporated area in the foothills of the Sierra Madre Mountains.

It was going on three when Tanaka arrived at Francelli's house. A long driveway led to a small white bungalow hidden from the road by a copse of eucalyptus trees.

Tanaka could see a large greenhouse around back. Moisture coated the windows. It looked like a grow-op to him.

A man crouched beside a gleaming Harley-Davidson motorcycle. He had a screwdriver in his hand when he stood up to greet Tanaka.

He was huge, at least six-four, weighing in at about three hundred pounds. He had a swarthy complexion and looked older than his stated age. His paunch hung over his belt buckle. A large spiderweb tattoo encircled his thick neck, and a second tattoo covered the rear of his shaved head. His hands looked like they could crush rocks.

"Mr. Francelli?" Tanaka asked. He was thinking, *I'm not going to be able to intimidate this guy. It'll take more than tae kwon do to do that.*

The guy nodded. "What can I do for you?"

Tanaka handed Francelli his business card. "I'd like to ask you a few questions."

"Who is it, honey?" a female voice asked.

They both turned toward the sound of her voice. She was walking toward them.

In her early twenties, with lots of blond hair teased out in all directions, she was diminutive compared to Francelli. Faded blue-denim jeans showed every nook and cranny. Her most striking attributes were her huge breasts. A white T-shirt with the words *Born to Please* emblazoned across the front stretched across them.

"It's okay, babe," Francelli said. "This gentleman's come to see me. You go back and relax on the porch."

"Okay, honey," she said.

They watched her until she was seated on the porch.

"Doesn't that get your juices flowing?" Francelli said.

"You got that right," Tanaka said.

"So? What can I do for you?"

"I'm looking into the death of David Earl Warren, and—"

"That creep's dead?"

Tanaka nodded.

"Good," Francelli said.

"Do you mind me asking you a few questions?"

"It's a free world."

"I understand you were harassing him before his death?"

Francelli raise an eyebrow. "What's it got to do with you?"

"We know Warren was murdered, so we're checking on everyone who had contact with him the weeks before he died."

"What's this we shit? If Warren was murdered, how come the cops aren't investigating?"

"They are, but I'm doing a little investigation on the side," Tanaka said.

"Must be big bucks in that?"

"Did you have anything to do with his death?"

Francelli roared with laughter. "I don't have to answer any of your questions. I know my rights. I studied law."

"You studied law?"

"Uh-huh, at Corcoran State."

"Corcoran State? I've never heard of that university."

Francelli smiled. "Corcoran State Prison, dummy. I'm a jailhouse attorney."

"Look, all I want to do is eliminate you from the list of suspects, I'm not out to get you."

"You're full of shit."

"Well, if you prefer, I could get the cops out here to speak to you. They might be interested in your garden," Tanaka said, looking at the greenhouse.

Francelli glanced at the greenhouse. His eyes narrowed when he looked back at Tanaka. "Don't threaten me, buddy," he said in a gruff voice. "I'll break your fuckin' neck and bury you where they'll never find your mangy corpse."

"Listen," Tanaka said, "it's not a threat, it's a promise. I can arrange for you to have a real bad day if you like. I'm sure the cops would like to know you've threatened me with bodily harm. How would that play with your probation officer?"

Francelli was silent for a few moments. He beat the screwdriver on the palm of his hand. "What do you want?" he finally said.

"Where were you on January the twelfth and thirteenth?"

"What days were they?"

"Thursday and Friday," Tanaka said.

"That's easy. I was working those nights, and sleeping all day."

"What kind of work do you do?"

"I'm a nightclub bouncer."

I might've known, Tanaka thought. "I'm sure you don't have to do much actual bouncing. They probably take one look at you and they're gone."

Francelli managed a smile, of sorts. "My babe is with me all the time—we're joined at the hip—so she can vouch for me. Isn't that right, babe?" he called out.

"What's that, honey?" she said.

"You and I were together all the time on January the twelfth and thirteenth," he said.

"That's right, Joey…we're always together."

Talk about a built-in alibi went through Tanaka's mind.

Francelli glared at Tanaka. "That useless attorney didn't do his job, so I ended up inside. He got what he deserved, but it wasn't me, it must've been some other dude."

Francelli gave Tanaka the name and address of the club where he worked.

As Tanaka turned to leave, Francelli called out, "If the cops come snooping around here, you're dead meat…and that's a promise."

Tanaka believed him.

CHAPTER THIRTY

It was still early when Tanaka got back to San Sebastian, so he dropped in to see PI Harry Whitfield. In his mid fifties, Whitfield specialized in the investigation of spouses for divorce proceedings.

Whitfield had put on weight since Tanaka had last seen him. His impossibly tiny feet rested on his green metal desk. Smoke from the cigar clamped in his mouth hung in a cloud over his head. His many chins rested on his chest.

"Hello, Harry," Tanaka said.

Whitfield lowered his legs and patted the orange-tinted toupee resting on the top of his egg-shaped head. He removed the stogie and placed it in an ashtray. "Well, bless my soul...if it isn't Tanaka."

"Long time no see, Harry. How've you been?"

Whitfield rubbed his hands together. "Excellent, excellent. Business couldn't be better, let me tell you."

Tanaka took a seat on the straight-backed chair next to Whitfield's desk. "I guess as long as there are adulterous people around, you'll be in business."

"Yes and no. Folks just don't seem to be marrying as much anymore, which cuts into my business. Of course, now that you queers are getting married, business should start picking up. I mean, you ever heard of a queer being able to keep his dick in his pants for longer than five minutes? I'm sure there's no such thing as a monogamous queer."

That was just the kind of comment Tanaka expected from someone like Whitfield. He took a deep breath and waited for ten seconds. "You have a special niche in the marketplace, Harry, and probably don't have too much competition either."

"Yeah, maybe so. What brings you here? Are you trying to get the goods on somebody? You haven't tied the knot again, have you? I heard about your, uh…lover."

"No. Still single."

"How come?"

"I like it that way," Tanaka said.

Whitfield lifted the top of a small dish on his desk and popped a candy into his mouth. "Want one?" he asked.

"No, thanks, Harry. Have to watch the waistline."

"Hey," Whitfield said. "Maybe you can help me. You've been around the block a few times. I've been reading about fags—trying to get ready for the influx of divorces—but I can't figure out how they decide who's the pitcher and who's the receiver? Do they draw straws, or is the one with the biggest dick automatically the pitcher? I mean, who carries the bouquet when they walk down the aisle?"

Tanaka shook his head. "They wrestle, and the one who wins gets to do the screwing."

"Hmm, very interesting," Whitfield said. "I'm looking for someone right now."

"You looking for a pitcher or a receiver, Harry?"

"Very funny," he said. "I'm strictly into pussy."

"I understand you did some work for David Earl Warren," Tanaka said.

"That the attorney that croaked?"

"Yeah. He drowned in his tub."

"What a shame…and all that money."

"So, did you?" Tanaka asked.

"Sure did. He had me follow his wife around for weeks. Made me a tidy profit on that one, let me tell you."

"Were you able to get the goods on her?"

"Oh sure. She's one horny broad. I had me a good old time on that case."

"Did you get any pictures of her and other guys?"

"Yeah, got some excellent footage. Some of the best work I've ever done. I would make a fortune if I started my own movie business, let me tell you."

"You used a video camera?"

"Got me some real good DVDs, let me tell you, and also some color prints."

"You keep any prints?"

Whitfield glanced at his filing cabinet and then back at Tanaka. "To tell you the truth I did keep a few, just for professional purposes, you understand. I don't want you to get the wrong idea."

Yeah, sure, scumbag, Tanaka thought. "Can I see them?"

"You know I can't breach client confidentiality. I mean, you're a PI, you should know that."

"Your client's dead. What's to breach…he'll never know."

"Yeah, I guess you're right, but I don't know. What if word gets around?"

"How's word going to get around? I'm not going to tell anybody. You can trust me."

"You'll owe me if I let you see them," Whitfield said.

"Right. I'll return the favor sometime."

Tanaka hoped that day would never come. He'd kill Whitfield before he would do him a favor.

Whitfield unlocked the filing cabinet and pulled out a stack of envelopes.

He thumbed through them. "Got me quite a collection, let me tell you."

"You sure have."

"Here we go. Margaret Warren," Whitfield said. "I've got a number ten on the envelope—I grade them from one to ten, so that should tell you how fine she is."

He sorted through the photos and passed one to Tanaka. "How do you like that one?"

Margaret was naked and sitting astride a male. Tanaka couldn't see the guy's face but could see what they were doing.

A look of rapture suffused Whitfield's face. "You should see the video. The things those two got up to. I got me a real sweet deal with a motel owner. He has an excellent setup, let me tell you. Always makes sure he checks my clients into the same room. He's got a room—"

"I really don't need to know all the details," Tanaka said, "and I don't need to see the guy's dick. Do you have any showing his face?"

"What? You don't like a little porn? On second thought, maybe not. If it were two guys, you'd probably be all for it."

"Sure I do. Not before dinner, though. I need to be in the mood."

Whitfield gave him a frigid look, then resumed leafing through the stack of photos.

"Does this one meet with your approval? I'd hate to mess with your sensibilities."

Tanaka looked at the photo. Margaret and her partner were still naked. Obviously postcoital this time. The male was Robert Sadler. *That switch-hitting breeder sure does get around* flashed through Tanaka's mind.

"You recognize him?" Whitfield asked.

"Yeah, I know the dude."

"You should've seen her working on him. Knew all the tricks, let me tell you. She's a real pro."

"Do you think I could have this copy?"

"Well, I don't know." Whitfield said.

"No one will know where it came from. Besides, it's for my private collection."

"Yeah, I can see why you'd want a picture of him in your private collection," Whitfield said. "You'll probably stick it up on the wall next to your bed. You wanna see the video? It's a real turn-on. I could lock up if you're interested."

The thought of watching a porno video with Whitfield turned Tanaka's stomach. "No thanks, the photo's all I need," Tanaka said.

"You better not be blabbing about where you got it," Whitfield said. "Otherwise there'll be problems, let me tell you."

"Sure, sure, Harry, you have my word."

"I guess it's okay, then. But don't forget, you owe me."

Tanaka felt like going home for a shower. He knew that wouldn't help, and anyway, he still had work to do.

CHAPTER THIRTY-ONE

Tanaka wanted to conduct another search of Warren's suite, so on Saturday morning he drove to Warren's condominium building. Bernier watched Tanaka enter the lobby door.

"Hi," Tanaka said. "You remember me?"

"Sure, you're that detective fellow. What can I do for you?"

"Last time I was here I asked if anyone had visited Mr. Warren on the Friday."

"Sure, and I said he didn't have no visitors."

"Right. We've decided to widen our investigation and are now interested in the Thursday. Were you on duty that day?"

"Sure. I remember that day clearly. One of the guys took sick, so they asked me to work a double."

"Do you know if there was anybody besides Mr. Warren in his suite on that day?"

"Let me think," Bernier said.

Tanaka waited while Bernier closed his eyes and meditated. "I…I think…sorry, I just can't remember anything," he said eventually.

"You were about to say something and changed your mind. What was it?"

"Nothing, man. That day's a total blank."

"What do you mean that day's a total blank? You just told me you remembered that day clearly."

Bernier scratched his ear.

"Whadda you want from me?" Bernier said.

"I'm trying to find out if anyone was in Mr. Warren's suite on the day before his death, and I think you're holding back something."

"Why would I do that? Honestly, I don't recall anybody visiting Mr. Warren on that day."

Tanaka handed Bernier a photo he'd taken of Robert Sadler at the garden center. "You ever see him in the building?"

"Sure. Him I seen a few times on the security camera. He was 'anging around the garage door. The first time I saw him I went to check, but he was gone when I got down there. The second time I went down there, he was still there, so I asked him what he wanted. He was real rude, told me to eff off. I told him I was going to call the cops. When I got back to my desk he'd gone, so I let it drop."

"When would that've been?"

"January. Yep, it would've been in January."

"Before or after Mr. Warren's death?"

"Definitely before. I've got a good memory when it comes to things like that. I have to be on my toes all the time. Those street people are always 'anging around the recycle bins, looking for empties. They're talking about moving them into the garage, and guess who'd have to move them out for collection? Me, of course."

"Do you think you could've seen him on the day before Mr. Warren's death?"

"I already told you I don't remember nobody on that day. What're you trying to do, confuse me?"

Tanaka said, "You have my number. If you think of anything, please gave me a call."

❖

Tanaka took the elevator to Warren's suite.

Entering the suite, he could see someone had been inside. Whoever had been in had dusted the furniture and vacuumed the floors. He checked the vacuum cleaner. The bag was new.

He booted up the computer.

Somebody had deleted Warren's MS Word files. He checked the Recycle Bin. It was also empty. There were no email messages. The stack of discs that had been in the desk drawer had vanished.

Shit, Tanaka thought, *I'm slipping. I should've reviewed those files on my first visit. Somebody has gone to the trouble of getting rid of them.*

He was walking away from the computer when he noticed the

blinking lights on a wireless router. A cable connected Warren's desktop to the Internet, which meant he probably had a wireless laptop somewhere.

There weren't any new messages on the answering machine.

Tanaka phoned Winifred.

"Have you been in your nephew's suite?" he asked.

"No. I've been back to the building, but you're the only one who's been in the suite since David's death."

"You've been back to the building?"

"Yes. After David's death, I went to the post office and put in a change of address for him. I wanted to make sure his bills were paid. I've been to the building a few times to make sure his mailbox was empty, but I just couldn't go into the suite."

Tanaka knew that feeling well.

"Was there any mail?" he asked.

"Yes, but just junk mail and fliers. I contacted all the utilities and credit card companies, so they're sending everything directly to me now. I also put a note on the box letting them know I didn't want any junk mail."

"Did David have a laptop?" he asked.

"Yes, a Toshiba. He used it all the time...much more than the desktop. He carried it around with him all the time. It should be in the suite."

"A Toshiba?" Tanaka said.

"Yes, I know it's a Toshiba because he loaned it to me once when he was on vacation and mine was in for repairs. It's the same password as his PC."

"Maverick, right?"

"That's it."

"I'll take a look," Tanaka said.

"How are things going?"

Tanaka told her what he'd found in Warren's suite.

"Oh, no. Does that mean you won't be able to find out who's responsible?"

"On the contrary," Tanaka said. "It means we're on the right track and I've managed to panic someone. They've done something stupid."

"So, what now?"

"I know it's a bit late, but I think you should get the lock changed."

"Can you suggest anyone?"

He gave her the name of a good locksmith.

The laptop definitely wasn't in the suite.

He called Sally Ferguson. She said Warren always took his laptop home with him, and it wasn't at the office.

❖

Tanaka went back down to the lobby.

"Someone's been in Mr. Warren's suite since I was last here. Do you have any idea who it might've been?" Tanaka said to Bernier.

"No idea. I don't work twenty-four hours a day, you know. It must've 'appened when someone else was on duty."

"Do you think you could check with the other guys?"

"Sure, I can do that."

"Thanks for your help. You still have my card, right?"

Bernier patted the breast pocket of his jacket and nodded.

"Please give me a call if you hear anything from them."

Chapter Thirty-two

Karen was behind her desk when he dropped into his office on Saturday afternoon.

"He sounds like a real sleazeball," she said when Tanaka finished telling her about his session with Whitfield.

"You got that right. I wouldn't be surprised if he's into a little blackmail on the side."

"Imagine if I'd started my career working for him," she said.

"Somehow I think you would've moved on pretty quick."

Tanaka showed her the photograph Whitfield had given him. She whistled. Her eyebrows arched. "They make an attractive couple. I can see why she'd be turned on by him. He looks so angelic in this photograph, like butter wouldn't melt in his mouth."

"Yes, but rotten to the core."

"She's no slouch either. You think she's into S and M?"

"Who knows?"

"Did you go back to the condo?"

Tanaka told her about his visit to Warren's building.

"So that gives sexy Sadler the opportunity," she said.

"Right, and there would've been enough time for Sadler to slip into the building without Bernier seeing him. If it was him, someone else must've been involved. I don't think he's got the brains to plan such an elaborate scheme."

She nodded. "What else you been up to?"

He told her about his trip to Ventura.

"Do you think Francelli could've been involved?" she asked.

"Could be. He had it in for Warren, and he certainly seems bright enough to have planned the murder, but he'll be tough to crack."

He gave her the address of the club where Francelli allegedly worked. "Please check on his alibi. If he wasn't at work on the two days, I'll have to get the police involved with him."

"That girlfriend of his sounds like a real dilly. You think she had breast implants?"

"I'm sure she did."

"Probably his idea," Karen said.

"I can't imagine any man wanting a woman to do that, but Francelli's got her eating out of his hand. I'm sure she'd agree to anything he said."

"Did you get to meet with Harrington about the insurance?"

He told her about his get-together with Harrington.

"That sure gives Margaret a motive. I mean, a million bucks isn't exactly small change, even to a rich bitch like her," she said.

"Margaret and Sadler are on the top of my list of suspects. Even if she didn't do it, she could still be an accessory, but I don't think we should be too focused on them and miss something else. We still have to eliminate Daniel Mitchell, Stanley Pearson, and Jeremy Townsend."

"That's true," she said.

"Did you find anything on Clive Andrews?"

"Yes," she said. "I had a hard time getting the info. I eventually found out he was a carpenter, so I pursued that avenue. I checked with the local carpenters union. He's a paid-up member. They wouldn't give me his home address, but they did say he was working for Mercury Construction on that massive project north of Mountain View."

"On Lighthouse Road?"

"Yeah. That's the place."

"I guess it must be real easy for a carpenter to get work with all the construction going on in the area," Tanaka said.

She nodded. "So what's next?"

"I think we should put Sadler and Pearson under surveillance for a couple of days to see if anything comes up. We need to concentrate on the two who have sheets. Odds are it's one of them because crime seems to be all they know."

"Right. They're a couple of slimebags."

"Pearson the primate hasn't seen you, so you take him on. But be careful," Tanaka said.

"What are you going to do?"

"I'll tail sexy Sadler. Perhaps we can come up with something," Tanaka said.

"I'll start watching Pearson first thing tomorrow," she said, then added, "So tell me, I'm dying to know, how did the squash game go?"

"It was a good game."

"And you thrashed him, didn't you?" she said with a smirk on her face.

"You sure know how to get me going, don't you? If you must know, he beat me three straight games."

CHAPTER THIRTY-THREE

Tanaka spent the rest of the day shadowing Sadler.
He was sitting in his car outside the garden center when Sadler came out and climbed into his car. Sadler drove straight to a house in south San Sebastian and entered a side door.

Tanaka sat and waited. He was bored. He hated this part of the job. He'd brought a thermos of coffee along, but had to watch how much he drank. It was hard peeing into a bottle while sitting in a car.

At seven, Steve called Tanaka on his cell phone, wanting to know if they would be getting together that weekend. He was miffed when Tanaka told him he would be working. Tanaka couldn't blame him. He managed to suppress his annoyance when Steve suggested that maybe it wasn't work that was occupying his time.

At 8:15 p.m., a taxi pulled up in front of the house. Dressed in tight leather pants, black body shirt, black leather jacket, and black boots, with his long blond hair hanging to his shoulders, Sadler swaggered out and climbed into the taxi.

Tanaka followed the taxi. He wasn't surprised when Sadler exited the cab and entered Andre's. Tanaka parked down the street so he could keep an eye on the entrance.

He was famished, so he took a chance and rushed to McDonald's for a Big Mac and fries. Hoping Sadler hadn't left while he was absent, Tanaka made himself comfortable in the car and ate.

Being the designated smoking area, the entrance to the bar was a busy spot. The smokers were enjoying themselves, taunting passersby and people entering and leaving the bar.

At 11:10 p.m., a cab drew up outside the bar and the driver went inside. Sadler and the older guy Tanaka had seen him with on the previous occasion climbed into the cab.

Tanaka tailed them to the same house on Mountain View Drive. After about fifty minutes of twiddling his thumbs, Tanaka decided hanging around was a waste of time—Sadler would probably be occupied all night—so he went home.

❖

At eight o'clock on Sunday morning, Tanaka was once again sitting outside Sadler's house. Tanaka didn't know if Sadler was home, so he called Karen.

"Where are you?" Tanaka said.

"At home. Why?"

"I'm outside Sadler's house and I don't know if he's home. Can you see if he's in the phone book?"

"Sure," she said. "Hang on."

She came back on the line and gave him a number.

"Thanks. How's it going with Pearson the primate?"

"He's been working long hours at the auto shop. It seems like a busy place. I think you're right about it being a chop shop. Last night a young guy drove a fairly new Camry in and walked out. Do you think we should let Sadowski know?"

"No, not yet. If we do that, we might never find out who did Warren in. We'll wait until the case is resolved."

"Okay. I'm getting ready to go down there now. This is going to cost Winifred a bundle," she said.

"She doesn't care how much it costs. Anyway, she can afford it. This will be chicken feed to her."

"See you tomorrow," Karen said.

"Yeah. Make sure you're careful. Pearson is dangerous."

"Will do, Katsuro."

Tanaka called the number Karen had given him. A drowsy-sounding voice answered.

"Yeah?"

"Is that you, Jack?" Tanaka said.

"No it's not. You woke me up, dude. Next time—"

"Sorry, buddy," Tanaka said, and closed his phone.

Tanaka opened his copy of Michael Connelly's latest novel. At 11:25 a.m., dressed in his leather outfit, Sadler came out and got into his car.

Tanaka followed him to the El Centro Mall parking garage. Tanaka slipped on a baseball cap and a pair of black-framed plain-glass spectacles. Sadler roamed through various stores, examining the merchandise. Every now and then, he'd stop and look at himself in a store window and comb his blond locks.

At 12:45 p.m., Sadler made his way into the food court. After buying something to eat at a Tex-Mex stand, he sat down at one of the tables.

Tanaka used the restroom, bought an apple fritter and a cappuccino at Starbucks, and took a table across the room. He watched Sadler make eye contact with a guy dressed in cement-stained coveralls and a hard hat.

Sadler's cell phone playing a tune put an end to the eye contact. What looked like a heated exchange took place between Sadler and the caller. Sadler looked at the construction worker, shrugged, and made his way out of the food court.

Tanaka casually followed Sadler out of the mall and into the parking garage. He was right behind Sadler when Sadler drove out onto El Centro.

Tanaka thought he knew where Sadler was headed when he turned north on Ocean Boulevard. Tanaka's assumption was correct. Sadler parked outside Margaret Warren's condominium and gained entrance after using the intercom.

CHAPTER THIRTY-FOUR

It was past four when Sadler swaggered out of Margaret Warren's building and drove off.

After a few minutes, Tanaka went over to the entrance and buzzed Margaret's suite.

"You forget something?" Margaret said.

"No, Margaret, I didn't forget anything. It's Katsuro Tanaka. Can I come up and speak to you?"

A long silence ensued. "I'm busy. I don't have time to speak to you."

"Well, I suggest you make time, because I'm not going away."

Another long silence followed.

The door buzzed.

When he reached her suite, she was waiting for him at her door. No leather outfit this time, just a flimsy transparent robe.

Without all her makeup on, Tanaka thought, *she looks a lot older.*

"What's so important you have to see me right away?"

"You want me to discuss your business out here in the hall, where all the neighbors can hear?"

She grimaced, stepped back, and held the door open for Tanaka. He followed her into the living room where she flopped down onto the leather sofa. He stood facing her.

A sneer covered her face. "So?"

"Did you enjoy your afternoon tête-à-tête?" Tanaka asked.

"What's that got to do with you?"

"I'm tired of playing games with you, Margaret. It's time we had an honest chat."

"What's that supposed to mean?"

"It means that unless I get some straight answers from you, I'm going to the police."

"The police? What could you possibly tell them?"

"For starters, why didn't you tell me about the insurance policy you had on David?"

"Because you didn't ask, and because it's none of your damn business."

"I don't think the police will see it that way. Like me, they'll see it as a strong motive for murder."

"What's the matter with you? I keep telling you that David's death was accidental. You really are thick, aren't you?"

"No, Margaret, I know he was murdered…and I'm going to prove it was you and lover boy who did the dirty."

"Me and lover boy?"

"Yes, you and Sadler."

"Sadler?" she said. "I don't know who you're talking about."

"I know he just left here, so cut the crap. I also know he was the reason for your divorce."

"You're crazy. I don't know what you're talking about."

"Not so crazy. I've got photographic evidence of the two of you in bed."

Her mouth clamped shut like a Venus flytrap.

"Would you like to see a photograph?" Tanaka said.

"So what? You've got a photo. What's that prove? We like screwing…does that mean we're murderers?"

"You certainly had the means, the opportunity, and the motive. Yes, I think I can prove you two are murderers. It must've been a real shock to you when you found out you weren't David's heir."

"You're full of shit. Anyway, I already told you I was away that weekend, and I can prove it if I have to."

"Yes, but do you have an alibi for the Thursday before David's death?" Tanaka said.

"The Thursday?"

"Yes, the Thursday. You or lover boy went into David's suite and doctored his insulin the day before he died. That's what killed him."

She rose, turned to the sideboard, and poured herself a Scotch.

Tanaka persisted, "So where were you on that Thursday?"

"Where was I?"

He locked eyes with her. "Yes."

"I…I can't remember," she said.

"You'll have to do better than that."

She leaned against the sideboard and glared at Tanaka. An edge of impatience crept into her voice. "I don't have to do anything."

He smiled at her.

She didn't smile back. "I want you out of here, now!"

He followed her when she walked to the door. "I've had enough of your crap," she said, holding the door open. "I'm not speaking to you anymore. If you want to speak to me again, see my attorney. Now get the fuck out of here."

"And who would your attorney be?"

When he moved into the hall, she slammed the door so hard the frame shook.

Tanaka couldn't prove anything, but maybe he'd scared her into doing something stupid.

He'd have to wait and see.

CHAPTER THIRTY-FIVE

That evening, Tanaka picked up a bottle of water and twelve red roses from a florist and drove to San Sebastian Burial Park.

It was a tranquil environment. Besides him, there was only one other living person around. The occasional noise of trucks on US 101 was the only thing disturbing the peaceful setting.

He emptied the vase next to the tombstone, filled it with water, arranged the roses, and sat on the grass.

For the umpteenth time he read the epitaph:

> In Loving Memory
> Patrick O'Reilly
> 1970 – 2010
> Gone but not forgotten

Tanaka had wanted to put more on the stone, something to describe how he felt, but had been dissuaded. It seemed sad to him to see forty years of life condensed into so few words. He still couldn't believe Patrick was gone. From the moment they'd met, they'd been soul mates. If it hadn't been for Tommy, Tanaka would have given up and ended his life to join Patrick in the afterlife.

For the hundredth time, the mantra *I'm sorry, Patrick, I should've been there for you* went through his mind.

An old man who had been tending a nearby grave, leaning heavily on his cane, made his way over to Tanaka.

The old man read the epitaph. "Your brother?" he asked.

"No, my spouse."

"He was young."

"Much too young," Tanaka said.

"He sick for long?"

Tanaka didn't want to get into it with him but he didn't want to be rude either. "He wasn't sick at all. He was killed by some low-life scumbag."

The old man took a deep breath. "I'm sorry, son."

"Yeah, me too."

"What happened?"

"I was working on a case. I found him when I got home. He had multiple stab wounds, and his throat had been cut."

The old man gasped. "You must've been devastated."

"Still am."

The old man was silent for a long moment. "You a cop?"

"Used to be."

"Did they catch the killer?"

"Yeah, eventually they caught the son of a bitch."

"He get the death penalty?" the old man asked.

"Yeah, but he's sitting on death row, getting maid service and watching TV."

The past came rushing back. Tanaka could feel Patrick's cold, lifeless body in his arms. He could hardly breathe. He looked up at the old man. He could see the concern in the old man's eyes.

"I'm sorry. I can see he meant a great deal to you. You must think I'm a nosy old man, but I'm not. I'm a retired social worker and tend to fall into a therapeutic mode without thinking."

"It's okay," Tanaka managed to vocalize through his constricted throat.

The old man sighed and squeezed Tanaka's shoulder. "Take care, son. I hope you'll be okay."

He watched the old man walk away. Tears ran down his cheeks.

Sometimes I wish I were religious, Tanaka thought. *Maybe God would be able to help me accept Patrick's death.*

❖

When he arrived home, the message light on the phone was blinking. He knew it would be a message from Mary, Patrick's mother. She always called on the anniversary of Patrick's death.

He picked up the phone and called her. It was after ten in Chicago. "Hi, honey," she said. "Did you just get back from the cemetery?"

"Yeah, sorry to call so late. How are Tommy and Mom?"

"They've gone to bed already, but they're both fine."

"Tommy have any questions about why they're there?"

"Not really, George is keeping him busy."

"I miss them already."

"I bet you do. How are things going with you?"

"I don't know. Sometimes I think things are improving, and then at other times, like today, I can hardly function without thinking about him."

"Kats, you've got to let him go. Patrick would want it that way. You're still young and you need to get on with your life."

"I know, Mary, but it's so hard. I still miss him so much."

"I know, honey, so do I, but life goes on."

"I wasn't there for him…it should've been me, not him."

"I know you still blame yourself, but there was nothing you could've done to prevent what happened. How were you to know that creep was going to kill Patrick?"

"I still blame myself."

"Maybe you need to see that doctor again?"

"You mean the psychiatrist?"

"Yes. Perhaps it would help?"

"I don't think so. I'm not that bad."

"You need to find someone else and move on."

"I have been seeing someone, but I feel so guilty, as though I'm betraying Patrick."

"I'm happy to hear you're seeing someone. It's about time. What's he like?"

He told her about Steve.

"He sounds really nice. Just promise me you'll always keep in touch with me, no matter what happens…you'll always be a son to me."

"Of course we'll keep in touch."

"We've decided we want to move to San Sebastian. We're sick of this weather."

"That's great. You'll be able to watch Tommy growing up."

"That's another reason."

"You know when you'll be moving?"

"We're going to drive to San Sebastian this summer and look around."

"Good...I'm looking forward to seeing you."

"I'll let you go now, honey. Take care of yourself."

"Say, hi to Mom and Tommy."

"Will do."

Exhausted, he headed for bed.

The following morning, Tanaka awoke feeling depressed and lethargic, so he didn't go into the office.

He called Chicago, spoke to his mother and Tommy, and promised them they wouldn't have to stay there for much longer.

He went up to his room and showered. When he opened his closet to find something to wear, an old flannel shirt that Patrick used to wear around the house caught his attention. He pulled it out and slipped into it. *Maybe it's all in my mind*, Tanaka thought, *but I'm sure I can still detect Patrick's scent on it.*

The phone rang while he was dressing. He let it ring. Steve left a message asking him to call.

He went down to the family room, popped open a Heineken, and settled down in front of the TV in an old recliner.

He watched *Madame Butterfly* on PBS. The tears were flowing, on and off the screen, when Puccini's masterpiece finally ended.

Later that day, Tanaka was in the kitchen making himself a sandwich when the phone rang.

"I don't want to scare you," George said, "but someone has been snooping around the house."

Tanaka gripped the phone and held his breath. He couldn't speak for a few beats. Beads of sweat popped out on his forehead.

"Is Tommy okay?" he managed to vocalize.

"Yes...he's fine."

"What happened?"

"I saw a guy in the yard. When I went outside, he took off. I could see track marks in the snow all round the house. You could see he'd been looking in the windows."

"What did he look like?"

"Couldn't really tell. He was dressed in a parka—it was snowing."

"I'm coming out there," Tanaka said.

"That's not a good idea, Katska. Tommy is safe. I'll keep him inside for now. As you know, I have bars on the windows and a security system. There's no way anyone can get in here. If they did, I'd let them have it. I'll sleep with my old gun in the bedside table."

"I'll feel easier if he's with me."

George sighed. "I know how you feel, Katska, but you need to stay home and find out who threatened Tommy. If you don't do that, you'll always be looking over your shoulder. You'll never feel safe."

Tanaka knew George was right. He had to control himself and keep at the case. "Can I speak to Tommy?"

"He's sleeping. I don't think I should wake him up. We don't want him to start worrying, do we?"

"You're right. I'll call tomorrow. You'll let me know if the guy comes back?"

"Of course. Try to get some sleep, Katska. You need to be thinking clearly."

❖

Sometime during the night, Tanaka awoke in a cold sweat. He had dreamed of seeing Tommy in a small coffin. He rose, changed his T-shirt, had a drink of water, and then climbed back into bed. It took a long time before he finally drifted off.

CHAPTER THIRTY-SIX

The next morning, Tanaka was back at Jeremy Townsend's apartment.

After they were seated, Tanaka said to Townsend, "There are a couple of things we need to clear up."

"Such as?"

"Well, you told me you were in Palm Springs when David died, and you had stayed at the Royal Columbia on Indian Canyon. Is that right?"

Townsend looked at his hands. "Yeah, that's right."

"No, Jeremy, that's not right. I've checked, and you weren't at the Royal Columbia on that weekend."

Townsend was silent for a few seconds, and tears started coursing down his cheeks. "Sorry...I shouldn't have lied to you. It's just that... it's just that...David was a very private person. He didn't want anyone to know about us."

Aha, the truth at last flashed through Tanaka's mind.

"David and I...David and I..."

"Yes?"

"We were in love."

"I thought so."

"Are you shocked?"

"No, why would I be shocked? You were both adults. So what happened on the weekend David died?"

"We were supposed to spend the weekend at Terrazzo, a gay resort in Palm Springs. I drove over on Thursday, and David was going to fly over and join me on Friday night. He phoned me at Terrazzo on Friday afternoon and told me he wasn't coming over because he wasn't feeling well."

"Was that the last time you spoke to him?"

"Yes. I tried calling him, but there was no answer. I should've come home to check on him. Maybe he'd still be alive."

He reached for some tissues, blew his nose, and blotted his tears.

"You were together for a while?" Tanaka asked.

Townsend's chin quivered. "We'd been seeing each other for years."

"It started before the divorce?"

"Oh yes, long before. David had always been gay…bisexual, really."

"But he chose to marry?"

"Yes, you know what it's like. David felt the only chance he had of being a success as an attorney was to appear straight, so that's what he did."

"He hid his sexuality."

"He wanted to make partner at the law firm and knew that would never happen if he was openly gay. Pratt, the senior partner, is homophobic. He'd never have hired David if he'd known."

"So the marriage was a cover-up?"

"Yes."

"Did Margaret know about him?"

"No, I don't think so. She was always accusing him of sleeping around, but I don't think she knew he was gay."

"What about Margaret? Did she have a lover?"

"I'm sure she did. David said she liked rough sex and wasn't averse to taking on two guys at the same time."

"You know, Jeremy, there isn't any doubt in my mind David was murdered. Someone doctored his insulin on the Thursday before his death."

"Oh, no! How could they? Who'd do such a thing?"

Townsend's hands covered his face. Tanaka knew exactly what Townsend was going through, he'd been there.

Townsend walked over to the window and stared out over Lighthouse Park.

Tanaka joined him at the window and put his arm around Townsend's shoulders. Townsend turned toward Tanaka and buried his face against Tanaka's chest. Tanaka held him and rubbed his back.

After a few moments, the sobbing abated and Townsend looked up at Tanaka. "Sorry."

"No need to be sorry," Tanaka said as he moved away from Townsend. "I understand."

Tanaka returned to his seat.

"I don't know about you," Townsend said, "but I could do with some coffee. Would you like a cup?"

"That would be nice."

Tanaka watched Townsend working in the open-style kitchen. "Did anything unusual happen in the days or weeks before David's death?" Tanaka asked.

Townsend was quiet for a few seconds. "Well, I did think the will thing was strange, but David wouldn't discuss it with me. I had the feeling all wasn't well, though. He said something to the effect that coming out of the closet would resolve some problem, but he wouldn't elaborate."

"Do you think someone was blackmailing him?"

Townsend rubbed his cheek. "I don't know. Surely he would've told me?"

"Did David have any belongings here?"

"Yes. He was never here overnight because he didn't want to keep his diabetic stuff here, but there are some toiletries and some casual clothes. The bag the will was in is still in the closet."

"Anything else in it?"

"I don't think so. I'll get the bag."

He left the room and returned with a small valise.

"It feels empty."

Tanaka watched Townsend check the side pockets of the valise.

Townsend pulled out a folded clipping from a newspaper and handed it to Tanaka. "This is all that's in it," he said.

It was an article from the December 27, 2009, edition of *The San Sebastian Gazette*.

Townsend sat next to Tanaka and they both read the article.

WOMAN RUN DOWN ON CROSSWALK

Dawn Hepburn, a San Sebastian resident, was run down at 8:00 last night while crossing El Centro at Ventura. When the police arrived at the scene, witnesses told them the 68-year-old widow was crossing on a green light when a black or dark blue foreign-looking car ran her down. The car stopped briefly and then fled the scene before witnesses could get a look at the tag number. The victim was announced dead at the scene. Police are asking that anyone with information regarding this incident contact Sgt. Ricky Alvarez at San Sebastian Central Police Station.

"What does it mean?" Townsend said when he'd finished reading the article. "It couldn't have been David. He'd never've left the scene of an accident."

"I'm not sure what it means. Do you know if David rented a car in December?"

"I don't know. I was away on a course in December, so he could've, but I'm sure I would've known if he had."

"Do you mind if I take this with me?"

"Of course not."

Townsend went back into the kitchen and poured two mugs of coffee. "You take cream and sugar?"

"No, black's fine with me."

He handed Tanaka a mug of coffee and then watched Tanaka over the top of his mug.

Sipping coffee, they sat in silence for a few moments.

"Is there anything else you think I should know?" Tanaka asked.

"No, I can't think of anything."

"If you do, you'll give me a call?"

Townsend nodded. "Were you able to get hold of Joey Francelli?"

"Yes, I did. He lives in Ventura."

"So why was he harassing David? You think he killed David?"

"I haven't decided yet. I'm still trying to work things out."

"Will you let me know if you find out anything?"

"Sure…I'll keep in touch."

"I'd like that," Townsend said.

When Tanaka finished his coffee, he left Jeremy's apartment and drove out to the garden center.

CHAPTER THIRTY-SEVEN

Tanaka didn't stop to speak to Sadler's mother. He went straight through to the rear of the garden center.

Sadler looked at Tanaka and quickly looked the other way.

"Sadler," Tanaka said. "We need to talk."

"What now? Can't you see I'm busy?"

"Why don't we step into your office?" Tanaka said, pointing to the small shed. "Unless you'd prefer to stay out here and have all your customers hear our conversation?"

Sadler threw down the garden hose he was using and stomped into the shed. He leaned up against a potting table, crossed his arms, and scowled at Tanaka. "I told you I didn't know...what's his name again?"

"You've been screwing his ex, and you don't know his name... give me a break."

"I don't know what you're talking about, dude."

"I've got a photo of you and her in bed, and you were the reason for their divorce. I also know you were with her on Saturday, so cut the crap."

"So what? It's a crime to have sex with a good-looking chick?"

"No, but it's a crime to murder her ex."

"You're full of shit. You can't prove that."

"No? We'll see about that."

Sadler glared at Tanaka.

"I understand you go for women and men. What's your preference?" Tanaka said.

Sadler's face turned a deep red. "Where'd you hear that shit? I'm straight, dude."

"Yeah, straight to bed, as long as they've got enough dough. Which way do you go when you're with men? Do you like getting or giving?"

Sadler's face contorted in rage. "You're crazy!"

"I've been following you around for days, *dude*. I know all about your visits to Andre's and Mountain View Drive."

Sadler's eyes opened wide and he looked to the right and left, like a rat trying to escape a rattlesnake. He pulled himself erect and peered over Tanaka's shoulder, as though checking to make sure they were alone.

"You're fucking crazy," he said.

"How about squaring with me? Did Margaret kill her ex? Did you kill him, or did you do it together?"

"I never killed that dude. Why would I? I didn't even know him."

"Why were you hanging around Warren's condo building if you didn't know him?"

"How would I know where he lived?"

"You're so full of shit, even an enema wouldn't get rid of it all. We've got you on a security camera tape, so you'd better come up with something better than that."

"I'm telling you the truth, dude."

"I'm tired of this bullshit. I'm going to send my buddy Sergeant Sadowski over to see you. Maybe he'll be able to get the truth out of you. You'll be back inside with your butt in the air in no time, but maybe that's what you want."

Tanaka turned to leave.

"Wait," Sadler said, grabbing Tanaka's sleeve. "If I level with you, will you stop bugging me? I've been straight since I've been out."

"Tell me what you know, and I'll think about it."

"Somebody asked me to keep an eye on his place."

"Why?"

"They wanted to know if Warren was seeing anyone."

"Who asked you to keep an eye on him?"

"Shit, dude, you're going to get me in a whole lot of trouble."

"You're in the shit already. Who was it?"

"Okay...it was Maggie."

"Maggie?"

"Margaret, Margaret Warren."

"I might've known," Tanaka said.

"You're not going to tell her about this, are you?"

"Why, you're scared of losing all that money?"

"We're close, dude, real close," he said, entwining his index and middle fingers. "We're thinking about getting hitched. She can't get enough of me."

"Why did she want to know if Warren was seeing anyone?"

"She wanted to make sure Warren wasn't going to cut her out of his will."

"And?"

"And what?"

"Did you get the goddamn information for her?"

"Yes. Some dude that I recognized had a regular sleep-over with Warren."

"Who was that?"

"Jeremy. I met him once at Andre's—but he didn't want nothing to do with me, thought he was the cat's meow."

Tanaka's estimation of Townsend went up a notch.

"What did Margaret say when you told her?"

"Told her what?"

Tanaka sighed. *This guy's brain is definitely fried.* "What the fuck did she say when you told her about Jeremy?"

"I didn't," Sadler said.

"Why didn't you tell her?"

Sadler was silent.

"Let me guess," Tanaka said. "You decided to cut her out and make some money at the same time. What did Warren say when you asked him for ten thousand dollars?"

"No way, dude. I didn't ask for no money. He gave it to me…as a gift, yeah, as a gift. Said I deserved it."

Tanaka couldn't believe what he was hearing. "What I don't understand is why you killed Warren after he paid you off. I guess you thought Margaret was going to inherit?"

"I've had enough of your bullshit, I'm not saying no more."

"If you didn't kill Warren but you know who did, you better start squealing before you're arrested as an accessory."

Sadler compressed his lips into a thin line and folded his arms across his chest.

"Here's my business card," Tanaka said. "Give me a call if you decide to come clean."

Sadler threw Tanaka's business card on the floor and stomped on it like an irate child.

Tanaka shook his head. What a waste of a life.

When Tanaka arrived home, he phoned Chicago. George assured him all was well. He spoke to Tommy and his mother. They were both upbeat.

CHAPTER THIRTY-EIGHT

Tanaka wanted to determine if Clive Andrews was responsible for his plunge over the cliff on Lighthouse Point trail, so he drove to the construction site on East Lighthouse.

Million-dollar mansions had sprung up in the gated community below the Sierra Madre Mountains. Looking like recently vacuumed carpets, the lush green fairways of a new golf course encircled the buildings. Groves of bigcone spruce and Jeffrey pine trees stood out against exposed rock.

It was going on noon when he parked behind Andrews's pickup truck beside three houses Mercury Construction was building. A plethora of tradesmen clambered over the unfinished houses. Trucks bearing lumber, concrete, and other supplies were coming and going.

A trailer emblazoned with the company logo sat in front of one of the houses. Two men wearing hard hats hovered over building plans. One of them had *Foreman* inscribed over the left side of his orange vest.

"Sorry to bother you," Tanaka said to him. "Is it possible to speak to Clive Andrews?"

"You'll have to wait until his lunch break," the foreman said. "This is a closed site. No unauthorized personnel allowed."

"Would it be possible for you to let him know I'm waiting? It's important I speak to him, and I don't know him," Tanaka said.

"Okay, I'll let him know. What's your name?"

Tanaka told him his name and went back to his car. He watched the foreman climb a ladder onto the roof of the house and speak to one of the workers. While waiting he took in the panoramic view of downtown San Sebastian and the endless Pacific Ocean. The view was what it was all about. That alone would send the prices of the new houses soaring.

At noon, a loud whistle sounded. The tradesmen dropped their tools and collected outside.

The worker from the roof approached Tanaka's car. He had an uneven gait, as if one of his legs was shorter than the other. He looked to be about six feet and weighed about a hundred and eighty pounds. He was all muscle and brawn. His exposed face and arms were tanned a dark brown. A hard hat shaded his eyes. He carried a canvas bag.

"What can I do for you?" he asked.

"You Clive Andrews?"

The guy nodded.

"I need to talk to you. Why don't you get in the car?"

Andrews stared at Tanaka for a while. "Why not?"

After making himself comfortable in the front passenger seat, Andrews said, "I'm gonna eat while we talk. I don't have much time."

"Do you know who I am?" Tanaka asked.

"Of course...the foreman told me," Andrews said through a mouthful of whole wheat.

"So you know why I'm here, then?"

"Haven't the foggiest."

"How come you were parked at Lighthouse Point the other morning?"

A sneer covered Andrews's face. "What? I should get permission from you? You're the parking czar?"

"I know it was you who pushed me. I have a witness."

"You're full of shit. I never left my truck."

"I don't believe you. I know it was you."

"Look, buddy. I don't care whether you believe me or not. I told you I never left my truck!"

"What were you doing in the parking lot?"

Andrews took a bite out of his sandwich. "I've been watching you, but I didn't push you."

"You were watching me?"

Andrews ignored Tanaka.

Tanaka tried a new tack. "Well, if you didn't push me, maybe you saw who did?"

Andrews stopped chewing. "Maybe I did and maybe I didn't. Whatever. I'm glad someone pushed you."

Tanaka clenched his fists and his breathing accelerated. He could hardly control himself. He wanted to grab Andrews by the throat and throttle him. "Are you nuts?" he said. "Why were you watching me, and why are you glad someone pushed me? I could've been killed."

Andrews turned toward Tanaka. "Could've been killed? What a shame. I wish the guy had succeeded. The world would've had one less prick."

"So you did see something."

Andrews took another bite. "Maybe I did."

"What's going on? If you saw something, why won't you tell me?"

"Look, asshole. I didn't see him push you, but the guy left in a hurry, so I figured something was up."

"What was he driving?"

Andrews looked out the side window and kept chewing.

"Please," Tanaka said. "I have to know."

Andrews shrugged. "No skin off my nose, I guess. He had an old Pontiac."

"A gold-colored Trans Am?"

"You know the guy?"

Tanaka nodded.

"I'm glad I'm not the only one wants you dead," Andrews said.

Tanaka shook his head. "While you're in a talkative mood," he said, "why don't you tell me what you've got against me?"

"If you don't know, then you're more stupid than I thought."

"This is crazy. I've got no idea who you are or what you're talking about. You've got me confused with someone else."

"I'm not confused, man. You're the one."

"Since I'm so stupid, why don't you tell me why I'm the one who's confused?" Tanaka asked.

"I've said all I'm gonna say," Andrews said.

Andrews collected the remains of his lunch and packed it into his bag as if he was getting ready to leave. *Maybe if I put some pressure on him he'll come clean?* Tanaka thought.

"I'm sure your boss would like to know you're an ex-con and can't be trusted," he said.

Andrews laughed again. "That supposed to scare me? You're blowing hot air, man. My boss knows all about me."

"And he still hired you?"

"I've done my time. Besides, I'm a good carpenter, and he needs all the help he can get."

Andrews opened the door and made a move to leave.

Tanaka grabbed Andrews's arm. Andrews wrenched his arm free and shoved Tanaka back against the door. "Don't touch me, you creep!" he yelled. "I don't want your filthy hands on me."

"What the fuck's the matter with you? Are you crazy?"

Andrews curled his lips and sneered at Tanaka. "Didn't he talk about me?"

"He? Who?"

"You don't recognize me?" Andrews said.

"Take your hard hat off."

Andrews took his time opening a can of Coke. He took a long drink and then removed his hard hat.

Tanaka stared at Andrews. He looked vaguely familiar. Tanaka had seen a picture of him, and the limp rang a bell. Suddenly he remembered. "You knew Patrick."

"Knew him? Yeah. In the biblical sense, you might say. We were lovers, man, until you came sniffing around and screwed everything up."

"You're the control freak Patrick couldn't get rid of. The one who was stalking him," Tanaka said.

"He had a strange way of showing it. He couldn't get enough of me." Andrews grabbed his crotch and sneered at Tanaka.

"You're disgusting," Tanaka said.

"Disgusting. What the hell you think you are?"

"You've just confirmed what Patrick told me. You were an abusive prick, and you're still one. What do you hope to gain by this? Patrick's been dead for two years."

"It was your fault, buddy," Andrews said. "If he hadn't married you, he'd still be alive."

"Don't you think I know that? There's not a day goes by I don't think about it."

Andrews turned in the seat and glared at Tanaka. "Good. Now you know what I went through, you goddamn Jap."

Andrews climbed out and slammed the door.

Tanaka's anger exploded. He sprang out of the car and ran after Andrews. He kicked Andrews behind the knee. The Coke can went flying in one direction and the canvas bag in another direction. Andrews hit the ground but bounded back up on his feet. He gritted his teeth and snarled.

A fist connected with Tanaka's jaw, and Tanaka sat down hard in the dirt on his aching rear end. Tanaka jumped back up and landed a solid right hook on Andrews's jaw. Andrews landed some good body punches of his own, and Tanaka was down in the dirt again. His ribs were still sore from his fall over the Lighthouse Point cliff.

Tanaka sprang to his feet and swung at Andrews. He couldn't stop. He was getting as good as he was giving, and getting winded and exhausted.

Things would've gotten a lot worse if some of Andrews's mates hadn't separated them.

"What's going on?" the foreman bellowed.

Andrews and Tanaka glared at one another. Blood oozed from Andrews's lower lip, and his right eye was swollen. He struggled to free himself. Two workers restrained him.

"He stole my lover," Andrews yelled.

"He's been dead for two years," Tanaka shouted. "Let it go."

"Enough," the foreman shouted at Tanaka, "I want you off this site."

Tanaka's body was aching and his knuckles skinned, but when he climbed into his car, he felt good.

He drove back into the city.

CHAPTER THIRTY-NINE

On the way to his office, Tanaka stopped at the McDonald's on El Segundo.

Karen was working at the computer when Tanaka came through the door. He wasn't pleased to see her. He'd been hoping she wouldn't be in the office because he didn't feel like discussing his escapade at the construction site.

She followed Tanaka into his office. "What've you been up to?" she asked.

Tanaka's fist and body ached from the fight.

"What happened to your hands?" Karen asked. "It looks like you've been in a fight."

"I have," Tanaka said, and left it at that.

"Well?"

"Well, what?"

"What happened?" she persisted.

He told her about his encounter with Clive Andrews.

She shook her head. "Just like two schoolboys in the playground. Do you think he pushed you off the cliff?"

Tanaka thought for a few moments. "No, he didn't push me. I think he would've been pleased to tell me if he had. I'm sure it was Pearson the primate. He told me he saw Pearson's car in the parking lot."

"Do you think that's the last you'll see of him?"

"I hope so. I've got enough on my plate without that good-for-nothing screwing things up."

"Let's hope so. I need this job."

Tanaka switched topics. "I think I've managed to eliminate one of the suspects."

"You have? Which one?"

"Jeremy Townsend. I told you I thought he was gay. He confirmed that he and Warren were lovers."

"Poor guy, he must've been devastated. They together for long?"

"Yeah. For years…according to Townsend."

"Did Margaret know about it?"

"Townsend didn't think so."

She shook her head. "Are there any straight men left in San Sebastian?"

"You care?"

She got back on topic. "What about Sadler? You been tailing him?"

He told her about tailing Sadler, and his subsequent meetings with Margaret and Sadler.

"She tried to pretend she didn't know Sadler?"

"At first, but when I told her about the photo she decided to come clean."

"She lawyered up after that?"

"Yes. That was the first intelligent thing she did," Tanaka said.

"How did Sadler react when you confronted him?"

Tanaka told her about the hard line he'd taken with Sadler.

"So now we know it was Sadler who was blackmailing Warren. He was easy prey because he didn't want to be outed," she said.

"Right."

"And Margaret didn't know about Sadler blackmailing him?"

"Right," Tanaka said.

"Shit. My head's spinning. My horoscope said I was going to have a bad day."

"What did it say for me?"

"That romance was going to sour."

"I hope not, that's all I need."

She winked at him. "So Sadler and Margaret could've still killed him, right?"

He nodded.

"You think they did?" she asked.

"It's looking more and more like it, but there are still some unexplained things. I mean…where does Pearson the primate fit into the equation? I'm sure it was him who pushed me and tried to run me down."

"I've been spending a lot of time following him around. The only thing out of the ordinary I've seen is the strange goings-on at the body shop."

"The other person who needs to be eliminated is Daniel Mitchell."

"That's true. How are we going on that? I mean, if the guy's psycho we might never be able to get to the bottom of those payments," she said.

"I'm going to try and see him again. Hopefully he'll be more forthcoming."

He showed her the newspaper article.

"What does that mean?" she asked. "Do you think Warren was being blackmailed because of the accident? Surely two different people weren't blackmailing him for two different reasons. It blows my mind."

"Who knows," Tanaka said. "It's just one more angle we'll have to investigate."

"Do you want me to keep Pearson under surveillance?"

"No, let's give it a break. We'll decide tomorrow what to do next. You go on home. I have some paperwork to catch up on."

"Sounds good to me. I should do some studying."

Tanaka looked through his notebook. "Anything on Francelli?"

"Yes. I checked at the club, and he was definitely on duty, so I guess that rules him out."

"Good. Now we can take another name off the list."

"I see the opera's in town. Are you going?" she said.

"I have an extra ticket—Steve is busy, you wanna go?"

"Are you kidding? I'd rather go line dancing, thank you."

"Break a leg," Tanaka said.

"Take it easy, Rocky," she said.

CHAPTER FORTY

That evening Tanaka was in his office catching up on his paperwork when a shadow fell across his desk.

Steve stood in the doorway. Tanaka's pulse quickened.

"Buy me a drink, sailor?" Steve asked in a sultry voice.

"Ah," Tanaka said.

"Ah? Is that all you can say?"

"You're so handsome and sexy, you leave me speechless."

Steve smiled. "I hope you're free, because I've made dinner reservations."

"Good, I'm starving. I'm just jotting down some notes."

"I called you yesterday."

"Yeah, sorry. It was too late to call when I got in. I was going to call tonight."

"What've you been doing to keep yourself so busy you couldn't find even a minute to call me?"

Here we go again, Tanaka thought. *I wish he wasn't so jealous.*

"Working on the case I told you about, Stevie. Nothing else." Tanaka walked around the desk and took Steve in his arms.

They hugged and kissed.

"You're making me horny, Stevie."

"I know, I can feel it."

"What are you going to do about it?"

Steve stepped back and looked up at Tanaka. "You ever done it in the office?"

"No, you wanna try it?"

"We don't have time now," Steve said. "Maybe after dinner we can come back here."

When Tanaka turned around to retrieve his jacket from the back of the chair, Steve slapped his butt.

"Ouch! That hurt!" Tanaka said.

"What's the matter with you?"

"I hurt myself."

"How'd you do that?"

Tanaka gave him an abbreviated account of his dive over the cliff. He certainly didn't tell him about his confrontation with Clive Andrews.

"Show me your chest," Steve said.

Tanaka unbuttoned his shirt and showed Steve the bruises.

"My God! That's terrible. You must be in pain."

"It's not that bad. I'll survive."

Steve was silent while Tanaka buttoned his shirt.

"I wish you'd find some other line of work, Kats. This one's getting too dangerous."

"It's not that dangerous, Stevie. Besides, I like what I do. It's what I've always wanted to do."

"Always? You mean ever since you were a kid?"

"Yeah, as kids, Rick and I used to watch all the old detective reruns—*The Maltese Falcon* was our favorite, and I have all of Dashiell Hammett's old books. Did I ever tell you that?"

"Yes, Kats, you've mentioned it one or two times."

"Anyway, since then," he continued, "I've wanted to do this kind of work."

Steve was quiet for a short time. "You could still find something else to do."

Tanaka sighed. *He doesn't understand at all*. "I don't want to find something else, Stevie."

"I wish you'd reconsider. It scares me when you get hurt."

"It's not a problem…really."

"I don't know if we can carry on as a couple if you insist on doing it. I just don't see any future for us. I can't stand it. You know how I abhor violence."

"I know, Stevie. This was a one-off. Nothing else is gonna happen to me."

"I'm not sure about that. That's what Anderson said before he was killed."

Steve was talking about his younger brother, killed in Iraq.

Tanaka took Steve in his arms and tried to kiss him. Steve tensed up and pulled away from him. "Look at the time. I didn't realize it was that late. We better get going."

Tanaka tucked his shirt into his pants and straightened his tie. "Where we going?" he asked.

"Camille's."

"Good...I'm starving," he said as he slipped into his jacket.

Steve was quieter than usual during the meal, and conversation was stilted. Tanaka watched him picking at the slice of prime rib on his plate while he devoured his T-bone. After a particularly long silence, Steve asked, "How's the Warren case going?"

Tanaka brought him up to date. He didn't tell Steve about the threat on Tommy's life—that would've been the last straw.

"It sounds like Pratt James Easton are making some organizational changes," Steve said. "Old man Pratt asked a colleague of mine if she'd be interested in a partnership."

"Are they adding a partner?" Tanaka asked.

"I don't think so. I think it's to replace Easton. Attorneys are beginning to act like he's already a judge, so I guess the rumors are true."

"Have you ever thought about joining a big company like that?"

"If I was with a big company I would have to take what they handed me. Now I can pick and choose my own clients. Like you, I like my independence."

They finished their meal and left the restaurant. They ambled across the park in front of the old Spanish colonial courthouse and settled on a bench next to the central fountain. Tanaka put his arm around Steve, but Steve remained stiff and withdrawn.

"Do you want me to go home with you for a while?" Tanaka said after a long silence.

"Not tonight. I have to be in court early tomorrow."

Tanaka walked Steve back to his car, then watched him drive down El Centro toward Ocean Boulevard.

CHAPTER FORTY-ONE

The next morning, Tanaka phoned Daniel Mitchell's case manager. She informed him Mitchell was back home and apparently stable enough to interview, so he made his way back to the run-down housing complex.

Mitchell opened the door wide this time. He looked more like his old photograph. The beard was gone, he'd had a haircut, and he looked clean.

"Mr. Mitchell, my name's Katsuro Tanaka. I don't know if you remember me, but I came to see you a while ago?"

Mitchell stared at Tanaka for a few seconds. "Sorry...I don't remember you," he said.

Tanaka handed Mitchell his business card. "I'm a private investigator. I'm looking into the death of David Earl Warren."

Mitchell looked at the card for a few seconds. "I do seem to remember something about this."

"I'd like to speak to you about Warren. Mind if I come in?"

Mitchell stood back so Tanaka could enter.

He'd cleaned his suite and had made his bed.

Tanaka sat on the chair and Mitchell sat on the bed.

"I understand you and David Earl Warren went to the University of San Sebastian together?"

Mitchell nodded.

"Did you know David had drowned in his bathtub while in a diabetic coma?"

"Of course. Where do you think I've been, on Mars?"

"I'm sorry, I don't mean to upset you, but last time we talked you denied knowing him," Tanaka said.

"I did?"

"Yeah," Tanaka said.

"I don't understand. Why are you asking about David? His death was accidental, wasn't it?"

"Actually, his aunt doesn't think it was accidental, and I agree with her."

Mitchell's eyes opened wide. "That's crazy, man. What do you think happened? You think he committed suicide?"

"No, I think he was murdered."

Tanaka watched Mitchell closely. Mitchell looked everywhere but at Tanaka. His hands shook so violently he had problems lighting his cigarette. "I think you're full of shit. Why don't you leave the guy alone? What's in it for you? You're probably doing this for the money."

Shit, Tanaka thought, *here we go again.*

"No, I'm doing it for Ms. Ross, and because I believe David was murdered."

They were silent for a few minutes.

"So, what do you want from me? A confession? I had nothing to do with his death."

"Can you tell me why David was paying you a thousand dollars a month?"

Mitchell gave Tanaka a sly look. "None of your business. Why do you want to know anyhow? You're probably in cahoots with Social Services."

"Daniel," Tanaka said, trying to keep his annoyance from showing, "this is just between the two of us. No one else knows about the money. I have to tell you it looks like blackmail, and if you can't come clean with me, then I'm going to have to get the police involved. I don't want to do that, but if necessary, I will."

"Go ahead, they won't find anything. I had no reason to kill David. We were friends, man."

"Well, if that's the case, why don't you level with me? It would seem to me if you were friends, then you'd want to help."

"Shit, can't you let it go?"

"No. Please tell me about the money, and I'll leave. It'll be our secret."

Tanaka could hardly breathe in the smoke-filled room. Mitchell got up and opened the window.

"He felt sorry for me," Mitchell finally said.

"What do you mean, he felt sorry for you?"

"We were real close at school and the University of San Sebastian."

"How close?"

"Close, man. We were best buddies."

"Are you saying the two of you were lovers?"

Mitchell gave Tanaka an appraising look. "You know about him?"

Tanaka nodded.

Mitchell flopped onto the bed. "He didn't want anyone to know, so we kept it quiet."

"Are you saying the two of you were still getting it on?"

Mitchell laughed.

"No way, man. We haven't done it since we were at university. Not since I, um…got sick and had to forget about grad school. Anyway, he was going steady with someone."

"With Jeremy Townsend?"

He nodded.

"So what was the money for, then?" Tanaka asked.

"I told you, he felt sorry for me. He had lots of bread, man. It upset him to see me living like this, so he tried to help the only way he could. He was good to me."

"Did you still see each other?"

"He used to drop by once a month to drop off the check and to make sure I was okay."

"When was the last time you saw him?"

Tears started running down Mitchell's cheeks. "A few weeks before he died."

"Did the two of you ever discuss problems he might've been having with anyone?" Tanaka asked.

"Sure, we were close, man."

"Can you tell me what you discussed?"

Mitchell let out a long sigh. "He said he was going to come out of the closet because some guy was blackmailing him, and it was the only way to stop it."

"Did he say who it was, Daniel?"

"No."

"Anyone else bothering him?"

"Uh-huh. There was a guy tailing him."

"Do you know who it was, or why the guy was tailing him?"

"Yeah. I found out who it was. David had me wait outside his office. He pointed out the guy. I followed the guy to a building downtown."

"You found out his name?"

"Yeah, it was Alec Garrison."

"Alec Garrison? You're sure?"

"Sure. He's the same as you...a private dick."

"What did David say when you told him?"

Mitchell sniffed a couple of times and wiped his nose on the back of his hand. "Never got the chance, man. I never saw David again."

"Thank you, Daniel. I appreciate your honesty."

"If he was killed, I hope you catch the son of a bitch. David was a good guy. There was no reason for anyone to do that to him."

Tanaka stood. "Look after yourself, Daniel, and make sure you take your meds."

Mitchell nodded and opened the door.

"If you can think of anything that'll help me catch David's killer, please give me a call."

"Will do," Mitchell replied.

CHAPTER FORTY-TWO

Tanaka parked in his usual spot downtown and walked over to Alec Garrison's office. Garrison worked for a big outfit that provided a number of services. The sign on the door stated the company specialized in security, surveillance, employee background checks, missing persons, and divorces.

Garrison was behind his desk entering data into a computer. He was small, about five-six, and probably weighed in at about a hundred and forty pounds. His brown hair was turning gray. Essentially, his nondescript appearance gave him the ability to blend into the background. His choice of clothes, a wrinkled gray suit, off-white shirt, and dark-blue tie, probably helped.

Garrison smiled when he saw Tanaka. "So, you've decided to come to the real professionals for help?"

Tanaka leaned over, shook Garrison's hand, and took a seat.

"Nice to see you, Alec…it's been a while."

"Yeah, not since that conference we attended in Seattle. What can I do for you?"

"I'm investigating a suspicious death, and I understand you had the subject under surveillance."

Garrison raised his eyebrows. "You're investigating a death?"

"It's one the cops gave up on."

"Who are we talking about?" Garrison said.

"David Earl Warren."

"You think his death was suspicious?"

"Yeah, I do. Can you tell me why you had him under surveillance?"

"How do you know I had him under surveillance?"

"A friend of Warren's saw you."

"Shit, I'm slipping."

Tanaka asked again, "So, can you tell me?"

"I'm afraid that's confidential, Kats. I can't talk about it."

"I'm sure the guy was murdered, Alec, but I don't have any hard evidence."

Garrison sat back, interlocked his fingers over his abdomen, and twiddled his thumbs.

"I'm spinning my wheels, Alec. Anything you can tell me about him will help."

"There's not much to tell. I only had him under surveillance for a couple of days before he kicked the bucket."

"Didn't that surprise you?"

"Why should it? His death was ruled accidental, and that's all there was to it."

"Who hired you?"

"I told you, that information's confidential."

"Remember the time you came to me for help? Well, it's my turn now."

Garrison sighed. "No one can know where this came from, Kats."

"You have my word."

"It was the law firm he worked for: Pratt James Easton."

"Pratt James Easton? Why would they have you check on Warren?"

"It's not unusual for companies to do background checks on their employees. Some companies do it before hiring and promoting employees. We've done work for Pratt James Easton before. Maybe they were thinking of making him partner?"

"Who specifically hired you?"

"I can't say for sure without getting out Warren's file, and I'm not prepared to do that. This is as far as I'm going."

"Did you discover anything out of the ordinary?"

"Nada. He was clean. I couldn't find a thing on him. Of course after he died, they terminated the request, so I didn't do my usual full investigation."

"Thanks, Alec. I appreciate your help. If you need my help at any time, give me a call."

Tanaka walked back to his small office.

CHAPTER FORTY-THREE

Tanaka needed to think, so he leaned back in his chair and put his feet up on the desk. He was frustrated. While he'd managed to eliminate a couple of suspects, he still couldn't get a grip on the case.

He decided to start at the beginning to see if he'd missed anything. The last time he'd interviewed Henri Bernier he had been sure Bernier wasn't being entirely truthful. Tanaka decided to pay him another visit.

When Tanaka arrived at Warren's condominium, Bernier wasn't behind the desk. A neatly dressed young man was in his place. He looked up when Tanaka entered the lobby.

"I'm looking for Henri Bernier," Tanaka said. "He not on duty yet?"

"He doesn't work for us anymore."

"Since when?"

"Since last week."

"I'm surprised. I thought he liked the job. What happened?"

"I heard he came into some money and quit."

"Really? Did he win the lotto?"

"I don't know where it came from. All I know is he seemed to be really happy. The last time I saw him he said he was thinking about moving back to Lafayette."

Tanaka handed him his business card. "Do you know where he lives? It's important I contact him."

The guy read the card and gave Tanaka the once-over. "What's it about?"

"Just a private matter we've been working on."

"We're not supposed to give out employee information. I could get fired."

"Please, it's important. Nobody'll know."

The guy deliberated. "I guess there's no harm. I mean, he doesn't work for us anymore."

He pulled a ledger out of a drawer and turned the pages. He turned the book so Tanaka could read. "Here we go."

Tanaka recorded Bernier's address in his notebook. "Thanks, I appreciate the help."

Tanaka drove over to Bernier's pad. He recognized the place. It was an old motel converted into so-called apartments. As well as long-term residents, it allegedly rented by the hour. The walls looked like they used to be blue but were now mostly bare concrete. The doors were a dirty gray color and rust-stained drapes covered the grimy windows. A used syringe lay on the ground beside Tanaka's car.

He knocked on Bernier's door. No answer. He banged louder. Still no answer. There wasn't anyone around. Most of the residents probably worked nights, so he slipped a credit card between the door and the jamb and sprang the cheap lock.

The room was musty and untidy. The bed was unmade. A packed suitcase sat open on a chair. The closet, bedside tables, and dresser were empty. A half-full bottle of Jim Beam sat on a bedside table. A couple of gray-tinged dry bath towels hung over the shower rod. Mildewed grout encircled the stained tub. The cabinet over the vanity contained shaving equipment, a dry toothbrush, toothpaste, Listerine, and Tylenol.

He couldn't find any personal papers or ID in the room.

To Tanaka it looked as though Bernier had just stepped out and would be back; however, the place seemed deserted.

To get assistance, Tanaka had to ring a bell on the desk in the management office. He could hear Judge Judy on a TV in a back room.

A morbidly obese middle-aged woman with bright-orange hair emerged from the back room. She was dressed in a floral muumuu. Silver-colored bangles jingled on her wrists as she moved. "Whadda you want?" she mumbled through the smoke rising from the cigarette dangling from her lips.

"I'm looking for Henri Bernier."

"You a dick?"

He nodded.

She glowered at Tanaka. "I haven't seen him for a few days. If you find the drunken bum, tell him I'm going to sell his crap if he doesn't pay his rent." She disappeared into the back room.

CHAPTER FORTY-FOUR

That afternoon, Tanaka was sitting at his desk reading the *Gazette* when he received a call from Warren's research assistant.

"I need to talk to you," Sally Ferguson said.

Her voice was so low Tanaka could hardly hear her.

"I've been doing some snooping—"

"That's not a good idea, Sally. It could be dangerous."

"I've been careful."

"You've found out something?"

"Yes, but I can't talk now. I'm scared the dragon lady'll hear me. I got heck from old man Pratt the last time. Said he'd fire me if I spoke to you again."

"Sorry about that, Sally. Would you like to meet somewhere?"

"It better not be at Starbucks, it's too close to the office."

"What about your place or my office?"

"No. I don't think that's a good idea."

He thought about alternative sites. "What about North Beach Plaza?"

"That would be okay. Where?"

"How about the Coffee Bean?"

"I finish at five. I could be there at five thirty. Would that be okay?"

"That's fine with me. Be careful, don't take any chances, and please don't do any more snooping, it could be dangerous."

❖

At 5:15, he was sipping a latte next to a propane heater on the patio at the Coffee Bean.

He spent a lot of time in the North Beach Plaza, usually at the Coffee Bean and sometimes in the local pub. The village had most of the services he needed. Sally still hadn't shown up by 5:45. Tanaka waited another thirty minutes.

I should've given her my cell phone number, Tanaka thought.

The evening wasn't a total loss, though. He was thinking about leaving when Jeremy Townsend appeared.

"Katsuro," he said. "What are you doing here?"

"I live in the area. I should be asking you what you're doing here."

"I was out for a ride, so when I saw you sitting here, I decided to stop for a caffeine fix. Mind if I join you?"

"Please," Tanaka said.

"You want another coffee?" Townsend asked.

"No, I'm fine, thanks."

Townsend was dressed in a tight Lycra bicycle outfit and a helmet, as if he was ready for the Tour de France. He dropped his helmet on the table and went inside to buy a coffee. Tanaka watched Townsend's muscular rear end as his bicycle shoes clomped across the tiled floor. *Get a grip on yourself*, Tanaka thought. *The guy's in mourning.*

When Townsend was seated and stirring his latte with a wooden stick, Tanaka asked, "How are things doing?"

"I really miss David. I feel lost without him."

"It's hard having to adjust to being alone, isn't it?"

"Yes, I'm taking one day at a time. I've been working a lot of overtime."

They talked about soccer, squash, and tae kwon do. A black Mercedes CLS pulled up to the curb. Two women exited the vehicle. The driver, a striking blond woman, looked familiar. Jeremy waved, and she waved back. The two women crossed to the other side of the street.

"Who was that?" Tanaka asked. "She looks familiar."

"It's Jennifer Easton," Townsend said.

No wonder she looks familiar, Tanaka decided. *I've seen photographs of her.*

"She a friend of yours?" Tanaka asked.

"She used to be, when she worked at the hospital, but that was before she married Easton."

"You mean the attorney?"

"Yeah, in David's firm."

"What kind of work did she do?"

"She was an RN on one of the medical units, but why she worked I don't know. It was common knowledge she inherited oodles of cash and lived in a mansion on Mountain View Drive."

"Some people just like the challenge of working," Tanaka said.

"I guess so. I called her after she left to invite her to a staff party, but she said she couldn't come because Easton wouldn't allow it. I guess we weren't good enough for him. I would've told him to shove it."

"Me too," Tanaka said.

"It was okay for him to enjoy himself outside the marriage, but she couldn't even go out with friends."

"Whadda you mean?"

"David told me Easton had had lots of women on the side. One woman even came into the office to confront him."

"Typical," Tanaka said.

Townsend looked at his watch. "I have to run. Maybe we can get together for a drink when this is all over?" he said.

"Sure…we can do that."

"Looking forward to it," Townsend said.

"I'll give you a call to let you know what happens."

They shook hands.

Back at the office, Tanaka checked to see if Sally had called. There weren't any messages on the machine. He looked her up in the phone book. He tried the number. After four rings, her answering machine came on. He recognized her chirpy voice.

"Hi, this is Katsuro Tanaka," he said. "I guess you got held up at work? Give me a call on my cell phone when you have a minute." He left his number.

Tanaka was concerned about Sally's no-show.

Where was she? Why hadn't she shown? She'd seemed so excited when she'd called him. He hoped she was all right.

CHAPTER FORTY-FIVE

The next morning, Tanaka called Pratt James Easton. Sally Ferguson wasn't at work. He tried her home phone. No answer again, so he left another message asking her to call him.

He sat as his desk and thought about Sally. *Where is she? Why hasn't she contacted me?*

A worm of fear turned in his stomach.

Later that morning, he was still at his desk. He felt like a juggler with too many clubs in the air. It was time to step back, forget what he was doing, and take a fresh look at the evidence.

The telephone saved him from further dithering. When he answered a female said, "Hold for Mr. Pratt, please."

After a few seconds, Pratt came on the line. "Tanaka?"

"Yes."

Pratt got right to the point. "I have discussed Warren's death with all our attorneys, trying to determine if there's any validity to your questions. Now, don't get me wrong, I still believe Warren's death was accidental, but one case did come to mind that I thought you might want to hear about."

Tanaka put his feet up on the desk and leaned back in his chair. Hopefully, this was the lead he was waiting for.

"Some time ago," Pratt continued, "Warren was involved in a lawsuit where a Paul Jackson gave evidence against one of Warren's clients. Warren proved Jackson committed perjury on the witness stand, which resulted in Jackson being charged and convicted. Jackson threatened to kill Warren because of this."

"Did Warren ever talk to you about Jackson?"

"He did mention he'd heard Jackson had been released."

"Do you know if Jackson contacted Warren after his release?"

"I think he may have."

"What makes you think that?"

"It was just a feeling I had. Warren seemed preoccupied about something; however, he wouldn't tell me what was bothering him. All he said was it had something to do with an old case."

"Were the police involved?"

"No. Not to my knowledge."

"Jackson is the only person you can think of who had a grudge against Warren?"

"Yes. All our attorneys concur. As far as we know, Warren did not have any enemies. He was liked by everyone."

"Do you have any idea where Jackson can be found?" he asked Pratt.

"I looked up his file. The last address we have for him is in Santa Barbara County. Do you have a pen?" He read the address to Tanaka.

"Do you know if he works?"

"No idea. It says in his file that he's an arborist. At the time of his arrest, he was working for Firs Unlimited. It's also located in Santa Barbara County."

"Thanks. I appreciate your call. I'll see what I can find on him."

"Where are you with your investigation? Have you reached any conclusions?"

"Nothing specific yet," Tanaka said. "You're probably right that Warren's death was accidental."

"I would appreciate it if you stopped harassing our employees. If you want anymore information about Warren, or our firm, please contact me directly."

"Who's...?"

The line was dead.

"Well, good-bye to you too, buddy," Tanaka said and banged the phone down.

Tanaka called Karen into his office and told her about the call.

"Well, at last we have someone with a reason to get rid of Warren," she said.

"That's true...but we'll see. Men of that ilk are more likely to use violence. Why would he try to cover up Warren's death? He could've mugged Warren on the street and no one would've known it was him."

"I guess you're right."

"All we know for sure is he threatened Warren," Tanaka said.

"What are you going to do?"

"I'm going to go back and see if Bernier has surfaced."

"What about me?"

"When you have time between classes, get back to tailing Pearson. Maybe something will come up. See if you can get a photo of him. Please, be careful, and don't take any chances with that weirdo."

Chapter Forty-six

After his discussion with Karen, Tanaka drove out to Bernier's motel room.

The door opened a couple of inches when Tanaka knocked on it and a youngish woman wearing baby-doll pajamas, eyes half-open, peered at him.

"You're too early." She yawned. "I said after four. You must be really horny."

Tanaka checked the door number. He had the right room.

"Sorry. I was looking for Henri Bernier. I understand this is his room."

"Oh, you're not into women?" she said.

"You got that right," Tanaka said, "but he's just a friend...not my type. I'm sure I have the right room."

She yawned again. "Not anymore. I moved in yesterday."

"Thanks, sorry to disturb you."

"No problem, cutie. Pity you're not into girls." She closed the door.

The insouciant, muumuu-encased receptionist sat behind the desk. "Yeah?" she asked.

"I'm looking for Henri Bernier."

"Oh, yeah...you're the cop that was here yesterday."

"I'm not a cop."

"I thought you said you were a dick?"

"I am. A private one."

Her eyes narrowed. "You knew I thought you were a cop."

"I see you've rented his room to someone else."

She lit a cigarette and blew smoke in his face. "So? What's it to you? You taking a census?"

"It's really important I get in touch with him."

Her lips screwed up and her nostrils dilated. "He's moved out."

"Moved?"

She took a long drag on the cigarette and again blew smoke in Tanaka's face. Her secondhand smoke turned his stomach.

"What are you, a parrot?" she finally said.

"Do you have a new address for him?"

"No."

"Did he collect his belongings?"

"He phoned and apologized. Said he'd come into money and didn't need the room no more. Told me to get rid of his junk."

"What about the rent?"

"He sent it to me."

"Did he pay by check?"

"What is this? I'm tired of answering your stupid questions."

"Sorry I'm bothering you. It's very important I locate him."

"Look, he's paid his rent…that's all I care about. He even included a little extra for me because I was so nice to him."

Sure, nice just like Attila the Hun, Tanaka felt like saying. "So, you've no idea where Bernier is?" he said.

Her brow wrinkled. "What? Are you deaf? Weren't you listening?"

"Thank you for your help," Tanaka said.

She took another drag on the cigarette. Tanaka stepped back out of the range of fire.

"You're welcome," she said.

❖

When he got back to the office Karen was getting ready to leave.

"You stink of cigarette smoke," she said.

Tanaka removed his jacket and hung it on the back of a chair next to an open window.

"You'll never guess who called," Karen said.

"I'm not in the mood for guessing."

"My, my…aren't you the grumpy one. And how was your afternoon?"

He told her about the prostitute working out of Bernier's room and about his conversation with Bernier's landlady.

"Do you think he won the lotto?"

"I hope so."

"If I lived in that dump, I would've done the same thing," she said.

"Me too."

He sighed. "You said someone called?"

"Yeah, Margaret Warren. She wants you to drop in and see her tonight at seven."

"Did she say why?"

"No, I couldn't get anything out of her."

"Perhaps she's decided to come clean?"

Karen picked up her keys. "Let's hope she has something useful for us. Anyway, I have to run. I've got a class tonight. See you in the morning."

At 6:45, Tanaka parked on Ocean Boulevard and walked to Margaret's condominium. A noisy crowd congregated on the street and sidewalk in front of her building. Onlookers packed the balconies. He pushed his way through the crowd. Margaret, dressed in jeans and a white blouse, lay dead on the sidewalk.

CHAPTER FORTY-SEVEN

Tanaka still felt compelled to check Margaret's wrist. There was no pulse, and she certainly wasn't breathing.

"What happened?" he asked.

A teenaged girl with eyes like a raccoon burst out, "It was awful, dude!" Her voice rose an octave. "We were walking along, minding our own business. All of a sudden, there was this God-awful screech and she landed, splat, right in front of us. If we'd been two feet closer she'd've squashed us!"

Tanaka looked up at Margaret's penthouse balcony, and back down to her body.

"Has anyone called 9-1-1?" he asked.

"Uh-huh," she answered.

He was hyperventilating. He had to concentrate to get his breathing under control. His stomach heaved and he could taste bile in his mouth. His legs felt weak. He had to get out of there before he made a fool of himself.

Tanaka crossed the boulevard and collapsed on a bench. He'd seen enough corpses during his years on the homicide team to desensitize him to death, but it hadn't happened. The psychiatrist told him it was the trauma of finding Patrick's body that brought on the panic attacks.

He sat on the bench and forced himself to take slow, deep breaths. He tried to push thoughts of Patrick out of his mind and concentrate on the case. It wasn't easy, but eventually his training helped him focus on the current crisis and overcome his panic attack.

He wondered what had transpired since Margaret had spoken to

Karen. He couldn't believe she'd jumped. *Why call me and then take her life?*

Tanaka pulled out his cell phone and called police headquarters. Sadowski wasn't on duty. He couldn't remember Sadowski's home phone number, so the person on the desk said he'd get Sadowski to call Tanaka.

In a daze, Tanaka wandered back to his car.

Flashing red lights of police vehicles and an ambulance screeched to a halt in front of Margaret's condominium.

Sadowski called while Tanaka was climbing into his car.

"What now?" Sadowski said. "Don't tell me you've chickened out of tonight's game?"

"I wish it was that simple."

"What's going on? What's all that racket?"

Tanaka told him about Margaret's demise and the fact she'd called him only a few hours before, and he didn't believe it was suicide.

Sadowski said he'd look into it and meet with him at Tanaka's office when he was done.

It was going on eleven when Sadowski finally showed up at Tanaka's office. It had been a long four hours. Tanaka had been reviewing the case, but couldn't concentrate. He kept seeing Margaret's broken body lying on the sidewalk.

Sadowski eased himself into the chair alongside Tanaka's desk. "She's Warren's ex, right?" he asked.

"Yes."

"Are you still working on that case?"

"Yes."

"So tell me why you don't buy suicide," Sadowski said.

Tanaka told Sadowski all he knew about Margaret and about her involvement with Robert Sadler. It took some time, and as Tanaka talked, his nerves calmed and he was able to get himself under control.

"You've no idea why she wanted to see you?"

"No. She wouldn't tell Karen over the phone."

"Do you have any ideas?"

"The last time I talked with her I told her I thought that she and Sadler had killed Warren, and she needed an alibi for the day before Warren's death. She wouldn't, or couldn't, come up with one."

"Why are you interested in that day?"

Tanaka explained his theory of the doctored insulin.

"Why didn't you tell me about this before?"

"It's all conjecture. I don't have any evidence. I was trying to come up with something specific before getting you involved."

Sadowski's left eyebrow rose. "Is there anything else you've neglected to tell me?"

"No, that's it. I'm still on the case, and if I do come up with something I'll be sure to let you know. Did you find anything in her suite?" Tanaka asked.

"You mean a suicide note?"

"Yes."

"No, no note. Her suite was clean. There weren't any signs of forced entry or of a struggle."

"Sounds like déjà vu," Tanaka said.

Sadowski didn't respond to the comment. "If she was pushed," he continued, "it had to be somebody who knew her. There was a stool on the balcony, but that could've been put there afterward. None of the neighbors heard or saw anything unusual. The only witnesses were two teenage girls on the sidewalk, who heard her screaming before she landed. You wouldn't expect a suicide to be screaming, would you?"

"Any signs of drugs?"

"No, but we'll see what they find at autopsy."

"You probably won't find any," Tanaka said.

Sadowski stood and sighed. "Why do I think you're still holding back?"

"I'm not, I promise."

"You don't happen to have Sadler's address, do you?"

Tanaka handed his notebook to Sadowski and watched while he recorded Sadler's address.

"If he tries to deny their relationship, tell him you have a photograph of them doing the naughty."

"You have a photo?"

"Yes."

"How did you get that?"

He decided to lie. "I found it in Warren's condo."

"Can I have it?'

"No, not now. If you need it later—for evidence, I'll give it to you."

"Fair enough. Don't lose it, and don't leave town," Sadowski added, with a grin. "I'll be in touch."

Tanaka couldn't think straight. He couldn't concentrate anymore and couldn't keep his eyes open. He didn't even feel like driving, so he called for a cab and went home to bed.

CHAPTER FORTY-EIGHT

It was nearly ten the next morning when Tanaka finally arrived at his office.

Tanaka hadn't been able to sleep. Every time he closed his eyes, he saw Margaret's broken body lying on the sidewalk—only the face was Patrick's. He felt drained and had a pounding headache.

"You started keeping executive hours?" Karen asked.

Tanaka went into his office and slumped into his chair. He rummaged through his desk, looking for his bottle of Tylenol. He swallowed two tablets with a mouthful of coffee from the mug Karen plunked on his desk.

"You and Steve have a good time last night?" she asked. "It's a long time since I've seen you with bags under your eyes."

He shook his head, "I wish it were so."

She settled in a chair.

Tanaka told Karen about Margaret Warren's sudden demise and his meeting with Sadowski.

The expression on her face mirrored his feelings.

"I feel somehow responsible for her death," Tanaka said. "Maybe if I hadn't threatened her she'd still be alive."

"That's crazy talk, Kats."

"I guess you're right, but that doesn't help with the guilt." He drank some coffee. "How did Margaret sound when she called?"

"She didn't sound anxious or anything like that. Do you think she was suicidal?"

"No, I don't. I think somebody helped her over the balcony."

"I guess that rules her out as Warren's killer."

"Not necessarily. Perhaps Sadler thought she was going to spill her guts, so he decided to get rid of her," he said.

"But they're a couple, surely he wouldn't kill her?"

"I don't think he would've given it a second thought. He doesn't strike me as someone with a conscience."

"You think he's a sociopath?"

"I don't know, Karen. Anyway it's in Sadowski's hands, not ours."

"So are we finished with the case?"

"We still haven't found out who killed Warren, so no, we're not finished."

She nodded.

"I've got a dreadful feeling that unless we can figure out who the killer is, this won't be the last death," Tanaka said.

She shuddered. "What's Pearson the primate's role in all of this?"

"That's one thing I'd like to know," Tanaka said.

"So I should continue tailing him when I can?"

"Until we can eliminate him."

"Will do, Katsuro," she said and disappeared into the outer office.

❖

He called Winifred and told her about Margaret Warren's death.

"That's awful. I know she was self-centered and obnoxious—but to die like that?"

"Yes. I'm sorry she's dead, and I wish I hadn't seen her on the sidewalk. It must've been terrifying for her."

"What does it mean? Do you think she committed suicide because she couldn't live with the guilt?"

"No, I think she was pushed."

"That's appalling," she said. "What do you think we should do?"

"I would like to continue with the investigation, if that's all right with you."

"Yes. I still want to know what happened to David."

"Winifred, I need to ask you something personal about David."

"What about?"

"Did you know he was gay?"

She was silent for a few seconds before saying, "Let's put it this way: I'm not surprised, but no, I didn't know for sure. When David was a teenager, I came home early one day and found him and a neighbor's boy in bed together. At the time, I put it down to youthful experimentation, but later on, I saw the signs. We never discussed it. At first, I blamed myself, wondering if it was because of the way I'd brought him up—and not having a father figure to identify with—but after doing a lot of research I realized it had nothing to do with it. Of course, when he got married, I thought I'd been wrong."

"So you probably had some idea about Jeremy?"

"Yes. Does this have any bearing on David's death?"

"It might."

"You're not saying that Jeremy...?"

"No. I think we can safely rule him out."

"Good. I'm very fond of him. In fact, I've been thinking of giving him David's condo. I think David would've wanted that. I don't need it, and I certainly don't need the money."

"That's really nice of you, Winifred. I'm sure he'll appreciate it."

After Winifred hung up, Tanaka called Pratt James Easton. The secretary who answered obviously hadn't been told he was persona non grata. She told him Sally was off sick. Her father had called in to let them know Sally had strep throat and couldn't speak. She was staying with him until she was well enough to return to work.

Tanaka's head was still throbbing and he wanted to go home to bed. But he still had work to do, so he persevered.

Chapter Forty-nine

Tanaka took US 101 south to Santa Barbara. He could've phoned to see if Paul Jackson worked at Firs Unlimited but he didn't like to let suspects prepare themselves for his visits. He liked to see the reaction on their faces when he questioned them. To watch for tells. He could usually tell when people were being untruthful. It was going on one when he arrived in Santa Barbara, so before looking up Jackson he stopped for a meal at Breakwater Restaurant.

It had been a few years since Tanaka had been in Santa Barbara. The last time he was there was for a yacht race. He'd crewed on a forty-foot cutter, in a race around Santa Catalina Island. They hadn't won; however, it had been a memorable weekend.

The Firs Unlimited office was a small corrugated iron shed at one end of a large lot. Wood chippers, backhoes, and an assortment of other gardening machinery occupied a large amount of space.

In one corner of the lot, the smell of rotting vegetation emanated from a large pile of soil. A variety of potted trees and shrubs took up the rest of the space.

A masculine-looking middle-aged woman wearing coveralls sat behind a desk in the office. She looked up at Tanaka when he opened the door.

"Help you?" she said.

"I'm looking for Paul Jackson. Does he still work here?"

"You a relative?" she asked.

Tanaka handed her his business card.

"Was he in trouble again?" she asked.

"How come you're using past tense?" Tanaka said.

She sighed, came out from behind her desk, and gestured to an armchair.

"Why don't you take a seat?"

Tanaka sat down and watched her. She closed her eyes and took a deep breath. He knew it wasn't going to be good news. She crossed her arms and perched on the edge of her desk.

"I'm afraid I have some bad news," she said. Her calloused hands fiddled with some pens in her breast pocket. "We had a terrible...um, accident."

He waited.

"Paul...had an accident," she said.

"Was he badly injured?"

She sighed. "Well...yes. I'm awfully sorry, but he passed away."

"He passed away?"

"Well, actually, he was killed."

"Please," Tanaka said, "tell me about it."

"You want the details?"

"Yes, please."

"It's not very pleasant. Are you sure?" she asked.

"I can handle it."

"We had a huge pile of brush in the yard. We could hardly move our equipment, so Paul decided to work some overtime. He was working on our big wood chipper when I left for the day."

"He had an accident with the chipper? You mean he lost an arm or something?" Tanaka asked.

"I'm afraid it was worse than that. We think he must've got caught on a branch or something, and was pulled into the chipper."

Tanaka covered his mouth with a hand.

"We're not sure when it happened. Some neighbors called the Santa Barbara Sheriff's Department at eleven to complain about the noise. When the deputy got here he couldn't find anyone around, so he shut down the chipper and phoned me."

"You mean...he was gone?"

"Yes. They found bits and pieces of him and his clothing in the wood chips."

Tanaka couldn't imagine what it would be like to die in that manner. The idea of being dragged into a wood chipper was horrifying.

"When did this happen?"

"Two weeks ago."

"Did he have any relatives?"

"Just his father, but he's not with it…Alzheimer's, I think. Paul was a loner. We couldn't find any friends."

"That's terrible."

They were quiet for a few moments.

"Why are you looking for him? How come you're asking questions about him?"

"It's got something to do with a case I'm working on. I don't think he was involved, though. I just wanted to clarify something."

"I'm glad to hear that, he was a nice guy. I had a memorial for him."

"Do you know where he lived?"

She pulled a ledger book out of a drawer, copied out Jackson's address, and gave him directions.

Tanaka rose to leave.

She placed her hand on his shoulder. "I'm sorry for the bad news."

He nodded.

❖

Tanaka drove to the address she'd given him. It was a small basement apartment in a dilapidated clapboard house. He knocked on the door. Nobody answered. Tanaka could hear a TV blaring upstairs, so he banged on the front door of the house.

A gray-haired woman stuck her head out of an upstairs window. "What you want?" she yelled.

"Did Paul Jackson live here?"

"You looking for a room?"

"No," he yelled. "Did Paul Jackson live here?"

"What're you shouting for? I'm not deaf, you know."

"Sorry." He tried again. "Did Paul Jackson live here?"

"He did. You heard what happened to him?"

"Yes, I've just come from Firs Unlimited."

"So what do you want, then?"

"Are his belongings still here?"

"The apartment came fully furnished. He only had clothes in there."

"Do you still have them?"

"I gave them to Big Brothers."

"Didn't he have any relatives?"

"His father didn't want them. Anything else? I'm missing *The Young and the Restless.*"

"Thank you, no."

Her head disappeared and the window banged closed.

Tanaka didn't believe Jackson had accidentally fallen into the chipper.

It just didn't sound right.

CHAPTER FIFTY

Tanaka drove back to San Sebastian. His mind was in a whirl. He was still trying to figure out what had happened to Paul Jackson and Margaret Warren, and he still felt guilty about Margaret's death.

Steve was expecting him for dinner. He went home, called Chicago and spoke to his mother and Tommy, packed an overnight bag, and drove to Steve's place.

Steve had just finished cleaning his house when Tanaka arrived.

"You timed that right," Steve said.

"I'm not crazy. I've been outside, waiting for you to finish."

Tanaka threw his bag onto the bed, went into the kitchen, and opened a couple of beers.

They settled themselves on the sofa with Sheba insinuating herself between them.

"Aren't you the jealous one?" Steve said.

"I don't mind sharing her with you."

Steve smiled. "I was talking to Sheba."

"You've been busy this morning," Tanaka said. "The place looks spotless."

"It needed it."

Tanaka put his arm around Steve's shoulder and ruffled his hair.

"What've you been up to?" Steve asked.

"Working…nothing else, really."

"You and Rick not been out drinking?"

"It's been a while since Rick and I've been out drinking. Anyway, I'm too busy with the Warren case."

"I heard about Margaret's death," Steve said. "You think she jumped?"

"No, I don't. I think she was pushed."

"God, what a mess. I hope you're taking care of yourself."

"I'm being careful, Stevie, I'm not taking any chances."

"You think her death has something to do with Warren's death?" Steve asked.

"I do. I don't know how, but I'm sure it does."

Tanaka didn't give Steve any details about the case. He didn't want him to get all upset again and ruin the day, so he changed the subject. "You been up to anything special?"

"Not really. One thing did happen, though, that you might be interested in. I ran into Jennifer Easton at the airport yesterday."

"What were you doing there?"

"I had to pick up a client."

"Was Jennifer coming or going?"

"It was a bit strange, really. She told me she was going to Dallas to visit her sister, but I saw her boarding a Chicago flight."

"I wonder why she did that?"

"Don't quote me, but I think she had a black eye. She'd covered it with makeup and was wearing dark glasses, but I could still see the bruising when she turned sideways."

"Did she say anything about it?"

"No. So I had to assume it was something she didn't want to talk about."

"Strange," Tanaka said.

"She seemed nervous while we were talking and kept furtively glancing over her shoulder, like she was anxious to be on her way and didn't want to be seen."

"What do you think was going on?"

"I've no idea. She seemed spaced out, as if she was on drugs or something. Maybe she was in an accident and just wanted to get away for a while. Maybe she was on pain pills. Who knows?"

Low, thick clouds darkened the sky. A sudden gust of wind rattled the deck chairs. Rain beat on the windows.

Steve ran into the bedroom to close the windows. Tanaka did the same in the kitchen. When Steve came back into the family room, he turned on the gas fireplace and popped a rented movie into the DVD player. The rain kept coming, a driving torrent that pounded the windows and deck.

❖

When they finally pulled themselves out of bed the next morning, the rain had stopped. They would've stayed in bed longer but Sheba wouldn't let them.

After lunch, Sheba brought them her leash, so they took her for a walk. The scent of pine permeated the surroundings. Sheba dragged them down a short street between Steve's property and his neighbor's property that dead-ended at the cliff edge.

The rain had done a lot of damage. An uprooted Western sycamore tree hung over the brink. A temporary yellow-and-black-striped warning barrier lay on a ledge about six feet down.

Tanaka's eyes focused on the crashing waves below the cliff. "That's kind of dangerous," he said.

Steve nodded. "Yes, they've been trying to shore up the cliff. It keeps eroding more and more with each storm."

"That's what happens when you cut down the trees."

It was too muddy to walk any farther, so they headed back to Steve's house.

Steve liked to give him massages, so they stripped and he lay on the bed. Steve sat astride Tanaka and kneaded his back muscles.

"The bruises are starting to fade," he said. "Is it still painful?"

"No, it feels great."

"I bet Patrick didn't do this for you, did he?"

Why does he insist on asking me questions about Patrick? Tanaka was thinking. "I don't want to talk about Patrick, Stevie. It would be the same if someone asked me what you and I do in bed. I would tell them to mind their own business."

"Sorry," Steve said. "I was just interested."

The mood was broken, and Tanaka wanted out of there. "What's the time, Stevie? I have to go home...I promised Tommy I'd take him for a ride."

He hated lying to Steve, but he couldn't think of anything else to say.

"It's only three, we still have time," Steve said.

"Three? I better get going, he'll be wondering where I am."

"Do you have to go?" he asked, when Tanaka started dressing.

"Yeah, sorry...I'll see you next week."

CHAPTER FIFTY-ONE

Tanaka was at his desk on Monday morning. Three weeks had passed since Winifred hired him, and he wasn't any closer to closing the case. Someone rapped on his door.

A tall slender woman, probably in her mid-thirties, stood in the doorway. Her hair, cut to the nape of her neck, had a coppery sheen to it. She wore the uniform of a Ventura County sheriff's deputy.

She looked vaguely familiar but Tanaka couldn't place her.

Her hazel eyes sparkled. "How're you doing, Kats?"

He leaned back in his chair and eyed her. "I'm trying to remember where we met."

She reached across Tanaka's desk and offered him her hand. "Elaine Nielsen."

"Oh sure, I remember now. We worked on a case together while I was still on the San Sebastian force."

She sat in the chair next to his desk. "You're looking good, Kats, just as handsome as ever, I see."

"You're looking pretty good yourself, Elaine."

"I try."

"What brings you into San Sebastian?"

"I'm working on a case, and your name surfaced."

"What case is that?"

"Do you know Henri Bernier?"

"Sure. I've interviewed him a few times. He was a concierge at the building where a client's nephew lived."

"What client is that?"

"Why don't you tell me what this is all about, Elaine."

She was silent for a few moments. "Bernier's body was found at the base of a mountain in Los Padres National Forest. He'd been there for a few days. If he hadn't left his car in the parking lot at the top of the mountain, we might never have looked for him."

Shit, not another one, Tanaka thought. *I knew something happened to Bernier.*

"Your business card was in his jacket pocket."

"You think it was suicide?"

"We've no reason to think otherwise. It looks like he drove up there and jumped. His body is with the Ventura County coroner waiting for autopsy. The examiner on scene said Bernier's neck was broken."

"No signs of foul play?" Tanaka said.

"Why do you ask?"

"I don't think he was suicidal. Why would he want to kill himself when he'd just come into money?"

"He came into money?"

The image of Bernier's squalid room, along with the muumuu-encased landlady and her story about a lottery win flashed back into his mind. Deputy Nielsen needed to know everything, so he gave her a detailed account of his investigation.

"So do you think he really did win the lotto?" she said.

"Not for a second. I think he saw something—or someone—at Warren's condo and tried a little blackmail."

"You really think Warren's death was a homicide?"

"Yes, and Margaret's. I think we're dealing with a psycho who will eliminate anyone he thinks is a threat to him."

"Hmm. It does look a bit fishy now that you've filled me in."

"You said Bernier's car was in the parking lot?'

"Yes. The keys were in his pocket."

"I guess that means—if he was thrown off—that there had to be at least two people involved. I can't see the perpetrator walking home from there, can you?"

"Maybe they arranged to meet up there and drove in separate cars?"

"That's possible," Tanaka said.

Elaine finished jotting notes in her small book and looked up at Tanaka. "Listen, if there's anything else you think I should know about, gimme a call. Maybe we could go out for a drink sometime?"

"I thought you were married?"

"Not anymore. Couldn't take any more of his abuse."

Tanaka shook his head. "Not another one."

"Yeah…well, I'm glad to be rid of the asshole."

They stared at each other for a while.

She raised her eyebrows. "So?"

She must be the only person in the two counties that doesn't know about Patrick, Tanaka thought. "I'm going steady, Elaine."

"That's too bad. If that ever changes, gimme me a call."

She wrote her phone number on his note pad, gave him a wink, and departed.

Tanaka shook his head, wrote her phone number in his notebook, and called Sadowski and told him about his meeting with Deputy Nielsen.

"What the hell, Kats. I've got enough to do without all this shit."

"Are you still investigating Margaret Warren's death?" Tanaka asked.

"Yes, but we're not getting anywhere with that. It still looks like suicide."

"Did you check on Sadler?"

"Yes, I personally interviewed him, he appeared to be devastated by her death, and he has an ironclad alibi for the time of her death. So that rules him out."

"Who gave him the alibi?"

"Some rich old fart on Mountain View Drive says Sadler was with him from five p.m. until midnight."

"Huh."

"What do you mean, 'Huh'?" he said.

"Did you ask what they were doing?"

"Why would I do that? The old geezer seemed pretty genuine."

Tanaka told Sadowski about Sadler and the old guy.

"So you think he might be covering for Sadler?"

"Who knows? I feel like I'm getting a migraine."

"Poor baby," Sadowski said. "By the way, I checked Sadler's prison records. Would you believe he shared a cell with Pearson, the other character you had me check?"

"Nothing would surprise me," Tanaka said. "I wonder if Pearson had anything to do with Margaret Warren's death?"

"I had the same thought. I'm going to visit him today."

"Have you found out anything else?" Tanaka asked.

"Yeah. We found a video in her suite. It's a ménage a trois…her and two guys. The one male is Sadler. We haven't been able to identify the second male yet."

"Where was the video taken?"

"We found a video camera set up in her bedroom closet. There's a see-through mirror in the door," Sadowski said.

"They were performing for the camera?"

"It looks like Margaret and Sadler were. I got the impression the second guy was unaware he was being taped."

"Now why would they do that?" Tanaka asked.

"Who knows? Maybe she was setting up the guy for blackmail?"

"Shit. Maybe that's why she took a dive?"

"Could be."

"Did you ask Sadler about the video?"

"Yeah, says he doesn't know anything about it."

"You believe him?"

"Not really. I'll get back to him when he's recovered from Margaret's death."

"I'm sure he's crying crocodile tears."

"When you get a chance I want you to look at the video to see if you recognize the guy."

"I'll drop by as soon as I can," Tanaka said.

"Thanks for filling me in. I'll give Elaine a call. Maybe she'll get together with me for a drink. I'm more her type, don't you think?"

"Very funny," Tanaka said.

"Don't forget to drop in to see the video. I'd like to find out who the guy is."

"I'll try and make it tomorrow."

"Good...now for my call to Elaine," Sadowski said.

Tanaka could hear Sadowski laughing when he hung up.

CHAPTER FIFTY-TWO

Tanaka hadn't fully recovered from the shock of hearing about Bernier's demise and was still doodling on his pad when he received his second visitor of the day.

This time a chubby, gray-haired man about six feet tall stood in the doorway. With his horn-rimmed glasses and thick gray mustache, he reminded Tanaka of his high school history teacher, but his uniform told another story.

"Tanaka?" he asked.

Tanaka nodded.

"Zach Denman," he said, reaching over to shake Tanaka's hand. "I'm with the San Sebastian County Sheriff's Department."

Oh, fuck! Not another one flashed through Tanaka's mind.

Denman took a seat and placed his briefcase on the floor.

"What can I do for you, Deputy Denman?"

"I understand you knew Sally Ferguson?"

Tanaka had a sudden sick feeling of dread. "You're talking as though she's dead."

Denman gazed at Tanaka for a while. "I'm sorry, she is."

"How do you know I knew her?"

"We found your business card in her apartment, and you did leave a couple of messages on her answering machine."

"What happened?"

"She apparently committed suicide."

"Apparently? It sounds like you have some doubts about it."

"Well, I'm sure you know the routine. We have to rule out homicide before settling on suicide. Besides, there are some things I'm not happy with."

"How did she apparently do it?"

"She shot herself in the head with a nine-millimeter Beretta pistol."

"That doesn't sound like something she'd do."

"How well did you know her?"

"I didn't really know her at all. We talked on a couple of occasions about a case I'm working on. The last time we talked was last Wednesday. We made arrangements to meet, but she never showed."

"The forensic pathologist figures she died sometime Wednesday evening."

"She wasn't depressed when she called me. She seemed excited about something," Tanaka said.

Denman rubbed his chin.

"Can you give me all the details of Sally's death?" Tanaka asked.

Denman gave Tanaka a long appraising look. "Why had you been talking to her?"

Tanaka told Denman about Warren's death, and about Margaret Warren and Bernier. He pulled Warren's appointment book out of his desk and showed Denman the entries Sally had shown him. He told Denman everything he knew about Sadler and Pearson.

"If you need someone to vouch for me, you can call Sadowski," Tanaka said.

"I've already checked you out with the chief."

Denman pulled a file out of his briefcase and paged through it. "The gun was at this angle." Denman demonstrated with his right hand. "The bullet entered in front, above her right ear, and exited below, behind her left ear."

"Strange angle for a self-inflicted gunshot wound," Tanaka said.

"Right. In the majority of suicides the entrance wound is in the right temporal area, and the exit wound is in the left temporal area."

"Especially for a left-handed person," Tanaka added.

"She was left-handed?"

Tanaka nodded. "Yes, we joked about it."

"The palm of her right hand contained gunshot residue—but not the back, which indicates she held the gun but didn't necessarily fire it, and there definitely wasn't any residue on her left hand."

"How did the entry wound look?" Tanaka said.

"It was a typical star-shaped contact wound. There was an abrasion collar and gunpowder blackening. Her hair was scorched."

"Did you find the slug?"

"Yes. It was in the sofa and did come from the Beretta."

"Where did the gun come from?"

"Her father has a collection of firearms in his cottage."

"Any fingerprints on the gun or casing?"

"Nothing we could use. Just smudges."

"She was found in a cottage?"

"Yes, it belongs to the family. It's in an isolated area, so the gunshot wasn't heard by anyone. Her parents were in San Diego for a week. When they returned, they found her body."

"When I called Pratt James Easton last week, they told me her father had called in to tell them she had strep throat and wouldn't be in to work."

"He didn't do that."

"Women don't usually shoot themselves in the head, do they?" Tanaka said.

"Right, that's more of a male thing. There was a full bottle of her mother's amitriptyline in the medicine cabinet, so if she was suicidal that would've been a more likely scenario."

"Were there any drugs in her system?"

"No. She was clean."

"Was there a note?"

"Yes, but very generic. It was typed and wasn't signed."

"What did it say?"

"Nothing much. Just that she couldn't face life anymore and was sorry to disappoint her parents."

"Were there any other findings?"

"She wasn't sexually assaulted, but we did find blood and pieces of skin under her fingernails and bruises on her wrists, so it looks as though she put up a struggle."

"I don't think she committed suicide, and I don't think you do either."

Denman sighed. "What a mess. It sounds as though it's time to get the different forces involved. I'll call Sadowski and Nielsen and set up a meet."

"I'm still on the case," Tanaka said. "If I find anything to help with your investigation, I'll give Sadowski a call."

CHAPTER FIFTY-THREE

Tanaka felt dreadful on Tuesday morning. On Monday night, in an attempt to block out the image of Sally Ferguson, he'd had a few too many Heinekens. He'd taken a couple of Tylenol and was still waiting for them to take effect. He needed some coffee.

Where's Karen? Tanaka was thinking when the telephone rang. It was Elaine Nielsen from the Ventura County Sheriff's Department. "We have the autopsy results on Bernier. Do you want to hear them?" she said.

"Not particularly, but I guess I better."

Tanaka was hoping she was going to say it was suicide.

"The cause of death was neurogenic shock precipitated by a forward occipitoatlantal dislocation, causing C1 on C2 subluxation, with transverse separation of the spinal cord. His aorta, liver, spleen, and heart were lacerated, and he had a fractured pelvis and skull, but those injuries were postmortem."

"Are you're saying his neck was broken and he was dead before someone threw him off the side of the mountain?"

"That's exactly what I'm saying. Glad to see you're not just a pretty face."

"Shit," was all he could muster.

"You can say that again. It's now officially a homicide case. Officers from the San Sebastian Police Department, the Ventura County Sheriff, and the San Sebastian County Sheriff are forming an integrated unit to investigate the deaths."

"Sounds like we have a serial killer on our hands."

"Please, don't use those words. Someone might hear you."

After she hung up, he found himself bouncing a brass paperweight. Without thinking, he threw it across the room. There was a crash of breaking glass when it landed on a small glass table.

"What's going on?" Karen yelled from the other room.

A moment later, she appeared in his doorway.

"What's your problem? You have PMS today?" she asked.

"Make some coffee, then I'll tell you about it."

"I knew there was some reason you'd hired me."

"Sorry. You know that's not the reason. I always screw up when I try to make the coffee. You have the feminine touch."

"Male chauvinist pig," she mumbled.

"I heard that."

Without further ado, she set about making the coffee, watching him out of the corners of her eyes. "Ah," Tanaka said, when she opened a box of Krispy Kreme doughnuts and took a big bite out of one, "just what I need."

He sipped the coffee and ate a doughnut.

"Well," she said, an edge of impatience creeping into her voice, "are you going to tell me or not?"

As he told her about the two visitors he'd had on the previous day and Elaine's call, he could feel his pulse racing and his voice rising.

"Oh shit," she said. "This is serious. I can see why you're upset."

"Upset? I'm outraged!" he yelled. "Some weirdo's going around killing people, and I'm too dense to figure out who's doing it."

"Whoa, Kats! Take it easy. We've been working our butts off trying to solve this case. What more could we possibly have done?"

"Maybe if I'd got Sadowski more involved, this wouldn't have happened."

"What could you've told him? We didn't know anything."

"I'm not sure about that," Tanaka said. "Bernier didn't deserve to die like that, but he only had himself to blame. But Sally...she was an innocent. I told her not to snoop, that it could be dangerous, but she was caught up in the excitement."

"I can tell you're feeling pretty hopeless at the moment, Kats, but logically, how could you have prevented her death?"

She's right, there's nothing I could've done, Tanaka thought, *but that doesn't make it any easier for me to accept.*

"I guess Bernier thought he could solve all his problems by blackmailing the killer," she said.

"Yes. He must've seen the killer on the Thursday before Warren's death...but who was it?"

"My money's still on Pearson the primate," Karen said. "He's evil. He tried to run you down and pushed you off the cliff, so he'd be capable of breaking Bernier's neck and throwing him off a mountain."

Tanaka took a swig from the mug. "I've been trying to remember everything Sally and I discussed."

"She gave you Warren's appointment book and told you about Warren's plans to meet Pearson and Sadler?"

"Yeah."

"What else did you discuss?"

"I showed her the key and the code, but she didn't recognize them. I also asked her about the car rental, but she couldn't shed any light on that either."

"Maybe she'd found out something on the car rental?" Karen said, her mouth full of doughnut.

"Could be."

He pulled out the bill from the car rental company and handed it to her. "When you have a minute, see what you can find out about it. We should've done it before."

"It'll be hard. They don't like giving out information...but I'll see what I can do."

"I guess you better get back to tailing Pearson too," Tanaka said.

"Shit, you think I'm superwoman? That's three things you want me to do. Which one's the priority?"

He smiled at her. "Actually I do think you're superwoman, but you're right. You can't be doing it all Let's concentrate on Pearson today. You can get to the rest later."

She drained her coffee and stood up. "Okay, I'm off."

"You be careful," Tanaka said.

"Will do, Katsuro."

She suddenly let out a scream.

Tanaka jumped. She was pointing at the window. A raven sat on the ledge staring at them.

"There's going to be another death," she said.

"You and your superstitions. It's only a bird."

She marched out of the office.

He was reviewing Karen's notes on other cases they were handling when the phone rang.

"It's me," Karen said. "I'm in the parking lot at Lighthouse Park."

"You're supposed to be working," Tanaka said. "Not taking in the view."

"I've been tailing Pearson. He's just met up with someone. I can't see who it is, but the person's in a black Mercedes CLS with dark tinted windows."

"You have the tag number?"

She read it off to Tanaka.

"Okay. Stay on his tail. I'll get Sadowski to check it."

He called Sadowski.

"I don't know why I don't quit my job and join you. I seem to be spending an awful lot of time doing work for you," Sadowski said.

"But how would we get all this information you're providing if you left the force?"

"That's true."

"I'll buy you dinner next week. You can name the place," Tanaka said.

"Sure, sure. Anyway, I'm too busy now looking into your murders. I'll get to it when I can."

"My murders?"

"You know what I mean."

Tanaka thought about Karen's call. He'd seen another black Mercedes CLS recently. *Is there a connection?*

CHAPTER FIFTY-FOUR

Tanaka was at his desk going through the mail. One envelope stopped him dead. Emblazoned across the top of the envelope were the words *San Quentin State Prison*. What did they want? Patrick's killer, Lawrence Ingram, was on death row in that facility. Feeling shaky and nauseous, Tanaka stared at the letter. *I hope he's dead* was the first thought that entered his mind. *Maybe they've given him his long-awaited lethal injection? I hoped to God he hasn't escaped.*

Tanaka's hands were trembling when he sliced open the envelope. It was a one-page handwritten letter. He checked the scrawl at the end of the letter. It was signed *Lawrence Ingram.*

Dear Mr Tanaka,

Im sure your shocked getting a letter from me and I want blame you if you chuck it in the garbage but please I want to tell you something. There's not a day goes by when I dont regret what I done to Patrick and how I messed up your life. I know theres no excuse. They say it was me but I cant remember cause I was high. I know this is hard for you but I want to ask you to forgive me. They say I have to do this before I can see my mistake.

Lawrence Ingram

Tanaka pounded his fist on the desk. The bastard...did he really think it was that easy? He felt like ripping up the letter and throwing it in the garbage, but didn't. He reread the letter three times before returning it to the envelope and putting it in his pocket.

Tanaka placed his elbows on the desk and rested his head in his hands. How would Patrick handle this if things were the other way round? He knew Patrick would've been able to forgive Ingram—that was the kind of person Patrick was—but Tanaka wasn't sure if he'd ever be able to forgive Ingram. He tried to blot it out of his mind, and went back to opening the mail.

Sadowski phoned while Tanaka was reviewing his Visa statement. Tanaka told him about the letter from Ingram.

"If you can forgive that sick bastard, you're a better man than me," Sadowski said.

"I'll think about it."

"I'm calling to remind you to come in to review the video we found in Margaret Warren's suite."

"I'll come in this afternoon, Rick."

After Tanaka hung up, he settled back in his chair and thought about Ingram.

❖

That afternoon, Tanaka was just about to leave for the San Sebastian Police Department when he received a call from Stanley Pearson. "You sent the pigs to see me," Pearson bellowed.

"The police have been to see you?"

"Like you don't know? You're full of shit, man."

"What can I do for you, Mr. Pearson?"

"Get the pigs off my back! I did nothing, man. Maybe I did in the past, but not now."

"I'm supposed to believe that? Give me a break."

"It's true, man, I'm innocent."

"Sure, like you didn't try to do me in?"

"You think you know everything, don't you? But you don't know nothing."

"Why are you calling me?"

Pearson was silent for a while and Tanaka waited.

Eventually Pearson said in a low voice, "I need help, man, and you're the only person I can think of."

"What kind of help do you think I can give you?"

"Not on the phone, man. They probably got my phone bugged. Come down to my place tonight. You won't regret it."

"What's it about? I'm not coming unless you tell me more."

"Fuck, man. It's about a car I painted in December. This is big, man. You might even want to pay me for this."

Tanaka considered Pearson's request. If he went to see Pearson maybe he'd learn something new.

"What time?" Tanaka asked.

"How 'bout seven. Come round back. You bring the cops, I ain't saying nothing."

"Okay, I'll be over."

Tanaka called Sadowski and told him about the call. He didn't want to lose his license. If he went to see Pearson, the police might interpret it as interfering in an active homicide case, and he didn't need that.

"No problem," Sadowski said. "Go ahead and see him, but don't go alone."

Tanaka called Karen on her cell phone.

"Where are you?" he asked.

"I'm at home. Pearson drove back to his workshop after leaving Lighthouse Park, so I thought I would come home and have a bite to eat before tae kwon do."

Tanaka told her about Pearson's call.

"Do you mind missing tae kwon do tonight?" he asked. "I think it would be a good idea if you came along."

"No problem, Katsuro. I'd like to see him close up for a change."

"Good. Meet me at the office around six forty-five."

"Will do, Katsuro."

Tanaka opened his safe and pulled out his 9mm Smith & Wesson pistol. The last time he'd used it was a couple of months ago at the practice range, so he dismantled and cleaned it. When he was satisfied it was in tiptop condition, he loaded it and slipped it into his shoulder holster. His black leather jacket hid it from view.

CHAPTER FIFTY-FIVE

It was dark when Karen and Tanaka pulled up outside Pearson's body shop. The rain had stopped; however, it was threatening to start up again. A thick fog rolled in from the ocean, leaving a salty taste in Tanaka's mouth.

Not the kind of place for a carefree stroll, Tanaka thought as he looked around.

The area was deserted, and the front of the body shop was in darkness. Tanaka could see a faint glow coming from the rear. He shivered when a grove of fir trees shimmied in the fractious wind. He felt chilled to the bone.

"What's that for?" Karen asked when he pulled out his pistol.

"Just a precaution. Who knows…maybe he's got the pit bull unleashed?"

Her hand shook when he handed her a flashlight.

"You ready?" Tanaka said.

She nodded.

They headed up the alley toward the rear of the building.

"What if—?"

"Quiet," Tanaka whispered.

Tanaka could hear Karen breathing behind him. Her hot breath sent shivers down his spine. A gust of wind rattled the rusty siding, and then the night was suddenly still. Not a sound came from the workshop.

They scanned the area with their flashlights.

"I don't see the pit bull, he's not in his usual spot," Tanaka said.

She grabbed his arm with her trembling hand.

"It's not here," Tanaka said. "It would've attacked us by now if it was."

She released his arm.

When they walked in the gaping door, Tanaka knew what they were going to find. He could detect the distinct rusty odor of blood. One dim overhead light swung back and forth in the gusty wind, giving the place an eerie look. The Honda Civic was still in the bay. The block and tackle was free of the motor. Pearson was leaning into the engine area, only this time he wasn't moving.

"Pearson," Tanaka shouted. There was no response.

Tanaka holstered his pistol.

They inched toward the car.

Karen shone the flashlight on Pearson. "Oh, God," she said.

Pearson's head was caught between the motor and the body of the car. Tanaka couldn't see Pearson's face but he recognized the blond ponytail—now bloody red—the greasy overalls, and the Dr. Martens boots.

Karen ran outside. Tanaka could hear her vomiting.

He went outside to check on her.

"I'm sorry," she said. "I've never seen anything like that before."

Tanaka put his arm around her shoulders. "That's okay," he said. "Don't think for one minute I don't feel the same. They say you get used to seeing death, but nothing can prepare you for what we've just seen. Wait for me in the car. Give Sadowski a call and tell him what we found."

Tanaka went back inside and did a quick tour of the place. He couldn't see anything unusual, and he didn't touch anything. He felt calm and analytical, like he used to feel before Patrick's death. The anxiety that had nearly overwhelmed him when he'd seen Margaret's body on the sidewalk had not resurfaced.

"Shit," Karen said when he joined her in the car. "If I'd stayed on his tail I would've seen who did it."

"Maybe it's a good thing you weren't around."

They were waiting in the car when Sadowski arrived.

"Wait here," was all Sadowski said.

After about ten minutes, Sadowski came out.

"I've called a team in to process the scene," he said. "You two might as well go home. I'll want you both at the station tomorrow to give written statements."

Tanaka dropped Karen off at the office so she could collect her car and headed home. It was too late to phone Chicago, but Tanaka was comforted by a message from his mother telling him they were both fine.

He sat on the edge of Tommy's bed and thought about his mother and Tommy. He missed them. He'd never felt so alone. Tommy's G.I. Joe wasn't there, but his Spider-Man pajamas were still under his pillow. Tanaka picked up the pajamas and held them.

It seemed like days had passed since he'd heard from Ingram, but it had only been a few hours. "What should I do about Lawrence Ingram, Tommy?" he said to the empty room. "I think your daddy would've forgiven him, but I'm having trouble with it."

When he finally started to relax, he climbed into his own bed and fell into a troubled sleep.

❖

The next afternoon Karen and Tanaka went into the police department and signed written statements.

"Well, so far it's looking like an accident," Sadowski said when Tanaka enquired about Pearson. "It looks like the block and tackle broke while he was working on the car. He never had a chance."

"You really believe that?" Karen asked.

"I'm keeping an open mind," Sadowski said.

"Did you find anything on the premises to connect him to the other deaths?" Tanaka asked.

"As a matter of fact, we did. We're still processing the scene—there's lots to go through—but we did find Warren's briefcase in a drawer."

"You're sure about that?" Tanaka said.

"Sure I'm sure. It's got Warren's files in it, and his address book."

"I knew it was him," Karen said.

Tanaka kept his thoughts to himself. He didn't believe it for a moment. It was all too pat. What was Pearson's motive for all the killings? It didn't make sense.

"Thanks for coming in, guys," Sadowski said. "I hope this puts an end to it."

Don't bet on it, Tanaka felt like saying.

"Oh, Kats, I have the name that those plates are registered to."

He shuffled through some notes on his desk. "It belongs to a Jennifer Easton."

Karen and Tanaka left Sadowski's office.

"Jennifer Easton?" Karen said when they were clear of the building. "What the hell's going on?"

"I don't know. We should've checked Easton's alibi. Can you go up to Carmel and make sure they were there?"

"Will do, Katsuro. I'll go up this afternoon. Is it okay if I spend the night there?"

"Winifred can afford it."

"Good, I'll take Jo with me."

On the way home, Tanaka remembered he still hadn't reviewed the videotape.

CHAPTER FIFTY-SIX

Tanaka called Steve and told him he would prepare dinner for them that night at Steve's place. Then he called Chicago and spoke to his mother and Tommy.

Tanaka spent a few hours at the gym, picked up two large pizzas from Pizza Hut and a couple of bottles of Merlot, and headed for Pacific Heights. It was sunny for a change, so he took Sheba for a long walk.

He had to watch where they walked because of all the mud. A couple of times he nearly ended up on his rear end. The guardrail was still missing at the end of the side street. He could see the waves crashing on the rocks below. It looked like an accident waiting to happen.

Steve smiled when he walked into the kitchen and saw the dinner Tanaka had prepared but didn't say anything. Tanaka pulled the pizzas out of the oven. They sat in the den, ate pizza, and sipped Merlot.

"I'm glad you called," Steve said. "I was beginning to wonder if you'd gone off me."

"Why would you think that?" Tanaka asked.

"I don't know. It's just…you seem preoccupied, like you've got something on your mind."

"I do. It's just the Warren case, Stevie. Nothing else."

Steve sipped his wine.

Tanaka was glad Steve didn't ask him about the case. He didn't need to burden Steve with the gory details and have him worry about him.

"Do you know Geoffrey McDonald?" Steve asked.

Tanaka thought for a few moments…the name didn't ring any bells. "No, I don't think so."

"He's an attorney. We were talking at the courthouse yesterday. He wants me to join him in a partnership."

"What do you think about that?" Tanaka said.

Steve took another sip of his wine before answering. "I'm not sure. I told him I would think about it."

"I know…you prefer being independent."

"Anyway, while we were talking," Steve continued, "Easton came walking past us. It looked as though he'd been in some kind of fight or accident. He had some scars on his face."

"What kind of scars?"

"You know…like deep scratches, nearly healed."

"I guess his wife is back?" Tanaka said.

"I don't know if she's back. Anyway, he nodded at us and said, 'Hartman, McDonald,' and kept walking. Geoffrey glared at him."

"He doesn't like Easton?"

"That's putting it mildly. He said he's known Easton since primary school, and Easton has always been an insufferable prig. They were in college and law school at the same time. Easton and Warren shared an apartment while they were in L.A. with another student. Warren wanted Geoffrey to move in with them, but Geoffrey didn't want to live with Easton.

"Warren thought about moving in with Geoffrey, but never got around to it. After law school, Easton took some time off and went on a European tour. Geoffrey joined Pratt and James. He was doing well at the firm and thought he'd make partner. Then Easton joined the firm."

"Uh-oh," Tanaka said.

"Uh-oh is right. Easton wanted the partnership. His father and Pratt were friends, so Easton felt he was entitled to the partnership. He did everything he could to undermine Geoffrey. He said Easton was controlling and manipulative and turned the staff against him. Geoffrey eventually left the firm and opened his own practice. All his clients went with him."

"I bet that didn't sit too well with Pratt and James?"

"I think Geoffrey's dreading the day when Easton's a judge and he has a case before him."

The wine bottle was empty, so Tanaka went into the kitchen and opened another one. His mind was in a whirl.

"Do you think Geoffrey would be willing to talk to me?" Tanaka said when he got back to the den.

"Why would you want to talk to him?"

"Maybe he can shed some light on Warren's background that'll help me," Tanaka said as he topped up the wineglasses.

"Hmm. I don't think he'd be very happy to hear I've been talking about him. I'm sure he thought he and I were having a confidential discussion," Steve said.

"Please try, Stevie. It's important to me."

Steve mulled it over for a while. "Okay, I'll give him a call tomorrow. He'll probably agree when I tell him about our relationship."

"I hope you're not going to tell him about the hot tub?"

"You're such a silly boy," Steve said. "Come with me."

He took Tanaka's hand and led him into the bedroom.

They seemed closer that night than they'd been for a while.

CHAPTER FIFTY-SEVEN

S teve called around ten the next morning. He'd spoken to Geoffrey McDonald, who had agreed to see Tanaka. It was noon when the secretary showed Tanaka into McDonald's office.

McDonald was short and delicate-looking, but had a firm handshake. With his shaved head and smooth face, he looked a little like Yul Brynner. McDonald steered Tanaka over to a seating area in the corner of his office. After they were seated, McDonald said, "Steve tells me you'd like to speak to me about David Earl Warren."

"Yes, and I'd also like to know more about Pratt James Easton too, if that's okay?"

"May I know the reason for your interest?"

Tanaka told him all about his investigation and his conclusions.

He was silent during Tanaka's monologue and remained silent for some time after Tanaka finished talking.

"I'm finding it hard to accept David was murdered, and yet it would seem, from what you've described, that that's exactly what happened. He never had a mean bone in his body. He was always pleasant and cheerful."

"That's what I keep hearing, and yet someone had it in for him."

"If it hadn't been for David, I probably would've dropped out of law school. He was bright and articulate and assisted me with my studies. He spent hours drilling me...helping me pass my final exams."

"Did you know David was gay?"

"Of course I did. We had no secrets. However, no one else knew. If Easton had known, he would've moved out of their L.A. apartment. Of course, Pratt and James never knew either, or they would never have taken him on."

"What kind of person is Easton?"

McDonald's eyes narrowed and he gave Tanaka a long, searching look. "You think he might've had something to do with David's death?"

"I don't know. I keep getting different vibes about him. He seems to be an enigma. He seems to have a public persona and a very different private persona."

"Don't we all?" McDonald said.

"Yes, to some degree. But there seems to be something more going on with him."

"You've heard the rumors he's going to be a judge?"

"Yes," Tanaka said.

"He's going to be a very powerful person. A person I can't afford to alienate. Not as an attorney."

"I understand. Whatever you tell me will be completely confidential."

McDonald closed his eyes and deliberated for a few moments before saying, "Easton's really malevolent, you know, and I'm sorry to say, he scares me."

"That bad?"

"Steve tells me you can be trusted, and I trust Steve, so I'll tell you some things I've never spoken about before. However, I need to be assured this will go no further."

"You have my word. This conversation is just between the two of us."

McDonald stared at Tanaka, as though he was trying to make up his mind. "Let me begin by saying I don't think he's an appropriate candidate for the appellate court, and that's the only reason we're having this discussion. I have thought about informing the State Bar of my doubts, but I do not have any evidentiary support to prove malfeasance on his part, and I have nothing to back any allegations I might make. It would be my word against his."

"I can tell you've done a lot of thinking about this," Tanaka said.

McDonald poured himself a glass of water from the carafe on the coffee table and took a long drink before continuing. "I've known Michael for a long time. We grew up in the same neighborhood and went to the same schools. He was always a bully and intimidated anyone who showed the slightest weakness, which included me. He was on the school wrestling team and lifted weights in his spare time, so he had the wherewithal to back up his threats."

"He doesn't look like a jock."

"But he is. He's also highly intelligent and treats peers and underlings like fools. He's a compulsive liar and is not averse to altering facts to support his assumptions."

"He sounds like a real...um, charmer?"

"A psychopath is more accurate. One incident, above all others, really showed me what kind of person he is. One day while we were in high school, I found him torturing a cat. When I confronted him, he laughed and said, 'You better watch it, Geoffie, or you'll be next.'"

"What kind of upbringing did he have?" Tanaka asked.

"I didn't like his parents one bit. They were very different from mine. They came across as cold and unloving, and his mother in particular seemed to be constantly belittling him. It's strange, now that I think about it, but that's how he treats his wife. I guess it bolsters his sense of self-worth to treat her like that."

"Growing up in that type of environment wouldn't be easy," Tanaka said.

"I tried to stay away from him after that, but unfortunately, we were also at the University of San Sebastian at the same time. Our paths kept crossing, and whenever we met he'd say, 'Remember what I said, Geoffie.' I know I wasn't the only one scared of him. There were rumors amongst the female students he'd forced some of them into sexual activities."

"What a scumbag."

"He joined the drama club and became a skilled actor. The acting classes allowed him to become an expert at deception. When he showed up at Pratt and James, I knew my days were numbered. I knew too much about him. So I took the road of least resistance and resigned."

McDonald looked drained when he stopped talking, and his eyes had taken on a haunted look.

"Thank you for telling me about him. I'm not sure if Easton had anything to do with Warren's death, but I'm going to do something about him. We can't let him be appointed."

Tanaka could see a look of panic in McDonald's face. "You're not going to get me involved, are you?" McDonald said. "If he's what we think he is, I'll be next on his list."

"No. I'll find some other way of dealing with him."

"Thank you. If I can be of any more help, give me a call."

Tanaka left McDonald's office feeling the case was drawing to a close.

Chapter Fifty-eight

Tanaka was starving, so he picked up a pizza and two cans of cola from Pizza Hut and carted them back to the office.

"I hope you brought enough for me?" Karen asked. "I was just thinking of going out for lunch."

"I have a large one," Tanaka said.

"So you keep saying, but I've yet to see any proof."

"Ha, ha," Tanaka said, and handed her a cola.

"I want to phone Chicago," Tanaka said.

"You want some privacy?"

"'Course not."

He chatted with his mother and Tommy. They were both fine. Karen took the phone from him and spoke to Tommy.

"I'm looking after your dad while you're in Chicago," she said. "So you don't have to worry about him…he's behaving."

Tanaka could hear Tommy laughing when she hung up.

"He sounds fine," she said.

He nodded. "How was your trip to Carmel? Did you find out anything?"

"Sure did. Easton hadn't registered at the Rendezvous for those days. They never heard of him. No one recognized his photo either."

"I just knew he was lying when I questioned him, he was too pat," Tanaka said.

"I phoned the State Bar yesterday afternoon, and they said Easton hadn't attended the event, hadn't even registered."

"Where did you phone from?"

Karen smiled. "Don't worry, I didn't phone from here. I went over to Easton's law office and told the receptionist I wanted to apply for a clerking job. She had me sit in an empty office to fill out the application, so I phoned from there."

"That was good thinking. One of these days you'll be leaving me to start your own business."

"You should've seen me. You wouldn't have recognized me. I even put on a dress, made up my face, and wore a pair of high-heeled pumps."

"I didn't know you owned a dress and high heels," Tanaka said.

"I don't. I borrowed them from Jo. I haven't worn a dress since I was forced to join the Brownies, and that didn't last too long."

"What line did you give the State Bar?" he asked.

"I told them we needed a copy of Easton's receipt for income tax purposes. She came back on the line and said there had to be a mistake because his name wasn't on the list of attendees. I apologized and hung up."

"So that probably means neither Jennifer nor Easton were in Carmel that weekend," Tanaka said.

They sat silent for a short while.

"So," Karen said, "How did your meeting with McDonald go?"

Her eyes were wide open by the time Tanaka finished giving her the details.

"What a bastard he is," she said. "I guess he's responsible for all the deaths. I used to think it was Pearson, but with him dead, it could only be Easton."

"Yes, but why? What was his motive?"

"Beats me," she said, "but I've got more info on him that might help."

"You have?"

"I managed to find out who rented that car in December. It was Easton."

"Aha," Tanaka said, "at last, a motive."

"So you think he's the one?"

"Yeah, I think his car was involved in the hit-and-run accident where the old lady was killed. Pearson repaired his car. Easton found out Pearson was about to spill the beans to me, so he got rid of Pearson," Tanaka said.

"That makes sense. Can we tie him to the other murders?"

"It would be hard to tie him to any of the murders. We don't have any evidence, it's pure conjecture on our part. We'll need more than that to pin the murders on him."

"I guess the whole thing started when Warren found out about the hit-and-run and confronted him with it," she said.

"Bernier must've seen Easton on the Thursday. I knew he was covering up something. He tried to blackmail the wrong person."

"What about Margaret?"

"At this point I can't think of a reason why he'd kill her."

"And then there's poor Sally," she said. "He must've heard her talking to you."

"Right, and it was probably the confrontation between Warren and Easton she overheard. The first time I spoke to her, I asked her if she knew anything about the car rental. I think she found out it was Easton."

"We don't have anything to connect Easton to her death either, do we?"

"I think she's the one death we can get the evidence on. I started to suspect Easton when Steve told me he had scratch marks on his face. I think if we can get a DNA sample from Easton, we'll find it was his skin under Sally's nails."

She opened the pizza box and pulled a face when she saw he'd taken the last slice. "How are we going to do that?"

"We'll need to think about it," Tanaka said.

"Are you going to tell the cops?"

"What's to tell? They're hardly going to arrest a future judge on our say-so. We need to get something definite on him before we can get them involved."

"Maybe I can tail him. If he stops somewhere for a drink, I might be able to pick up the discarded container."

Tanaka was feeling out of his depth. "I feel so stupid. I'm not sure I'm cut out for this job. I told Winifred I didn't think I was the right person, but I let my ego get in the way. I should've refused to take this case."

"And how would that've helped? Warren would still be listed as an accidental death."

"Yes, but the others would still be alive," Tanaka said.

She sighed. "Kats, you can't think that way. We've done our best. I don't think anyone else could've done any better. You're a good investigator. If you weren't, I wouldn't be sitting here."

The telephone interrupted Tanaka's self-analysis. It was Sadowski. "I thought you'd like to know the person you assumed was Pearson wasn't him at all," he said. "It was Sadler."

"Sadler?" Tanaka said.

"That's right. He's the one that was pinned under the motor. With his head squashed the way it was, I can see why you misidentified him. The fingerprints are definitely Sadler's."

"So that means Pearson is still alive?" Tanaka said.

Karen's eyes opened wide.

"There's no flies on you, Sherlock," Sadowski said.

"Smartass," Tanaka said.

"We know they knew each other, they were cellmates, so I suppose we shouldn't be surprised Sadler assisted Pearson. Now, was it an accident, or was it intentional? If it was intentional, was Sadler the target, or did the perp also mistake him for Pearson? Or was Pearson the perp?" Sadowski said.

"It's a conundrum," Tanaka said.

"Well, your vocabulary sure has improved since you left the force."

"It's the company I'm keeping these days."

"Do you have any more bad news for me? No more deaths to report?" Sadowski asked. "I'm having a slow day."

"Not today, Rick."

"Make sure you keep it that way," Sadowski said before hanging up.

"What was that all about?" Karen asked.

Tanaka told her about the mistaken identity.

She shook her head as if trying to clear her brain. "I can hardly keep up with these twists and turns," she said.

Tanaka sighed. "I'm still hungry. Any doughnuts left?"

"No, there aren't. What a time to be thinking about eating."

"It helps me think," Tanaka said.

She leaned back in her chair with an exasperated look on her face. "So we're back to square one, then?" she said. "Maybe it's Pearson after all."

"I still think Easton killed Warren. Pearson doesn't have the brains to plan anything so elaborate. Maybe he assisted. However, Easton should still be our primary focus."

Out of a drawer, Tanaka pulled the envelope containing the key and code he'd found in Warren's car. "What do you think this key's for?"

Karen shrugged. "Beats me."

"I have a feeling about this key. I think it may be for Easton's house. Winifred told me Warren used to look after the Eastons' house when they were on vacation, so he probably had a key. What do you say we give it a try?"

"You mean break in?"

"I'd hardly call it a break-in if we have the key. I know it's not legal, but who's going to know?"

"I'll know," she said.

"Sometimes in this profession you have to bend the rules to get to the truth." He waited to see if she'd object. She didn't. "I'd like to try the key after dark. Why don't you set up surveillance on Easton's house? Call me after dark if the place is deserted. But keep out of sight, and be careful. Remember who we're dealing with."

"Don't worry about me, my horoscope said things weren't going to go well, so I'll watch it."

She picked up her jacket and a book, and left.

Tanaka called Sadowski. "What do you want now?" Sadowski said. "People will start talking about us."

"Sorry, Rick, something's just come up, and I won't be able to make the game tonight."

"You'll do anything to get out of paying me the bet, won't you? Make sure this is the last time you cancel. My ego can only take so much rejection, you know."

"Your vocabulary has improved since I left the force. You been taking psychology classes?" Tanaka asked.

"Smartass."

He hung up on Tanaka.

CHAPTER FIFTY-NINE

At 8:00 p.m., Tanaka called Karen on her cell phone. She didn't answer.

Maybe her phone battery is dead, Tanaka thought.

Tanaka waited another thirty minutes before trying again. She still didn't answer, so he drove to Easton's house. Some of Easton's house lights were on, and a Mercedes was parked in the driveway. There was no sign of Karen's car.

Surely she'd've called me if she'd had to leave?

He had a terrible premonition. He drove to her apartment building and used the intercom. Jo, Karen's partner, answered.

"It's Kats," he said. "Is Karen home?"

"No, I thought she was working?"

"Can I come up?"

"Sure," she said, and buzzed him in.

"You going out?" he asked when she met him at the door.

"I just got in. Haven't had time to take my coat off. What's going on, Kats?"

"I don't know. Karen was supposed to have someone under surveillance, but she's not there."

"What do you mean she's not there?"

"I don't know, Jo. Is her car downstairs?"

"No."

"Has she been home this evening?"

"I'll check," she said, and walked into the bedroom.

"Could she have gone to a class?" Tanaka said.

"No," Jo called out from the bedroom. "She didn't have any classes scheduled for today."

He took a seat on the sofa.

"There's a message on the phone," Jo said.

He joined her in the bedroom while she listened to the message.

"It can't be," she said, and sat down on the bed.

He waited until she'd hung up, and then asked, "What's wrong?"

"It was a message from the ER at the medical center. They want whoever checks the message to call them." She sat looking at the phone, as though she was in a daze.

"Well," Tanaka said. "Are you going to call them?"

"I'm scared, Kats."

He sat next to her on the bed and put his arm around her shoulders. "Me too, Jo, but you better call."

She nodded, checked the message again, and wrote down a name and phone number. She called the number and spoke to someone. Tanaka was frustrated only getting one side of the conversation. Whatever was being said didn't sound good.

"What's up?" he asked when she hung up.

She started crying. "It's Karen. She's been in an accident. She's unconscious and in the intensive care unit."

"We better get going," he said.

Jo moved like a zombie when Tanaka led her to the apartment door.

"You have your keys?" he asked.

She picked up her purse and they headed for Tanaka's car.

The drive to the hospital seemed to take forever.

When they arrived at the ICU, the nurse in charge asked if they were next of kin.

"No," Jo said, "but I'm her partner."

"You married?"

"No."

"I'm sorry," the nurse said, "we need to contact the next of kin. Do you know who it is?"

"Yes, I'll call them after I've seen her," Jo said.

"Before you go in I need to tell you what's going on," the nurse said.

They sat in a small interview room.

"I'm sorry," she said, "but it's not good news. We've done an EEG and—"

"What's that?" Jo asked.

"An electroencephalograph," she said. "It measures brain activity. Karen's brain is not showing any activity."

"What does that mean?" Tanaka asked.

The nurse looked at Tanaka. "I'm sorry, but it means there's no life. When you see Karen, she's on life support. We are keeping her on a ventilator until we do another EEG and until we know if she's an organ donor."

Jo let out a high-pitched wail and collapsed against Tanaka. When she was under control, he assisted her as the nurse led them to Karen's bedside.

Tanaka didn't recognize Karen. It looked like a stranger lying on the bed. Karen's face was swollen and bruised, her eyes were taped closed, and IVs dripped into the veins in her arms. A tube taped to her mouth and connected to a ventilator made an eerie sound as it breathed for her.

Jo and Tanaka held Karen's hands. They were ice cold.

Tanaka felt weak and disoriented. He wanted to scream but he had to be strong for Jo.

They stood like that for a while, and then the nurse led them back to the interview room.

❖

Jo called Karen's parents in Santa Barbara, and Tanaka called the police.

The police informed Tanaka Karen had driven over the side of Lighthouse Point.

He didn't for one minute believe it was accidental. Someone had deliberately killed Karen.

At 1:30 a.m., they disconnected the ventilator and allowed cardiac arrest to occur. Jo went home with Karen's parents, and Tanaka dragged himself home.

CHAPTER SIXTY

Tanaka spent the next day at home. If he'd gone into the office he would've been reminded of Karen, and that was too painful. He couldn't believe she was gone. *I shouldn't have let her watch Easton,* he kept thinking.

Tanaka phoned Chicago and spoke to Tommy, then his mother, and told her about Karen. He could hear her crying on the other end of the line when he hung up.

Tanaka felt like packing it in, but he knew he had to stop the out-of-control killer.

When it started to get dark, Tanaka changed into black jeans, black sneakers, a black toque, and a black slicker. His pistol was in the safe at work. He thought about picking it up on the way to Easton's house but decided he wouldn't need it that night.

El Niño was in full force. Warnings were out about potential mudslides in the areas devastated by wildfires the previous summer. It was the kind of night when sane people stayed indoors, but Tanaka couldn't afford that luxury. He had to act. The rain came down in torrents. Gusting wind blew pellets of stinging water into his face when he ran out to the car. Low-lying areas of the streets were flooded, the culverts unable to deal with the downpour, so he took his time driving to Easton's house.

When he arrived, he parked across the street. The place was dark and looked deserted. The garage doors were closed and there weren't any cars in the driveway. The wind buffeted Tanaka's car and rain streamed down the windows. He waited for an hour. He phoned Easton's home number. No one answered, so he figured it was safe to make his move. He would've felt better if Karen had been with him.

He pulled on a pair of black silk gloves, climbed out of his car, and took a flashlight out of his trunk. The wind destroyed his umbrella when he tried to open it, so he threw it back into the trunk.

The mansion was dark and quiet. He jumped when a huge branch crashed to the ground in front of him. The crunch of the gravel beneath his feet sounded loud enough to waken the dead, so he moved onto the lawn. He could hear water rushing down a culvert alongside the driveway.

Tanaka was soaked when he reached the front door. He could hear the chimes sounding inside when he pressed the button. He hadn't thought about what he might say if someone actually answered, so he hoped that wouldn't happen.

No one responded, so he took the key out of his pocket and, with a shaking hand, inserted it into the lock. The key turned easily and the door swung open.

He moved inside and shone his flashlight over the entrance hall. He could see the red light flashing on the security alarm. Holding his breath, he went over and entered the code from the envelope. The flashing light went off and the deactivated light came on. He took a deep breath. Even though it was cold, he was sweating.

Tanaka stood quietly for a while, listening for noises. All was quiet, so he removed his toque and slicker and left them in the hallway. He cringed when his wet sneakers squeaked on the granite floor of the hallway. He did a quick tour of the house, checking all the rooms. The house was empty. He breathed easier.

A study overlooked a garden at the rear of the house. Expensive mahogany bookshelves filled with leather-bound, law-related tomes lined the walls. It seemed like a logical place to start his search, so that's where he began.

A computer was in a prominent position on the huge mahogany desk. An Apple laptop sat on the credenza. He looked in the desk drawers, cupboards, and credenza; however, he couldn't find anything unusual.

He went back upstairs. The Eastons were using separate bedrooms. In the first—Jennifer's—he found a cardboard box containing a small mirror, a razor blade, and some rolled-up twenties for snorting drugs. There were also a number of small plastic baggies filled with white powder. A bag of marijuana, rolling papers, and a couple of rolled joints lay next to the baggies.

Talk about being prepared, Tanaka thought. *Maybe it's the only way she can abide the abusive pig.*

Tanaka found a Toshiba laptop hidden under some clothes in a drawer in Easton's bedroom. He pulled it out and started it up. When it asked for his password, he entered *Maverick.* Sure enough, it worked. He shut the laptop down and put it back in the drawer.

He looked through the remaining drawers. A blood glucose meter, a security box key, Warren's old will, divorce papers, and an insurance policy were in one of the drawers.

Headlights flashed across the ceiling. Tanaka's heart was pounding when he dashed over to the window and looked out. A car drove into the garage next door. He breathed a sigh of relief.

Tanaka resumed his search. His blood ran cold when he found Sally's onyx cameo. *The bastard. I'll get him for this.*

Tanaka had enough evidence to put Easton away for life.

His cell phone rang.

He jumped with fright. It was Steve calling.

"I'm right in the middle of something, Stevie. Can I call you back?"

"I have to see you tonight, it's really important. Can you come over?" Steve asked.

"Tonight?"

"Please, Kats, it's important."

"Okay, I'll be over as soon as I've finished this," Tanaka said.

Steve hung up without another word.

It's time to leave anyway, Tanaka thought, *I've found what I came for. I'll have to think of a way to get Sadowski in here before Easton destroys the evidence.* He checked to make sure everything looked undisturbed. He could see a few wet spots and a puddle on the entrance hall floor, so he wiped them up with paper towels from the powder room and stuck the towels in his pocket. On his way out, he reset the alarm and locked the door.

CHAPTER SIXTY-ONE

The drive to Steve's house took longer than usual. The wind and rain continued to bombard the coast. The water was at least six inches deep on some stretches of the road. When he crossed the San Sebastian River, normally a placid stream, he could see the turbulent water rushing out to sea. Debris backed up against the bridge.

The road that ran past Steve's property was in complete darkness. He had to drive around downed trees and branches littering the road. Across the road from Steve's driveway entrance a large cedar tree lay across the severed power lines, which danced in the wind and sent sparks flying in all directions.

Just as well the trees are soaked or we'd have a fire, Tanaka thought as he parked next to Steve's car.

I wonder why he didn't park in the garage? Tanaka was thinking as he climbed out of his car.

He was soaked when he got to the door. Steve, holding a candle, opened the door. He never said a word. Didn't even try to kiss Tanaka. His face was pale and haggard.

What's bothering him? Where's Sheba? were two questions that popped into Tanaka's mind.

He stepped inside and the door slammed closed.

With a gun in his hand, Michael Easton materialized out of the darkness. He pointed the gun at Tanaka's chest and glared at him.

"You took your sweet time getting here, Tanaka. I was beginning to think you wouldn't show up," Easton said.

"Kats," Steve said, "I'm sorry. I couldn't do anything. He threatened to kill me if I didn't call you."

Tanaka put his arm around Steve's shoulders.

"You faggots make me sick," Easton said.

"What's going on?" Tanaka said to Easton. "What's the meaning of this?"

"Like you don't know," Easton said.

"You're crazy," Tanaka said. "I don't know what you're doing here."

Tanaka scanned Easton's face. It was showing nothing but anger.

"If you don't know why I'm here, then you're dumber than I thought you were."

Tanaka knew Easton was going to kill them…they knew too much for him to let them live. Tanaka had to get some time to think. "Since I'm so dumb, why don't you enlighten me," he said.

A maniacal cackle erupted from Easton's lips.

Tanaka could feel Steve trembling. He wanted to say something to comfort him, but he didn't want to antagonize Easton.

"I know that you know," Easton said, in a singsong voice, "who ran down that old lady in December."

"You're wrong," Tanaka said. "I don't know for sure who ran her down, but my guess is it was your wife."

Easton blinked. "You mean Sally didn't tell you?"

"No, she didn't tell me," Tanaka said.

Easton paused and stared at Tanaka for a moment. "Oh, well. I had to get rid of her anyway."

What a pig, Tanaka thought. *If he didn't have that gun in his hand, I'd strangle him.* He tried to keep his voice calm. "So Jennifer got Pearson to repair the car?"

"He was in the car with her and persuaded her to leave the scene. She should never have listened to him." Another inappropriate laugh emanated from Easton.

"Warren found out about the hit-and-run and threatened you with exposure. When he confronted you, you knew you had to get rid of him because you'd never make judge if something like that came to light," Tanaka said.

"Warren deserved what he got. He should've kept out of it," Easton said.

Keep him talking, keep him talking. Maybe help will arrive in time to save us, Tanaka thought. "Jennifer helped you with the plan," Tanaka said. "She knows all about diabetes and insulin."

"She objected at first, said it was against the Hippocratic Oath.

It was a brilliant scheme, wasn't it? If only that old aunt of his hadn't interfered. Don't worry, though, she's next on my list."

"Pearson pushed me over the cliff and tried to run me down," Tanaka said.

"Apparently, he stupidly thought he could scare you off. That didn't work, did it? He misjudged your tenacity. I never sanctioned those acts."

"What happened? Did Pearson try to blackmail Jennifer? Is that why you tried to kill him, but killed Sadler by mistake?" Tanaka said.

"I had to get rid of him. He was a loose cannon. Fortunately Sadler was someone else I needed to get rid of."

"When I appeared on the scene, you knew you had to get rid of everyone who might be able to finger you," Tanaka said.

"Pearson was very good at carrying out orders. Mind you, how Jennifer tolerated him I have no idea, but I guess that's what happens when you get hooked on coke."

"So how come you're out here? Where's your henchman?" Tanaka said.

"I'm afraid he won't be going anywhere again. I couldn't take the risk of him running around."

"You mean you've—?"

"Yes. I've eliminated the threat." Easton related the facts in a cold, offhand manner, as if he was telling a story, as though he wasn't personally involved.

Tanaka felt Steve's body stiffen when Tanaka said, "Why did you kill Karen?"

"The silly girl. When I saw her sitting outside my house, I knew you were getting close. Pearson helped me stage her accident. That was his last good deed."

"Karen didn't die right away, she was conscious for a while. I heard she'd spoken to the cops."

"You think I'm dumb enough to believe that crap? She never regained consciousness."

"Where's Jennifer? Is she still alive?"

"Oh yes. She's in rehab. She'll be back to normal by the time I get appointed to the appellate court."

Over my dead body, he felt like saying. "You'll never get away with this. The police are investigating the threat you made on Tommy's life."

"Don't be ridiculous, they'll never be able to pin that on me."

"Don't be so sure. We have your DNA from the envelope."

"Stop fantasizing, you ridiculous man. I never used my saliva. Now, inside, you stupid faggot," Easton said, waving the gun in the direction he wanted them to take.

Tanaka followed Steve into the living room. With just the one candle, it was hard to see. The cold steel of Easton's gun pressed against Tanaka's spine. He knew he would have to do something. Easton had to kill them both, especially now they knew all his secrets.

As they entered the living room, Easton stepped in front of them. "Never let it be said I shot somebody in the back. No, this is going to be a murder-suicide. On the couch, faggot," Easton said to Steve.

Steve suddenly pushed Tanaka to the side and threw the candle into Easton's face. The noise of the gun going off was deafening.

Steve screamed.

Tanaka had to make a split-second decision in the total darkness.

Steve helped him make up his mind. "Get out! Get out!" he yelled.

Tanaka felt he was abandoning Steve when he ran toward the French doors, but knew he was doing the right thing. His shins contacted the coffee table, and he went sprawling across the living room floor.

As he lay facedown on the floor, the gun exploded again and the glass French doors shattered above him. Tanaka's ears were ringing and an acrid cordite smell hung in the air. *Shit...I should have brought my gun*, Tanaka thought as he groveled on the floor. He crawled through the shattered French doors onto the deck. Glass shards dug into his palms and knees. He felt his way to the stairs, stood up, and raced down to the lawn. Another shot echoed across the lawn. In total darkness, Tanaka headed for the other side of the house.

He pulled his cell phone out of his pocket and was about to press the 911 button when he tripped over something and took a nosedive onto the muddy grass. The phone flew out of his hand. He felt around. Sheba's dark, furry body lay unmoving on the grass.

Tanaka got to his feet and raced in the direction of his car.

Easton fired a shot. The bullet clanged when it hit his car. Tanaka changed direction and raced toward the road. Easton climbed into the car in the driveway. It was his Mercedes, not Steve's.

Easton turned on the headlights.

Tanaka had to get help.

He dodged around a fallen tree and continued to run. Easton's headlights guided him as he tore along the road toward the closest neighbor's house. Easton's Mercedes turned around in the driveway and raced toward Tanaka.

Tanaka's heart pounded and adrenaline pumped through him as he gasped for air.

He ran faster than he'd ever run before.

The downed trees slowed Easton's progress, but he was gaining on Tanaka.

Another shot rang out.

Tanaka turned into the dead-end road and sped toward the precipice.

I hope he stops and gets out of the car, Tanaka thought, *then I'll be able to wrestle the gun from him and throw him over the cliff.* He speeded up as he neared the edge. *Easton isn't going to stop, he's going to run me down* flashed through Tanaka's mind as he threw himself over the side of the cliff onto the ledge he'd seen on his walk with Sheba. Easton was going too fast to stop on the muddy road. The car's engine roared as it passed directly over Tanaka.

Tanaka watched as the car cartwheeled in the air and plunged swiftly into the dark waters of the Pacific Ocean a hundred feet below.

The rain, the wind, and the crashing waves were too loud for him to hear the impact. He could see the headlights glowing through the water as the car sank beneath the surface. Thunder shook the earth and lightning flashed across the sky. Complete darkness followed.

For a few seconds Tanaka couldn't move. His thoughts refocused. He rushed back to Steve's house. At one point he tripped over a downed tree limb and landed flat on his face.

When he ran through the front door, he could see a faint glow coming from the living room.

"Stevie?" he shouted. "Are you okay?"

"I'm in here," Steve called from the living room.

A lonely candle cast a feeble light over Steve.

Thank God, he's alive, Tanaka thought. *I'll never put him in danger again.*

Steve lay on the settee, a bloodstained towel pressed to his left upper arm. He was pale and clammy, like he was going into shock.

"Oh God, Stevie, you're wounded." Tanaka said. "I'll phone for help."

"I've already called the police and ambulance," he said. "Where's Easton? Is he coming back?"

"No, he won't be back," Tanaka said.

"I don't know where Sheba is," Steve said. "Have you seen her?"

"I'm sorry, Stevie…she's dead."

Tears streamed down his cheeks. "He killed her?" he asked.

Tanaka nodded. "I found her outside." Tanaka went to his knees beside Steve and gently stroked his hair. "You saved us, Stevie."

"I knew I had to do something," he said.

"Is it bad?" Tanaka asked.

"I'll live."

"It's all my fault, Stevie. I should've been here for you."

Tanaka could hear sirens approaching.

"Go and let them in," Steve said. "Be careful. I don't want them to think you're Easton."

Tanaka went to the front door.

Headlights flooded the area.

Tanaka held his arms in the air. "He's in there," he said.

"Who are you?" the police officer asked.

Tanaka told him who he was and explained how Easton had tried to kill them.

Using flashlights to illuminate the scene, a paramedic cleaned and dressed Tanaka's hands and knees while another one worked on Steve.

They loaded Steve into the ambulance. Tanaka wanted to accompany him, but the police officer wouldn't let him because Tanaka had to show them where the car went over the side.

A police office carried Sheba into the garage.

The police finished with Tanaka just before one a.m. They informed him they'd be back at daylight to search for the car.

Tanaka called the hospital to check on Steve. They were preparing him for surgery. A bullet had lodged in his left triceps muscle. He was lucky. The bullet had missed his major blood vessels, and there wasn't any nerve or bone damage. The nurse suggested Tanaka wait until morning to visit.

He found some plywood in the garage and nailed it over the broken French doors. He pulled off his wet clothes and hung them up to dry. He dried himself and then, exhausted, threw himself onto Steve's bed.

CHAPTER SIXTY-TWO

The next morning, Tanaka awoke to the sound of traffic and chain saws. He looked out the window. The rain had stopped, and the sun was shining. That didn't improve his disposition. Parked along the road were four police cruisers.

A utility truck was parked next to the damaged power line, and someone was using a chain saw on the downed tree.

When he called the hospital, he was informed that Steve was fine.

It was time to put things right. First he called a friend in the construction business and asked him to come out and repair the damage to the French doors. He called Steve's dog-sitter, who promised him she'd come out and spend the day at the house. When he called a pet crematory service, they said they'd take care of Sheba. His next call was to Sadowski. It took a while to tell him everything. And at last he phoned Winifred. She listened calmly as Tanaka told her the name of the person who had killed her nephew.

"Kats," she said, "I had faith in you from the start. I knew you'd discover the truth. I knew you wouldn't be able to rest until you had. You're like me that way. Now, thanks to you, I can put the past to rest."

But can I? Tanaka thought.

The power and the water were off, so Tanaka was unable to shower. Steve had a supply of bottled water, so he was able to brush his teeth and give himself a quick sponge-down. He put some fresh Band-Aids on his palms and knees. His clothes, though dry, were soiled beyond belief. He dressed in one of Steve's shirts, but he had to wear his own soiled pants because Steve's were too short.

He found his ruined cell phone in the mud and walked down to the dead-end road, which was still muddy. That hadn't stopped some of the inquisitive neighbors from walking down to the police tape across the road. They looked surprised to see him in his mud-covered pants.

"What's going on?" an elderly man asked.

Tanaka shrugged.

Two huge tow trucks parked at the dead end had cables dangling over the cliff. A police officer who had been on the scene the night before came over and raised the yellow tape.

A police Zodiac circled the area where the car had entered the water. Farther out, a Coast Guard vessel stood at anchor on the calm ocean.

"We've got divers down there attaching cables to the car," the officer said.

"Any sign of Easton?" Tanaka asked.

"There's someone in the car, so we're assuming it's him. We'll check when we get the car up."

"Good."

"Are you going to hang around?" the officer asked.

"No. I'll be at the medical center if you need me."

CHAPTER SIXTY-THREE

He went home to shower and change. He spent a long time in the shower, letting the warm water soothe his aching body.

The house was quiet and lonely. He would phone Chicago later and tell them to come home.

❖

Steve was sleeping when Tanaka arrived at his private room. An IV dripped slowly into his uninjured arm. His wounded arm was elevated on two pillows.

Tanaka sat next to the bed and held Steve's hand.

Steve was still out for the count at lunchtime. It had been a long time since Tanaka had eaten, and he realized he was ravenous. He knew Steve would be all right. He sat in the cafeteria, devoured breakfast, and drank three cups of coffee.

When he got back to the ward, Sadowski stood at the entrance to Steve's private room.

"The nurse said you'd be back," Sadowski said. "You look in worse condition than Steve."

Tanaka looked at Steve. He was awake.

"How you doing, Stevie?" Sadowski asked.

"I'll live," Steve answered.

Tanaka walked over and kissed Steve on the forehead. "You okay?" he asked.

"Did you get Easton?" Steve asked.

"Yes, we've recovered the car," Sadowski said.

"Recovered the car?" Steve said.

"He doesn't know?" Sadowski said to Tanaka.

Tanaka told Steve about Easton chasing him and plunging into the ocean.

Steve closed his eyes and shuddered.

"We found Pearson and his dog in the trunk," Sadowski said.

Steve groaned. "You looked after Sheba?" he asked.

"Yes, Stevie," Tanaka said.

"Rick," Tanaka said, turning to Sadowski, "have you managed to locate Jennifer Easton yet?"

Sadowski shook his head. "We've been in touch with the Chicago police. They're checking rehab centers."

"I hope she hasn't left the country," Tanaka said.

"When did you realize she was involved?" Sadowski asked.

"I never knew for sure, I just assumed she'd been the driver of the hit-and-run car."

"What about Easton? How long've you known about him?"

"When Steve told me about the scratches on Easton's face, I was sure he'd killed Sally Ferguson, so I had my sights on him. But again, I didn't know for sure until Easton admitted it to Stevie and me."

Tanaka didn't tell Sadowski about the things he'd found in Easton's bedroom—he didn't think he would approve of his unlawful entry and illegal trespass—however, he did say, "I'm sure, if you search the Eastons' house, you'll find the corroborating evidence."

Sadowski gave him a penetrating look. "You sound like you know that for sure."

"It's just an educated guess," Tanaka said. "How would I know for sure?"

"So the only proof you have is what Easton told the two of you?"

Tanaka nodded.

Sadowski was silent for a while. "So you're suggesting he got rid of Bernier as well?" he asked.

"I think Bernier saw Easton at Warren's condo the day before Warren died, and decided to blackmail him. Easton probably got Pearson to help him get rid of Bernier. It would've been dead easy for Pearson to snap Bernier's neck and then pitch him off the mountain."

They were quiet for a minute or two, thinking it over, and then Sadowski said, "I think I know the reason why Margaret Warren was killed."

"Why?" Tanaka asked.

"I don't think it had anything to do with the other murders or the hit-and-run. You remember I told you we'd found a video in Margaret's condo?"

"Yeah. Sorry I didn't get around to reviewing it."

"I recognized the second guy when I saw Easton's body. It was him," Sadowski said.

Tanaka thought about his initial meeting with Easton. Margaret must've phoned Easton and warned him. *He was prepared for my visit.* "You're saying they were having a ménage à trois and Margaret Warren tried to blackmail him, so he got rid of her?" Tanaka asked.

"Right. I don't think that's the kind of thing that looks good on a résumé," Sadowski said.

"There might be one other reason," Tanaka said.

"What's that?"

"Margaret told me she didn't have a key to Warren's condo, but I think she did. I think she looked for it after I confronted her about the Thursday, and when she couldn't find it, she realized Easton had taken the key, and that's why she wanted to see me. If she'd challenged him, he would've immediately got rid of her."

Sadowski nodded. "That sounds more plausible than my suggestion."

"I think you'll find there's at least one more death attributable to them," Tanaka said.

"Who might that be?" Sadowski asked.

Tanaka told Sadowski about Paul Jackson. "I'm sure if you get forensics to sift through the wood-chipper debris, you'll find it was a slug that killed him. I think they shot him and then threw his body in the chipper," Tanaka said.

"Why did they kill him?" Sadowski asked.

"Jackson was a red herring Easton threw out to confuse me. To him, poor Jackson was just another expendable. Easton was a psychopath with no conscience, and Pearson was no better. He didn't think twice before eliminating people he perceived as a danger. Easton wanted to be a judge, and nobody was going to prevent that from happening," Tanaka said.

"I'll ask the Santa Barbara sheriff to look into it," Sadowski said.

"Good."

"Well, enough chitchat," Sadowski said. "I've got work to do. If you have any more insights, give me a call. In the meantime, stay put.

We've had more murders in the last month than we normally have in a year."

❖

Steve had been listening to the discussion in silence.

When Sadowski left the room, Steve said, "Sometimes I think I don't know you."

"Stevie, I—"

"No, let me speak," he said. "I told you your job was dangerous, but you wouldn't listen. Now look what's happened. We were both nearly killed."

"Stevie, I—"

"I need time to think, Kats. I can't take any more of this."

"Stevie, I—"

"Please," he said, holding up his good hand to stop Tanaka. "I need time to think. I'd like you to leave now. I'll give you a call when I get home."

When he bent over to kiss him, Steve turned his head away.

Tanaka turned and walked out of the hospital room. He'd had doubts about himself when he'd first taken on the case. He now felt stronger and more settled. He'd been hanging on to Patrick's memory for too long. He finally realized he couldn't bring back a lost love—but he could open his heart to a new love.

He would drive up to San Quentin and meet with Lawrence Ingram—he knew he'd be able to forgive Ingram. What Ingram had done to Patrick would always haunt him, but he needed to live for the present and the future, not hang on to the past.

About the Author

Donald Webb has had numerous erotic stories published in gay magazines and anthologies. He lives with his partner of forty-five years in Victoria, BC. Donald can be contacted at: andon402@shaw.ca.

Books Available From Bold Strokes Books

Death Came Calling by Donald Webb. When private investigator Katsuro Tanaka is hired to look into the death of a high profile lawyer, he becomes embroiled in a case of murder and mayhem. (978-1-60282-979-4)

Love in the Shadows by Dylan Madrid. While teaming up to bring a killer to justice, a lustful spark is ignited between an American man living in London and an Italian spy named Luca. (978-1-60282-981-7)

Asher's Fault by Elizabeth Wheeler. Fourteen-year-old Asher Price sees the world in black and white, much like the photos he takes, but when his little brother drowns at the same moment Asher experiences his first same-sex kiss, he can no longer hide behind the lens of his camera and eventually discovers he isn't the only one with a secret. (978-1-60282-982-4)

In Between by Jane Hoppen. At the age of fourteen, Sophie Schmidt discovers that she was born an intersexual baby and sets off on a journey to find her place in a world that denies her true existence. (978-1-60282-968-8)

The Odd Fellows by Guillermo Luna. Joaquin Moreno and Mark Crowden open a bed-and-breakfast in Mexico but soon must confront an evil force with only friendship, love, and truth as their weapons. (978-1-60282-969-5)

The Seventh Pleiade by Andrew J. Peters. When Atlantis is besieged by violent storms, tremors, and a barbarian army, it will be up to a young gay prince to find a way for the kingdom's survival. (978-1-60282-960-2)

Cutie Pie Must Die by R.W. Clinger. Sexy detectives, a muscled quarterback, and the queerest murders…when murder is most cute. (978-1-60282-961-9)

Going Down for the Count by Cage Thunder. Desperately needing money, Gary Harper answers an ad that leads him into the underground world of gay professional wrestling—which leads him on a journey of self-discovery and romance. (978-1-60282-962-6)

Light by 'Nathan Burgoine. Openly gay (and secretly psychokinetic) Kieran Quinn is forced into action when self-styled prophet Wyatt Jackson arrives during Pride Week and things take a violent turn. (978-1-60282-953-4)

Baton Rouge Bingo by Greg Herren. The murder of an animal rights activist involves Scotty and the boys in a decades-old mystery revolving around Huey Long's murder and a missing fortune. (978-1-60282-954-1)

Anything for a Dollar, edited by Todd Gregory. Bodies for hire, bodies for sale—enter the steaming hot world of men who make a living from their bodies—whether they star in porn, model, strip, or hustle—or all of the above. (978-1-60282-955-8)

Mind Fields by Dylan Madrid. When college student Adam Parsh accepts a tutoring position, he finds himself the object of the dangerous desires of one of the most powerful men in the world—his married employer. (978-1-60282-945-9)

Greg Honey by Russ Gregory. Detective Greg Honey is steering his way through new love, business failure, and bruises when all his cases indicate trouble brewing for his wealthy family. (978-1-60282-946-6)

Lake Thirteen by Greg Herren. A visit to an old cemetery seems like fun to a group of five teenagers, who soon learn that sometimes it's best to leave old ghosts alone. (978-1-60282-894-0)

Deadly Cult by Joel Gomez-Dossi. One nation under MY God, or you die. (978-1-60282-895-7)

The Case of the Rising Star: A Derrick Steele Mystery by Zavo. Derrick Steele's next case involves blackmail, revenge, and a new romance as Derrick races to save a young movie star from a dangerous killer. Meanwhile, will a new threat from within destroy him, along with the entire Steele family? (978-1-60282-888-9)

Big Bad Wolf by Logan Zachary. After a wolf attack, Paavo Wolfe begins to suspect one of the victims is turning into a werewolf. Things become hairy as his ex-partner helps him find the killer. Can Paavo solve the mystery before he runs into the Big Bad Wolf? (978-1-60282-890-2)

The Moon's Deep Circle by David Holly. Tip Trencher wants to find out what happened to his long-lost brothers, but what he finds is a sizzling circle of gay sex and pagan ritual. (978-1-60282-870-4)

The Plain of Bitter Honey by Alan Chin. Trapped within the bleak prospect of a society in chaos, twin brothers Aaron and Hayden Swann discover inner strength in the face of tragedy and search for atonement after betraying the one you most love. (978-1-60282-883-4)

Tricks of the Trade: Magical Gay Erotica, edited by Jerry L. Wheeler. Today's hottest erotica writers take you inside the sultry, seductive world of magicians and their tricks—professional and otherwise. (978-1-60282-781-3)

Straight Boy Roommate by Kevin Troughton. Tom isn't expecting much from his first term at University, but a chance encounter with straight boy Dan catapults him into an extraordinary, wild weekend of sex and self-discovery, which turns his life upside down, and leads him into his first love affair. (978-1-60282-782-0)

In His Secret Life by Mel Bossa. The only man Allan wants is the one he can't have. (978-1-60282-875-9)

Promises in Every Star, edited by Todd Gregory. Acclaimed gay erotica author Todd Gregory's definitive collection of short stories, including both classic and new works. (978-1-60282-787-5)

Raising Hell: Demonic Gay Erotica, edited by Todd Gregory. Hot stories of gay erotica featuring demons. (978-1-60282-768-4)

Pursued by Joel Gomez-Dossi. Openly gay college student Jamie Bradford becomes romantically involved with two men at the same time, and his hell begins when one of his boyfriends becomes intent on killing him. (978-1-60282-769-1)

Timothy by Greg Herren. *Timothy* is a romantic suspense thriller from award-winning mystery writer Greg Herren set in the fabulous Hamptons. (978-1-60282-760-8)